Atlas' Last Stand
By J. Channing

Part One:

Hearts and Minds

Chapter One

Aboard the Tranquility
Orbiting Judgment, third planet (G-1726) of Sword Belt, within the
Great Orion Nebula System
Farthest human-occupied planet from Earth

"I know you. I know who you were," Captain Green's voice crackled through Mephista's cochlear implant. "You don't have to do this," he pleaded.

"Orders, ma'am?" the *Tranquility*'s weapons officer called from his station.

On the glowing panel of her holoscreen, Mephista could see the SSC corvette *Mercy* push its plasma thrusters until they shone white hot. Captain Green was trying to put distance between his small patrol ship and her larger cruiser. She watched his vessel slide above Judgment's ochre surface for a moment, and considered her counterpart. The *Mercy* was only designed for light reconnaissance and orbital assistance. It would never survive an engagement with them, and Captain Green was well aware of that fact, and he was also well aware that the *Tranquility* could turn them into nothing more than a footnote in the SSC's ship registry in no time at all. His only chance was to appeal to her sense of reason, but she'd long ago turned her back on Sol and on whatever the despised authorities there might consider rational.

"How far away is *Mercy*'s sister ship?" she asked. *Mercy* and *Fate's Winds* accounted for the total SSC presence in the system. She could easily handle them both separately but preferred not to be surprised if the other ship should happen to come to Green's aid.

"*Fate's Winds* is two days out, ma'am," the nav officer called back to her. "It's currently in orbit around Gertie."

"Good. Are we jamming the *Mercy*'s communications?" she asked.

"Yes, Captain," her communications technician responded. "But if they manage to get to the far side of the planet, our jamming will become ineffective, and they'll have a window to transmit a distress call."

"Helm, set course to overtake the *Mercy*," Mephista ordered. "Thrust to point-three-five. Weapons officer, ready the missiles."

"Yes Captain," the weapons officer said tentatively as he tapped the controls on his display. His name was Statin. He was barely twenty when Mephista had made the desperate leap to the Sword Belt after Sol Space Command's final incompetent betrayal of her mission. She heard the hesitation in his voice, wondering if these past two years of piracy had hardened him enough for what was to come. She'd been young once, and knew all too well the bitterness that came when youthful idealism was driven out by practical realities, but forging an alternative to Sol's failing government required a willingness to do battle. The time to test her crew's mettle had finally come.

"They're launching countermeasures, ma'am!" Statin said anxiously as he continued to stare at the readouts on his display.

A field of sparkling mirrors spread from the *Mercy's* hull, followed by the tiny flicker of electromagnetic pulse mines designed to confuse the *Tranquility's* missile guidance systems.

For a moment, her heart went out to Captain Green. His was a desperate struggle. Patrolling an entire system on the fringes of human-occupied space with only two scout ships was an impossible task, and he'd done the best he could. She'd shared his sense of duty once, but that was before she realized she'd merely been grist for Sol's mill.

"We're entering missile range now Captain," her tactical officer called.

"Arm the magna cannons. Fire when ready," she ordered, but Statin didn't respond.

"Missiles incoming!" her nav officer said with a nervous urgency.

"Evasive maneuvers!" Mephista shouted. Then she released the restraints which kept her tethered to her station, and floated free in the zero-G environment. She grabbed the back of her chair and quickly flung herself toward Statin, sailing over the dozen other bridge crew who faced the ship's main holoscreen. The *Tranquility* accelerated into its evasive maneuvers, and as it did the deck rose toward her, causing her legs to crash into the back of her startled communications ensign.

"Carry on!" Mephista growled.

Untangling herself, she seized a handrail and timed her launch to coincide with the next thruster firing. Her timing was dead on, and she quickly flew over to Statin's station, just in front of the main screen. The weapons officer's magnetic boots kept him frozen to the deck during the ship's maneuvers, so she grabbed his shoulder and used him to halt her momentum. As she dug her fingers into his pressure suit, a red flush of discomfort clouded his face. He'd never been this close to his captain before.

"Execute your orders Lieutenant!" she snarled.

"But, Captain...," he said as he nodded toward the massive enlargement of the *Mercy* that hung in shimmering light before them. "That's an SSC ship."

"We're clear of the projectiles," her helmsman called. "Their thrusters are at maximum, but we're gaining."

"Mephista, please," Captain Green's voice pleaded over the comms link. "This won't bring anyone back."

"Cut off that channel!" Mephista shouted as she shoved Statin aside and punched the glowing bar of light that charged the magna-cannons. Four yellow indicators appeared in the air beside her. The status lights blinked green, and the *Tranquility*'s hull shuddered as the ship's thrusters compensated for the cannons' massive recoil. On the main holoscreen, four ultra-dense osmium projectiles hurtled into the *Mercy* at one-third

To my Mosey Pals from Columbia River High in Vancouver, WA.

"It's better to burn out, than to fade away."

Prologue: Beyond The Gate

Outside human-occupied space
17 AUs beyond the Great Orion Nebula
1,344 light years from Earth

Hotaka hadn't slept for three days, and the headache he carried with him onto the *Ichikari*'s bridge was only growing worse.

"You look terrible, Hotaka," Third Mate Akiyama observed. "Need another trip to the lounge, eh?"

Hotaka grimaced and rubbed his eyes. It was late, and the skeleton crew that manned the mining vessel's bridge was exhausted. Now, especially at this time, he needed to control his temper. His smugglers had spent a long year illegally collecting metals in Bwain space, and the strain was telling.

"What I need is to get off this shift. Either that, or I need to get my body back onto a normal solar cycle," Hotaka said sleepily.

"You find the Captain a protoplanet that's got iridium or astatine, and he'll promote you from fourth to *third* mate. Just think. All this could be yours," Akiyama said, grinning to himself as he glanced around the bridge, spreading his arms wide to indicate the bridge's flickering holoscreens, its rusting joints, and the cracks and scratches in its dingy gray paint.

The *Ichikari* was nearly a century old, but she still turned a profit. For those who pushed beyond the safety of Sol Space Command (SSC), profit was all that mattered. The SSC provided a measure of security, but this far from Sol it was better not to take unnecessary risks. The *Ichikari* had already searched farther afield than many of her crew would have liked.

"I'd rather we set a course back through The Gate," Hotaka grumbled.

"Then hurry up and get those holds filled," Akiyama said. "You're just about in position for the next mineral scan. The systems are all running up to spec. Reactor two is still down for repairs to the cooling manifold, but...Hotaka?"

Hotaka shook his head. His vision blurred for a moment, and suddenly he was seeing the *Ichikari* from the outside. Somehow his mind had separated from his physical form, and he was able to view the ship's massive hull from the void of the empty space surrounding it. The ship wasn't much to look at, but then again, it wasn't designed to be aesthetically pleasing. It was designed to do a job, which it had done quite well during his tenure as a member of the crew.

Something started nagging at him as he floated there, and suddenly he realized what it was. There was a rasping, insistent voice that broke through his consciousness and dragged him roughly back to his senses.

"Ours," he thought he heard it say.

"Ours? Sorry, what?" Hotaka asked as he blinked his eyes and tried to regain his focus.

Akiyama's eyebrows arched in concern. "I swear, you're losing it. After your shift, you'd better go and see Kaylee in the lounge. That's an order."

"You serious?" Hotaka asked, still bemused by the strange vision. The voice had seemed so real...so present. It was as though it had emanated from the very walls of the ship. No, that wasn't possible. Could it have all just been in his head? Maybe a whole year out here chasing space rocks and trying to stay sane was really too long after all.

"Damn right I'm serious. Besides, this is her first tour, so her fees are still reasonable. Here," he said as he held out his hand for the cash transfer. His shirtsleeve rose to reveal the Kanji tattoos that covered his forearm. They were the only physical scars he had from the dozen prisons he'd escaped from. The markings ended with a set of double flags across Akiyama's wrist, which represented The Gate – the churning gas pillars that bordered the single safe path through the Great Orion Nebula's deadly radiation. The glowing path had reminded Hotaka of a child's hologame when he had first passed through it a year ago on his way out of human-occupied space.

They were in Bwain territory now, so there was no one to help if they got into trouble, and no one to talk to other than a few hundred other smugglers. The Gate imprinted on Akiyama's wrist reminded him always to stay on this side. A voyage outside The Gate didn't quite guarantee him a prison cell, but it was its own punishment.

"Consider it my finder's fee. It was you who originally brought her on board," Akiyama reminded him. "Or, if you'd prefer not to spend the evening relaxing with a gorgeous and gifted courtesan, I'm sure I could find reason to question your fitness for duty when writing my watch report."

Scowling, Hotaka tapped his data ring against Akiyama's finger. Three hundred credits, enough for one night with Kaylee, flowed from his account. The money was worthless until they reached a human-colonized planet back on the other side of The Gate, but the girl might actually help with his insomnia. Besides, Hotaka reminded himself, he was following orders from a superior.

"You're a con man," Hotaka muttered. In truth, he knew Akiyama to be smarter than the average smuggler, and he occasionally wondered what sort of trouble he'd been in, and what forced him into a life like this. Was it because he'd been convicted of committing a genuinely serious crime, or could the harsh sentencing he'd received just have been a whim of the SSC? He'd talked to a lot of outcasts over the years, and from what they said, the ratio seemed about even.

"A little enterprise helps pass the time," Akiyama said, waving the comment away. Many of the men ran businesses on the side, usually involving drugs or alcohol. Not many were in Akiyama's trade however.

Girls were scarce out here in deep space, and they required sensitive management.

"Sirs," a crewman's drowsy voice called from the *Ichikari*'s battered sensor station. "We're in position for the mineral scan."

"Well Hotaka, let's see if we can earn back some of your money," Akiyama said, smiling to himself as he turned to face the crewman. "Begin the scan."

Tapping a glowing button on his holoscreen, the crewman sent infrared pulses cascading through space. The sensor waves would reflect off of anything in their path, returning signatures that the mining computers would analyze for the telltale reflectivity of precious minerals. The scans provided some rare moments of excitement on the otherwise tedious voyage.

Hotaka's headache continued to intensify. He closed his eyes to try and dull the pain. The image of a vast, unending chain formed in his mind. Its glowing links reached out from the darkness of space to encircle the *Ichikari*, closing in like some ancient kraken clawing for his heart.

"Hotaka!" Akiyama shouted as he grabbed him by the shoulders and shook him awake. When he opened his eyes however, he saw a slender, reptilian image superimposed on the third mate's face. He pushed Akiyama away, shouting in horror as he stumbled backward.

Surprise filled Akiyama's face. The holoscreens behind him glimmered to life, showing the mineral scan's results. Unfortunately, the scans didn't find any minerals. Instead, they showed a sudden horde of angry red signatures closing on them fast.

"We are come," the otherworldly voice rasped in Hotaka's head.

"Sir, we're reading a swarm of unknown ships, heading straight for us!" the pale crewman said anxiously. The man turned in his chair to face his officers, his face full of fear. "They appear to be Bwain, sir."

Akiyama's eyes held Hotaka for a moment longer, narrowing with uncertainty.

"Hotaka, go wake the captain," he ordered, and then he turned back around and began barking orders at the crew. "Battle stations! Helm, get us back through The Gate as fast as you can. Weapons, launch the electromagnets."

While the crew around him fumbled to bring up the *Ichikari's* ancient defenses, Akiyama grew hideous and deformed before Hotaka's eyes. Horrifying images of reptilian skin and fleshy membranes hung from Akiyama's throat. The sight of it was more than he could bear. He turned quickly and tried to run, but he didn't make it very far before he collided with the sealed entrance of the bridge.

"No," Hotaka whispered to himself, half concussed from the impact. Sirens wailed through the old ship and pounded on his brain like a hammer. "No, no, no…"

"They're stationary sir," a crewman called, seemingly unaware of the hideous transformations that Hotaka was witnessing. "They appear to be waiting for something."

A keening wail escaped Hotaka's throat. He leaned back and smashed the back of his head into the metal of the bulkhead once more. The pain was a distant sensation however, as though it were being felt by someone else in another body.

"Get yourself together Hotaka, or I'll have you thrown out of the airlock!" the thing that had been Akiyama shouted to him.

Hotaka could only wail as the visions in his mind dragged him down into a void deeper than any nebula. His last sight was of Akiyama's distorted face as the third mate approached him, and his only thought was that he had to kill the abomination before it was too late. As he swung and clawed at the hideously deformed Akiyama, Hotaka knew that he'd already failed. The knot was getting tighter.

the speed of light. Warfare in space was a savage thing. It was a struggle of computing power and physics. Mass and acceleration equaled force, and Mephista always struck with as much force as she could. It was the only way her pain would ever stop.

Huge sections of the *Mercy*'s carbyne and steel hull vaporized under her projectile's kinetic force. Violent depressurization blasted debris into space as the ship's atmosphere erupted. The corvette's inducers kept firing for a few moments longer, tearing the *Mercy* into molten strips that tumbled through space like a deflated balloon.

Somehow, one of the *Mercy*'s crew had survived. The holoscreen automatically zoomed in on the body floating outside of the ship. Mephista watched as the survivor pinwheeled her arms and legs in a doomed attempt to swim through the vacuum. The crewman's mouth gaped, and her eyes sizzled as the heat of the Sword Belt's sun blistered her skin.

Mephista turned back to Statin. He was a good officer, snapping to attention to accept whatever discipline she chose to deliver. She could see the dying crewman reflected in his eyes.

"We're on our own out here Lieutenant," she commented as the *Mercy*'s survivor finally stilled and drifted with the rest of the debris. "That's a lesson you must never forget."

* * *

Above Belize City
Earth

From where his helicopter chopped the air high over the Drowned Cays, Major Atlas Carter watched the *Narcos* tear his life apart.

"*Dios!* Are we just gonna let 'em die?" a frustrated officer asked over the radio.

Atlas silenced the dissenter. "Our orders are to hold here and prevent a breakout," he reminded the junior officer. "Now keep the channel clear. That's an order."

The surface naval ships under Atlas' command floated underneath him like so many gray-colored, toy sledgehammers. Waves the color of the bloody sunrise pummeled the coast, while beyond the white buildings of Atlas' home city, everything burned. He zoomed in on his holoscreen, scanning the *Calle Boxer* district while bullets chipped away at the ramshackle buildings of his childhood. There was the *gimnasio* where he'd trained to fight; the dirt field where he'd played *fútbol* with a ball made out of coconut fiber, and the alley where a young *Narco* who'd called himself Cazador had first offered him mango liquor, and later became someone he'd thought was a friend.

Narcos. Sol meant the name as an insult, but the rebels were eager to adopt it. They were poor, but they lived outside of Sol's grip. Regardless of how they funded their independence, it was still something they could be proud of.

Cazador had risen from jungle exile and obscurity to become the most dangerous of men – a charismatic psychopath. He had seen potential in the young Atlas Carter, the child of a *Narco* leader, and had groomed him to infiltrate Sol's military. Cazador could be gentle, charming even. He'd looked out for Atlas after his father disappeared.

"The Navy's gonna be your ticket outta this place," Cazador had promised. "You're a smart kid, and you got a lotta potential. I mean, think about it. What's left for you here on Earth?"

Atlas knew that Cazador's motives were largely unspoken. A competent, loyal spy within the Sol navy would promptly alert him to any forthcoming Sol offensives against the *Narcos* and their bid to be free of the giant, stifling bureaucracy. The Bolivian's sweet talk was convincing, though in truth, Atlas had been in Cazador's pocket for years.

The younger, more naïve Atlas had taken Cazador's charity during hard times, and thus the crooked Bolivian thoroughly exploited him. Atlas was expected to wave through Cazador's secret shipments of weapons for the *Narcos*, on pain of being exposed as a spy, a fraud. He wouldn't be the first promising officer to take bribes, but Cazador could also prove that Atlas was complicit in the murder of a rival *Narco* gang leader who rashly opposed Cazador's authority. Atlas had been a puppet to this demagogue, who actually believed he could hold off the power of Sol's fleets, drones, and missiles, in order to bring about a popular revolution. He insisted there was enough drug money to keep them afloat, and Atlas had even believed it for a while, but neither of them had anticipated the newly-minted Major Carter's rapid promotion. Now, Atlas found himself in command of a giant fleet that was tasked with pushing the *Narcos* out of Belize, and out of Central America as a whole, once and for all.

He'd placed a secure call to Cazador in the days before the *Narcos*' bid to push Sol forces from Belize. "I'll try to keep the fleet from intervening, but you've got to get my wife and my family to safety."

"You can trust me," Cazador had told him. "You do your part, and I'll do mine. You have my word."

Carter stared intently at the zoomed-in image on the holoscreen he balanced before him in the whirling aircraft. He could now clearly see Cazador standing on the roof of Atlas' own house, holding a knife to his wife's throat. The man's brazen lies, his callous betrayal. What could Atlas do? Turn his helicopter on his brother officers and their men? He'd be cut down in seconds. He gritted his teeth in anguish as he watched, helpless to intervene.

It was as if, between the draconian thugs of Sol and the senseless, profit-crazed *Narcos* had made a list of the most important things in Atlas' life, and were now erasing them, line by line.

The house-to-house battle engulfed the street where almost all of his memories had been made. The *gimnasio* collapsed in a shower of cinderblock and timber as a tank that was grinding its way up the street stopped to blow it apart. The *Narcos* were fighting what remained of the

Belizean Army. Gunfire cut the palm trees in his garden into kindling, and as he watched, the tank's turret swiveled ominously toward his house. A Belizean soldier scurried across the brick street that had now been reduced to rubble, and raised an olive tube to his shoulder. The bazooka lanced wide of the tank that prowled *Calle Boxer*, and instead struck a transformer that exploded into a shower of spark and flame. Had they targeted his house specifically, knowing full well that he'd be watching?

Atlas had his binoculars fixed on the rooftop. Aida was struggling, kicking over the pots that held the tomato plants that they'd planted together. Her hair slashed back and forth as she wrestled against Cazador, but the struggle was pointless. Atlas had fought him in the ring more than once. The man was mad of little more than muscle and scar tissue, and possessed a strength that she was no match for.

With all the power of Sol at his command, he sat there watching it all play out, completely powerless. If he shot, Aida would die. If he didn't shoot, and if Aida survived, she would be captive to a regime with Cazador at its center.

"You bastard," he muttered darkly, forgetting that his mic was still open.

"Sorry Captain, I couldn't quite make that out. Say again?" a voice said in response.

"Belay that," Atlas replied quickly. His attention was entirely focused on *Calle Boxer*, despite the pillars of smoke rising from the city. In the distance, heavy storm clouds filled the horizon, and a strong, sudden wind buffeted the helicopter. Atlas momentarily lost sight of his house and its rooftop. When the pilot finally regained control, Atlas saw that his neighbor's house had been hit. It was now on fire and belching out massive clouds of thick smoke that further obscured his view as he struggled to make out the tussling figures of Aida and Cazador.

His radio crackled again as the disorganized Sol forces tried to understand the battle. Orbital assets, drones, and a host of aircraft were flying over Belize City, but the smoke and confusion were hampering Sol efforts to pin down the advancing *Narcos*. Unbelievably, against the might of a system-wide military machine, the grassroots rebels were carrying the day.

Atlas had orders to only engage if the rebels threatened to expand beyond the city's borders and into the jungle where the *Narcos* would be in their element. None of that mattered to him though in the face of what happened next. As he watched helplessly, the same tank that had blown apart his neighbor's house, tore his house asunder as well.

Less than a second after the tank fired, the house exploded in an orange wash of flame. Windows melted from their sashes, running in a molten drool across the brick, and the structural damage caused what was left of the house to collapse in on itself. The tank's smoking muzzle swept the street, searching for survivors, but no one moved in the rubble.

"Carter, report," General Kale demanded.

"General the...the situation here is..."

"Carter? I said report!" the general shouted into the radio.

Atlas' throat had clamped shut. His wife was dead, and the home they'd shared together had been utterly obliterated. "Sir, the situation here is..."

"Are there casualties, Carter? Civilians?"

"Yes sir. The *Narcos* are two-thirds through the city, and there's been heavy casualties."

"All right, I'm ordering an immediate withdrawal," Kale growled. "Units four and seven, provide rearguard. Carter, deploy your air assets for search and rescue operations. We lost this one. I want you back here in exactly three hours, and I want a full report on what went wrong."

* * *

The Ichikari

The ship lurched, throwing Kaylee into the embrace of the soft cushions. The futon was warm and comfortable, and Kaylee would have been more than happy to simply just sink into for a while, but before she knew what was happening, a pale hand seized her arm and pulled her upright.

She quashed the urge to resist, as she'd been forced to do a thousand times before. She'd detested this existence long before the arrival of whatever new chaos was overtaking the ship. Since being torn from her own bed back on Earth and forced into this life of remote servitude, she'd dreamed only of getting away. The constant pressure to behave as though these miners were her ideal men gnawed at her ceaselessly. They were uncultured nobodies, and having to falsely praise their fetishistic indulgences as though they were models of virtuous restraint made her physically ill. Perhaps all this sudden chaos would present her with some other options.

"It's those idiots on the bridge," Mirabelle said as she helped Kaylee to her feet. "They've been flying us around out here like we're a truckload of pigs headed off to market."

The cabin, which had been painted a deep purple color, was darker than usual. The shaking and lurching had knocked out several of the ceiling spotlights. They were designed to cast discreet shadows, ensuring some measure of privacy. They barely provided enough light as it was, but now that several of them were no longer working, she had to strain her eyes to see what was going on around her.

Kaylee steadied herself, then took a moment to smooth out the sensuous silk folds of her kimono, and then returned to tidying the cushions in the lounge's main area. The circular conversation pit was where the *Ichikari*'s crew came to lose themselves in drink and women before slipping off into the private cabins that ringed the large chamber. That's how things usually worked anyway, but it was already late in the afternoon, and as of yet there had been no customers.

"Something ain't right Mirabelle," Kaylee said, a worried expression clouding her face.

The madam's impeccably lined lips flinched. Her black hair was pulled severely back into a tight bun, and in her white makeup she could have been a doll. She was kind, at least in her own way, and she watched over her girls with a mixture of motherly attention and a drill sergeant's attention to detail.

"Kaylee dear, you're just too…oh, what's the word? Sour? Depressing? The men on this ship come to us so that they can lose themselves for a while – to forget their work and the frustrations of day to day life out here in space. It's difficult for them to do that however when the person they're with is lacking the appropriate level of empathy. This is why they choose the others over you."

"I don't care what they think," Kaylee said irritably. "When we get back to Earth, Akiyama's promised to release me, and my family's debt will be paid in full."

"That'll be a long time from now," Mirabelle noted. "You may not realize that a ship like the *Ichikari* carries enough supplies to be out here for years. We only have one antimatter charge for the Alcubierre drive to jump us back to Sol, so the captain's gonna make sure the holds are filled to bursting before we head back. You need to start thinking of this ship as your home, otherwise it's gonna be a very miserable existence for you."

"Is it yours?" Kaylee asked.

"My home is with my girls," she said as she chopped the last cushion with her hand, causing the back corners to stand up like ears against the settee.

Suddenly they heard the lounge door groan open. Kaylee took the position that Mirabelle had taught her, standing with her chest half turned to the door, and one pale leg slipping out from under her kimono. She hated that a provocative posture had become a reflex, but Mirabelle was a strict teacher. Kaylee had learned from the other girls that there were worse ways for a woman to be used on an illegal mining ship, so perhaps she should start trying to look on the brighter side of things.

She waited there like that for a few moments, but when no one came in, she glanced over and saw that the doorway was empty.

"Yes?" Mirabelle called. "Will you join us in relaxation?"

A few of the other girls gathered next to Kaylee. The girls kept ten percent of their fees, and whenever they managed to save enough, they could use that money to buy a few days off of themselves. There was often competition for customers, but other than Kaylee's friends Atsuko and Rika, none of the other girls would think twice about stepping in front of her, or of showing more of their bodies than she was.

They waited in silence for a few moments more, but still, no crewman entered.

Frowning, Mirabelle shuffled toward the door in the unsteady manner that she claimed the men of the crew desired.

"We have herbal tea and warm stones to soothe...," she said, but she stopped and gasped in horror as a bloody hand reached inside the doorway. Akiyama's sweating face and wild eyes came next. The man who'd taken Kaylee from her parents staggered into the lounge, trailing a wrenched ankle behind him. His jacket was blackened and torn, and his face was a mess of bruises and dried blood. He stumbled toward Mirabelle with the blade of a utility knife clenched in a red-stained fist.

"Girls!" Mirabelle called as she kept the futon between herself and Akiyama. "Girls, get your privacy screens up!"

The girls around Kaylee acted quickly, flying back to their bunks and triggering the metal dividers that rose to shield their chambers, just as Mirabelle had taught them, but Kaylee couldn't move. This was the man who'd promised to set her free. She needed to know what was happening to him.

"They're coming!" Akiyama howled.

"Akiyama-san, what's happening?" Kaylee demanded.

"Kaylee, call Yamada-san," Mirabelle said urgently. "He must come quickly!"

Akiyama's sweating face twisted toward Kaylee as he shuffled around the sitting area. Kaylee ran to the ancient communications console and slammed her hand down on the power switch.

"Mr. Yamada," she gasped to the computer. "Hurry, please."

The screen showed their overseer's quarters. The man who'd long been their protector from drunken miners wasn't alone. A growling officer was beating Yamada with a fusion pistol, cursing loudly and sweating profusely. The attacker's eyes widened suddenly, and then he staggered backward. Yamada's battered face filled the screen, and Kaylee's heart rose as she waved at him urgently.

"Mr. Yamada? Are you alright? We need, uhhh..."

The old man paid her no attention at all. Howling with rage, he rose quickly, spun himself around and stabbed his thumbs into his attacker's eye sockets.

Kaylee screamed and turned away from the console, but Akiyama had already reached her. A strange swelling distorted his face, and his eyes seemed almost distended as he breathed in heaving gasps.

"My head," Akiyama groaned. He paused, slumping against the wall. When Kaylee tried to rush past him, he seized the sheer silk of her collar with a sweating hand. She beat against his arm to try and break his grip, but Akiyama ignored the blows.

Chapter Two

"The Sword Belt": Great Orion Nebula planetary system (G-1726)
Gertie: Capitol planet (G-1726-3RT)

"You know we're innocent!" the prisoner screamed into the pure morning air. "Tannin, I know what you're doing! He's going to —"

One of Landfall's militiamen slammed the butt of his fusion rifle into the man's stomach. The prisoner bent over, gagging and trying to catch his breath while the colony doctor seized his hair, jerked his head over sideways, and injected a sedative into the side of the man's neck. The man would wake on Judgment, free to scream his accusations against Tannin's colonial government while scratching a living out of the desert with his fellow criminals. It was hard justice, but it was the only kind that worked in this backwater system. Administrator Tannin was almost as much an exile as the criminals on Judgment.

"This colony will prosper when we are rid of those who selfishly put their own needs first. And I intend to...," Tannin shouted to the farmers and colonists who'd come to view the proceedings, but his little speech was interrupted when a plasma bolt suddenly erupted from the end of the line of prisoners. Somehow free of their electro-cuffs, a man and a woman sprinted off down Landfall's main street toward the rolling grasslands that lay just outside of town.

"Sergeant-at-Arms!" Tannin bellowed. The instant the words left his mouth, Vartan shouted profanity laden orders at his men as his eyes fell to the dead militiaman who was laying in the street near where the prisoners had broken free. Without another word, several of his men abandoned their posts to chase after the escaping prisoners.

A part of Tannin wanted the idiot prisoners to turn a corner and duck into one of the squat, factory-printed houses that filled Landfall. The criminals would be found regardless, but at least the search would keep the people occupied. Fear was a powerful motivator, and it kept the colonists from asking too many questions.

Vartan's men aimed and fired at the escaping pair. The militiamen weren't really trained soldiers however, so most of their shots streaked harmlessly through the air overhead and off to each side, but one of the bolts of superheated plasma managed to hit the mark. It struck the fleeing man right in the center of his back and sent his smoldering corpse tumbling to the ground. The woman staggered on, clutching her thigh where another close shot had cauterized a chunk of her flesh. Her luck ran out however when Vartan stepped up and fired his pistol at the back of her head. An instant later her body fell to the ground in a heap, smoke rising from what was left of her skull.

"An excellent shot Vartan," Tannin noted dryly.

The militia leader glared at Tannin for a moment, his heavy eyebrows tightening in anger. "This is getting out of hand," he grumbled.

"We cannot let fear consume our population," the administrator replied. "It was a better death than starving on Judgment."

Grunting, Vartan turned away to supervise the remaining prisoners. One by one the doctor injected them with the sedatives, and the militia would then carry their limp bodies up the ramp to the waiting orbiter.

The space plane's nose was scored and darkened by years of atmospheric reentries on both Judgement and Gertie. It crouched on the landing pad beside Tannin's administrative compound. The compound itself was a white three-story building that gave Tannin a perfect view of the prison's ragged streets and ugly buildings that made up his colonial capital.

Danny Xiao, the lieutenant who jumped from the orbiter to join Tannin hid his own disfigurements much more deeply. The *Fate's Winds* officer had broad, full features, heavy brows, and puffed cheeks, but he couldn't have weighed more than a hundred and fifty pounds. It was as if when puberty came around, Danny couldn't decide whether to grow or shrink. His acne and the sprawl of his hair gave off the sullen appearance of youth, but his face was strangely expressionless. Even now, as Gertie's blushed sun filled the boy's face, he barely even squinted.

"Why do you think they resist?" Tannin asked when the lieutenant joined him.

"Why? Because they're innocent," he answered.

"*No one* is innocent," Tannin said in a hard, raspy voice. "Do I make myself understood?"

Vartan dragged the last of the surviving prisoners into the orbiter as a few curious colonists poked their heads cautiously out of their houses, hopeful that the latest unpleasantness had ended.

"Captain Green's last message to the *Fate's Winds* warned us that something wasn't right," Danny noted. "After that, the *Mercy* was blown to pieces. This isn't the time for heavy-handed tactics and rounding up starving colonists."

"What do you care?" Tannin asked with a cocky grin. "You'll be a rich man soon. Provided of course that you stick to our agreement."

Danny watched two of Vartan's men drag the corpses off the dirt road. "Oh, I will. But Captain Green's dead, and now Aric, his replacement, is gonna be watching me."

"Just do what I tell you. Your job is to make sure that array stays offline," Tannin reminded him. "Things are going to move very quickly from now on, but if you keep your eyes open and your mouth shut, you'll have nothing to worry about."

Danny glanced at him with the same dead look he'd given the prisoners.

"Or...I suppose I could always inform Acting Captain Aric of your activities," Tannin added smugly. "The requisitions. Your little plan for the security array. My payments of course would have to stop in that event, but what else can one do?"

"Don't worry, I'll keep funneling your material requisitions to Hal Yellowknife, and he'll keep honoring 'em, just like he always has. Dullards like him are good at taking orders, so don't worry about it," Danny said flatly. He took every chance to reassure Tannin that the risky agreement they'd made, was in fact going to hold. He depended on the corrupt bureaucrat a good deal more than was wise, but at this point he had little choice. "I can't even guess why you'd need all that stuff, but that's not what worries me."

"So just what *does* worry you Danny?" Tannin asked.

"Only that your checks clear," the officer called back over his shoulder as he turned and headed of back to his ship.

* * *

Hal Yellowknife craned his neck to look up at Gertie's pink sky. Even in the full afternoon sun, the light from Orion's nebula filled the air with a perpetual streak of salmon tint that still felt unnatural to him. He'd come here from Earth a full five years prior, but a man never forgets the skies of his home, and these skies were definitely different.

The music that swirled around him was ancient, but something about it comforted him. It was an ancient song from a simpler time, long before the first of the human colonies were built on the Earth's moon, and it seemed like an appropriate song to fill his brain with while he drank the day away.

"Clowns to the left of me, jokers to the right...," Hal sang in a hoarse, off-key voice.

"You have to do it, Hal," Victor interrupted from the stool beside him. "Tannin's ordering you to."

Victor Sheddick, the colony's Head of Agriculture, took a sip from his glass of nightcrawler, and rested the glass back on his thigh. Gertie's native night-ripening berries made a passable gin, and the liquor was one of the few escapes available to the colonists. The planet was beautiful, full of rolling grass-covered hills and clear blue waters, but the colony itself felt like it was sliding backward, and lately Hal had been much more interested in nightcrawler than in his job as Head of Colonial Construction. He'd come out to Gertie in order to punish himself for ruining one life back on Earth, so why not go two for two?

"I don't understand it Victor," Hal replied thoughtfully. "I mean, I've had the nanos and printing factories re-tasked for Sol Space Command's Emergency Requisition Usage for the better part of a year. The whole thing is ridiculous. They're still harvesting by hand on the south continent, and without excavating equipment we won't be able to get the irrigation canals on Judgment dug before summer. When are we gonna stop shipping everything we make into orbit, and start keeping some of it for ourselves?"

"Hal, the pirates just took out the *Mercy*," Victor said. "I think you can leave the agriculture decisions to me."

Hal swirled his glass. The sweet liquor numbed his lips and burned his throat as he swallowed, chipping away at the tension he'd felt building in him for the better part of a year.

"Tannin isn't the greatest at explaining himself, I'll grant you that, but he's doing his best. With all the pirate activity in this system..."

"Where the hell are all the parts goin'?" Hal asked. "That's what I wanna know. I'm tellin' ya Shed, Tannin's not bein' straight with us."

"Now, Hal, we all shipped out on the same boat, remember? We know some of it's being used for the intelligence array, and we did elect him fair and square to be the administrator. You think we elected a liar?" Victor asked.

Hal sighed. A cool breeze fluttered the grass at their feet, sweeping across the far hills like some kind of an invisible roller. The orderly rows of rectangular printing factories hummed with their quiet work in front of him. If he slipped on his special goggles, he'd see swarms of his microscopic robotic workers carrying granules of carbon and iron ore from the planet's incredibly mineral and ore-rich hills to each printing station. The nanobots deposited their haul in the factories' forges, where the raw materials were precisely fused into carbyne steel, microprocessors, or components for the intelligence array.

"That Sol-blasted array better be good for somethin' after all the work it's taken to put it together," Hal murmured bitterly. "I'll get started programming the designs for the parts tomorrow."

"That's all Tannin's asking."

"Listen Shed. I came here to build something, and I know you did too. Eventually we're gonna have to start thinkin' about ourselves."

Victor was a slender man, so when he tilted his head back to look up at the sky, his Adam's apple created a sharp wedge in his throat. "You know Hal, I've been stuck on this planet for five years now. That's more than long enough for me to know I've been marooned."

"Marooned?" Hal asked.

"Heh. Don't worry about it. It's just that there comes a point where you realize that all the dreams and idealism you once had may not be as realistic as you'd once hoped them to be," Victor said as he glanced over at Hal and gave him a tight-lipped smile. "Like I said, don't worry about it. Let's just get this stuff done for Tannin. The sooner we finish, the sooner you can get back to your normal production."

"Yeah, all right," Hal said with a heavy sigh. "You want another drink?"

"Sounds good," Victor said as they turned and headed back to the office together.

* * *

The Ichikari
Two AUs Outside The Gate

"Kaylee, I don't feel good. I feel sick," Atsuko whispered.

Kaylee anchored herself against a railing in the empty passageway and then helped Rika and Atsuko to come to rest beside her. A feverish dampness slicked Atsuko's narrow face, and her pupils had dilated so much that they'd nearly consumed her irises. She shivered under the translucence of her day robe, and she clutched at her waist as if trying to keep from vomiting.

"Wait here," Kaylee whispered. She pulled herself along the hallway's cold railings toward a flickering intersection. The distant shrieks of the crew slaughtering each other had faded, but she kept alert for the sounds of sweaty palms slapping against the bulkheads. In the past few hours, she'd become used to moving around in the zero-G environment, so she flipped herself around so that her legs could absorb the impact of her landing. The key was to move slowly, but it had been hard to fight the terror that threatened to overwhelm her.

She steadied herself against the last railing before the intersection, took a deep breath, and then peeked one eye around the corner. A body floated face-down in the hallway with a coagulated stream of blood dangling from its neck. She stifled a scream so that it came out as little more than a startled gasp, and then quickly pushed herself back toward her friends. The yellow arrow she'd been looking for was on the bulkhead just beyond the crewman.

"The life pods aren't much farther now," Kaylee told her friends when she returned. "Can you make it, Atsuko?"

The girl grimaced, and Kaylee saw a hint of the same strange look in her friend's eyes that she'd seen in Akiyama's eyes. The girl drew her robe more tightly around her waist, forced her hands to steady, and then nodded at her weakly.

"All right," Kaylee said, trying to sound confident. They pushed toward the intersection together, slowly floating toward the passageway's far wall.

"Close your eyes," Kaylee instructed when they neared the corner.

"But I can't see," Rika whispered. Panicked, the girl missed her grip on a handrail and bounced off the wall. She looked up, saw the corpse spinning toward her, and screamed.

"Rika!" Kaylee hissed. She settled against the wall next to Atsuko and kicked forward. "You need to be quiet. What if –"

Laughter bubbled from around the next corner. Rika's eyes widened. She slapped the corpse away from her, but the body stalled her momentum and left her stranded in midair.

Heavy panting grew louder from the other passageway. Kaylee's heart pounded.

"Hide!" Atsuko squealed.

The girl pushed to the opposite side and tried the door of a bay they'd just passed, but the hatch was sealed. The cabin next to Kaylee didn't open either when she spun and slapped its door control.

Boots and hands rang against the metal, the sounds growing ever closer, but then the laughter choked to a halt.

"I hear little feet," a man's voice slurred. "Are you trying to run?"

Atsuko curled into a whimpering ball against the bulkhead. Kaylee scanned the path they'd come, desperately looking for some means of escape, but there was none. The only other door in the corridor was welded shut, so there was no other choice. She grabbed Atsuko's ankle in a death grip, and then desperately tried to get enough leverage to push them back the way they'd come.

"We tried to run from the Bwain," the strained voice called to them. "That's what we did wrong. We shouldn't have been out here in the first place, but we were, and now we're paying the price."

"Kaylee, don't leave me!" Rika begged.

The other girl was trying to swim in the middle of the hallway, but with no momentum, and nothing to push against, she had no way to reach safety.

"It's the metal!" the voice cried as a hideous clanging began. "That's why you've got to go out this far. So many credits to be had, but I suppose none of that matters now, does it?"

A deformed shape floated into view behind Rika. The leering man had once been one of the *Ichikari*'s officers, but now the sight of him was simply terrifying. Lubricant, sweat, and blood greased his uniform. A plasma cutter, and a giant, gore-slicked knife dangled from his waist. Strips of flesh and hair hung from his scalp as if he'd dug his fingers into his skull in an attempt to quiet whatever was happening to his mind.

Hotaka stopped himself against a railing, tilting his head to watch Rika like some sort of a blood covered gargoyle.

"Nothing matters now, but that's all right. You girls can comfort me," he said with an insane look in his eyes as he lunged toward the helpless girl.

"Kaylee!" Rika screamed.

Kaylee forced Atsuko to wrap her fingers around the cold railing, and then with every bit of strength that she had, she sprang toward the space where the man would intersect Rika. Unfortunately, she was too late. The officer closed his eyes and pressed Rika against his bloody cheek as she floated screaming into his grasp.

Kaylee looked behind her helplessly as her momentum carried her toward the life pod. The younger girl had pulled herself to a stop, and her face crippled with fear.

"I can feel the others now," Rika said as she grimaced and reached up to hold the sides of her head. "There's so many of them. So much anger. They'll never stop. Never…"

"No!" Kaylee screamed.

Rika blinked her eyes hard and summoned the last vestiges control she still had over her own mind.

"Kaylee, go! Take the pod and get outta here. I'll try to keep them away," she said, the fear obvious in her voice as she waved a terrified goodbye and then turned to face the onrushing crew.

Kaylee hesitated for just a moment, but then she pushed herself the last few meters and banged into the life pod's access hatch. Reaching out her fist, she hammered the button to open the door, and then pulled herself inside. The hatch began to close as soon as she passed its electronic eye, and she turned back just in time to see the first of the crew reach her valiant young friend before the bulkhead sealed itself.

Her stomach felt as though it were going to fall through the floor as she pulled herself down into the seat. Rika had sacrificed herself so that she could escape. It was a debt that she'd never have the chance to repay.

Quickly she locked herself into the chair's restraints, tapped the launch controls, and then squeezed her eyes shut as the pod's boosters fired. In that moment, she knew what had happened to the crew. An image suddenly filled her mind that was both vivid and nauseating. It was an unwelcome peek into the collective mind to which they were now eternally bound. She visualized an endless knot, coiling into infinity. It was some sort of a symbol, or an icon, or even the center of power itself. She really didn't know, but the image assailed her painfully, and she screamed as her life pod hurled her into the endless void of space.

Chapter Three

Personal Logbook: Captain Atlas Carter
Entry 4 - Exiting Earth's orbit

So, they're sending me away.

General Kale is to be executed for his utter failure at Belize City. I told the inquiry I thought his orders were to stand by and provide search and rescue, not to dive into the fighting. I intimated that he was bribed by the *Narcos* to belay or confuse commands to engage. More lies to save my own skin, which resulted in yet another needless death.

After the insanity was over, I tried to find the rest of my family, but I couldn't find them anywhere. The city is free from the dominance of Sol, but it's certainly not better off. Cazador is now the Prime Deputy in New Belize, and I'm sure he's already got plans on how he's going to someday climb to the top rung of the ladder, so he can assume the role of Executor. I wonder who came up with that title? In any case, it seems to be a fitting title for the "elected" leader of that damned, dying city.

I felt sure he'd send men after me, so I decided to put some distance between Cazador and myself. The Navy's been helping me with that, albeit inadvertently. I've been reassigned. With my family presumed dead in the carnage of Belize City, the advocate that had been assigned to my case was able to make a convincing argument in my defense, and also that leniency should be shown since I'd just lost my entire family in the fighting. In the end, the high command decided not to punish me for anything more than my own inaction and stupidity. I was demoted and shipped off to a new assignment far away, where they probably figured I couldn't do much harm. There were some lingering suspicions that perhaps there'd been some treason at play. They couldn't prove it of course, but it was enough to guarantee that they'll never allow another *Narcos* into their elite ranks, no matter how high their scores are on the entrance exams. It was just too much of a risk.

To be honest, I thought long and hard about telling the whole truth and taking my place next to Kale out there on the receiving end of a firing squad. The advocate knew just how compromised I'd been, and how I'd been little more than an actor trying miserably to play two roles at once, but he told me to just keep my mouth shut and accept the reassignment. After all, he reasoned, I can't atone for my mistakes if I'm dead.

SSC is sending me to G-1726. The database says it's a remote system with one colony planet named Gertie, and a prison planet called Judgement, that seems far more appropriately named. From the mission reports, it sounds like both planets are surrounded by pirates, but not much else. Maybe this post will be a blessing in the long run. The smugglers probably haven't met an officer who doesn't care if he lives or dies, so who knows? Maybe I'll have a chance to do some good there, or at least a lot more good than I ever did back on Earth.

I look at the deep black of space, and I see your face reflected in the viewports. I wake up in the transport ship's tiny cabin, and I believe for a moment I'm in our bed. What a tiny, meaningless world I lived in; one that could be blown to bits in an instant. I'd do anything to go back there and have it be like it was before. I'd even become a Cazador's slave if that's what it took to get my old life back, but it's all beyond my reach now. Sometimes we just can't control what happens to us in life, so we have to learn to live with it, no matter how painful it is.

Why, Aida? Why did this have to happen? Wherever you are now, can you see into Cazador's soul? What did he gain from murdering the only woman I ever loved? I mean, I was following his plan. Did he really think I'd unleash the fleet on his rebels when your life was literally in his hands?

I doubt I'll ever make it back to Earth, but I swear to God, if I ever do, I'll find him, and I'll make him pay for what he's done.

I think maybe the SSC was right after all. Life, not death, is the worst punishment they could give me.

* * *

Fate's Winds
Four AUs from The Gate

Boots pounded down the cargo gangway toward where Lieutenant Danny Xiao, the *Fate's Winds'* supply officer was crouched down in front of the open mirror case. He dropped the micro chisel he'd been using on the satellite component, kicked the tool under a storage rack to hide it, and then slammed the case closed just as Pandith and Granger appeared from the science lab.

The two were close friends but also a study in opposites. Pandith, their environmental engineer, was a lighter-skinned Malaysian with wide, thoughtful eyes, and rather mild demeanor. Granger, the ship's science officer, was a tall, gangly man with a shaggy head of hair that nearly brushed against the top of the corridor.

Of the two, Danny only had strong feelings about Granger, who seemed to be endlessly nosy. Granger's curiosity, unbeknownst to him, often threatened to expose the arrangement he had with Tannin, which was why he hated to see the science officer approach with a question on his unshaven face.

"Danny?" Granger called out to him with a surprised look on his face. You should have left twenty minutes ago. The tests are about to begin."

"It's Lieutenant Xiao to you Mr. Granger," Danny barked. "Don't let your discipline slacken just because we have an *acting* captain now."

"Oh, uhhh...sorry about that Danny. Errr...Lieutenant Xiao," the science officer stammered. Beside him, Pandith simply blinked and remained silent. They had met at the prestigious SSC Science School. Granger had received a Sol Scholarship, which was quite an honor for a poor boy from the outskirts. In contrast, Pandith came from a wealthy family, which was the more traditional way of gaining admittance into the school. He could have had a commission anywhere, but Pandith chose to go with

Granger. They were the only two crew members who knew each other before boarding the ship to the Sword Belt. The rest had all been strangers.

"Where are you two going in such a hurry anyway?" Danny asked.

"We've had a serious breakthrough!" Granger replied excitedly. "The probes have found something!"

"Those little things?   I didn't think they'd even work."

"They did, and thanks for helping with the parts by the way. I need to tell Aric."

Danny almost let the pair pass through his supply hold but reconsidered, staying in the middle of the gangway as Granger inched forward.

"What do you need to tell Aric exactly?" he asked, his eyes narrowing as his voice suddenly turned cold. Glancing down at the case below him, he saw that the chisel's handle was just visible under the edge of the storage rack.

"You know, I'm not really sure exactly. We found Majorana particle readings out beyond The Gate, and we thought he should know."

"Pirates have just destroyed our sister ship, and you think it's a good idea to bother the acting captain with your hobby experiments?" Danny growled.

"But Danny, something might be out there!" Granger said with a hurt look, and an almost pleading tone to this voice.

Danny glanced at the open crates of tools, the jumbled cables, and the spare parts that had been haphazardly tossed everywhere. The *Fate's Winds* was a newer ship, but the crew's malaise had hurt their discipline, and Aric himself was overmatched as its acting captain. It was the perfect setup to exploit when Tannin needed Danny to lose inventory, or to report fake repairs. Where all those components went after they were printed by Gertie's factories, Danny didn't know, and more to the point he didn't care. The money was all that mattered.

"Danny, is this about Aric's promotion?" Granger asked. "He's a good officer. What happened to Captain Green and the *Mercy* wasn't his fault."

"Of course it wasn't, but if things were normal, Aric would be down here on Level Two with us helping us maintain things. We can barely keep up as it is."

Pandith blinked in discomfort, and then turned to Granger.

"I'm just saying that Aric's got a lot on his mind right now, and you and I both know how he feels about Captain Green's last message," Danny said.

Granger's eyes fell on the crate next to Danny, and he gave a slight nod of his head as he let out a heavy sigh.

"You're right Danny. We'll wait until it's a better time."

"That's good thinking, gentlemen," Danny said with an imperceptible sigh of relief. "We all need to help each other out on this boat."

Danny stood in the gangway for a moment longer, watching the two specialists pick their way back to their stations at the rear of the ship. Once they were gone, he stooped down to retrieve the chisel, and then picked up the crate before hurrying off to the airlock with it as fast as he could. He was already dangerously late, and if he didn't disable that damned security array before it fired successfully, Tannin would skin his chicken.

It was a silly expression, but it was something from his childhood that brought back fond memories. It was a saying his mother often used that made both him and his sister laugh in their childish innocence, but that was before the Bwain had come and crippled his sister's mind. Before she stopped laughing for good.

The truth was, if Tannin's money stopped, Danny couldn't afford his sister's life support. She was his only family, so if he had to lie to Granger and Pandith, and everyone else on the ship for that matter, that's what he would do. His family mattered to him more than anything else in this Sol-blasted system.

* * *

"Magnetic containment is holding steady," Ensign Bryon Purcell called from his weapons station on the *Fate's Winds'* bridge. "We're at a hundred percent gain, and ready to torch whatever gets in our way."

Purcell was practically dancing with excitement. A red-headed streak of muscular enthusiasm, the weapons officer often seemed to be the only crewman who actually enjoyed being assigned to the Sword Belt.

"The mirrors all appear to be in alignment Captain," the navigation officer reported.

"They *appear* to be, or they are?" Aric asked, not happy about the ambiguous nature of the report.

Danielle Hoff turned her smoldering eyes to him. She was beautiful, with shiny brown hair falling to her slender shoulders, and hips that swelled just right against her flight suit. Danielle was drawn to power, but command didn't come easy to Aric. He preferred to remain in engineering, solving the problems of Alcubierre drive's antimatter consumption, or optimizing the onboard fusion reactor's efficiency. He was as a natural at being a science officer as he was unnatural being a captain.

Captain Green's last warning of something rotten in the Sword Belt echoed constantly in his mind, and he had no idea what to do with it. Aric found the pressure to fix every little problem, and to do so with a crew that was already more or less falling apart, a nearly impossible task.

"Well how am I supposed to know?" Danielle asked snarkily as she turned back to her console to look over the readings once again. "Isn't that Danny's department?"

"Ms. Hoff, please watch your tone," Aric replied evenly. She glanced back at him for a moment, cocked her eyebrow at him, and then turned back around to resume her duties.

Aric sighed as he enlarged the holoscreens in front of him to show the entirety of the security array. He stared at it for a moment, and was awestruck by the magnitude of it all. The Orion Nebula's brilliant rainbow of gas and dust was millions of times larger than the Earth. Against the cloud's background, the array's fifty-meter-tall mirrors looked like white little pinpricks. The laser array would allow a single set of instruments to monitor all of the activities and communications in the Sword Belt, and in doing so, would hopefully reveal the hidden pirates that had been a constant plague upon the system, and the *Fate's Winds* in particular. Now if the crew could just get the Sol-blasted thing working…

Movement on the display caught Aric's attention, and he squinted at the sight of a small black figure jetting away from the laser closest to The Gate. Aric tapped the figure in the display, though he didn't need the computer's extrapolation to tell him who was out there.

"Danny, your orders were to be back on your station an hour ago," Aric said, his voice breaking into the quiet of the bridge more loudly than he had intended. "What the hell are you still doin' out there?"

The transmitter implanted into Aric's jaw captured his voice and routed it to its intended target. A few seconds later, Danny's response crackled through Aric's cochlear implant.

"Someone really ought to talk to engineering about these Casimir inducers," the supply officer's radiation-garbled voice responded. "It's great they don't need fuel or anything since it makes my job a lot easier, but they're slow as all hell."

"You and I both know the suit's speed. If you'd left when you were supposed to, you'd be back on board by now. Explain yourself," Aric demanded.

"I was admiring the view, *Lieutenant*."

"I'm warning you Danny, don't push me. I've got enough crap to deal with without having to deal with yours as well."

"Ok, fine. One of the mirrors was damaged by micrometeorites. I thought I had time to swap it, but, it turns out I was wrong,"

"On whose orders?" Aric asked.

The channel groaned with shifting static. For a moment, Aric thought Danny would finally abandon the sullen cockiness that he'd worn like a cloak ever since he'd come on board. He was quickly becoming impossible to work with, and Aric wondered if Captain Green hadn't been referring to the *Fate's Winds'* own supply officer when he'd transmitted his final warning.

"Is this gonna be another pissing contest Aric?" Danny asked, his voice tinged with sarcasm. "Because it's gonna be really awkward doing that in this suit."

Aric watched the tiny figure shielded in ultra-black carbyne mesh for a moment, and a thought came to him. Danny looked like the tiniest star in an ocean of giants as his EVO suit shimmered with nanobots. The microscopic machines drew power from the trillions of photons crashing into them every second, and they had the ability to instantly repair any damage to the fabric. They were an engineering triumph, a massive technological leap forward that had saved countless lives.

Left to an engineer like Aric, problems quickly became reduced to their simplest components. The solution to a faulty fuse was to simply take it out.

"They're coming, but I'll spare you from having to see it," he said, smiling as he pushing her down to her knees.

Blood varnished Akiyama's teeth as his knife rose, but then he gagged, and blood began to pour from his mouth. He let out a gurgling cough, and the blade suddenly fell from his hand as a second, fatal stab under his rib cage pushed the last breath from him.

He fell to his knees, and then toppled over onto the floor, shuddering in his death throes. Mirabelle stood above him as he gurgled once more, and then finally fell silent. She held the bloodied knife with unconcealed defiance, but her face remained clenched in the impassive mask of the geisha.

* * *

Kaylee and the other girls dragged Akiyama's body out into the corridor, sealed the door of the lounge, and then waited while the ship descended into madness. At first they heard a rush of orders and announcements through the ship's intercom, and for a while it seemed as though they might be getting things back under control, but by the time the evening rolled around, all they heard from the ship's comm system were the screams of what was left of the crew. Finally, Mirabelle turned off the intercom so they wouldn't have to listen to it anymore.

"I told you something was wrong," Kaylee said.

Mirabelle's calm demeanor was showing signs of strain. "This is not the time," she snapped.

"We could take the life pods and get ourselves off the ship," Kaylee offered.

Mirabelle had tucked the cleaned knife she'd killed Akiyama with into her obi. Its handle jabbed at Kaylee when the madam pulled her close.

"The life pods are at the other end of the ship. How would you suggest I keep you and the others safe along the way with what's happening out there?" she asked. She looked into Kaylee's eyes for a moment, and then released her.

In her usual, almost motherly fashion, she smoothed the fabric of Kaylee's blue obi, and tried to smile at her reassuringly. Kaylee could see the wrinkles of age in the white makeup at the corners of her madam's eyes.

"We're not all as brave as you are Kaylee," Mirabelle sighed as she straightened and padded across the tatami toward Rika, who was trying to make them all some tea, though she was finding it difficult with her hands trembling the way they were.

"No, but we need not be slaves to our fears either," Kaylee said firmly. Mirabelle looked at her for a moment, and then she nodded slightly as she considered the words.

They sat in a circle and drank Rika's green tea while the corridors outside echoed with the howls of crewmembers that had been affected by whatever was happening to them. They all seemed to have gone out of their minds for some reason, but there was no clue as to what had caused it.

"It's getting colder," Atsuko noted listlessly. She was the youngest, and at times, the most terrified of their little group. Kaylee sat with her, and the two warmed their hands on a shared mug of tea.

"The ship's heaters always were useless, but hopefully it'll all be over soon," Mirabelle said as she started handing out blankets to the girls.

"And what if it isn't?" Kaylee asked. "We'll all die here."

Mirabelle considered Kaylee for a moment with calm eyes. The madam seemed about to say something, but instead curled her legs on the futon. "Why don't we tell each other a story from back home?" she suggested with a forced brightness. "That's always a good…"

"My head hurts," Atsuko interrupted as a pained look took over her features and she reached up to massage her temples.

"You're probably just tired. Why don't you lie down and rest for a bit?" the madam suggested.

Metal clanged against the lounge's doors, while Atsuko pressed her palm against her forehead, the look of pain on her face intensifying. The other girls all scattered to their cabins in an attempt to hide from whatever danger was coming, though no door would be a match for a cutting torch. Not for long anyway. Atsuko was unable to move, so Kaylee stayed with her terrified friend, determined to protect her no matter what happened.

The banging continued for a time before eventually slackening into a raking squeal. A few moments passed before one final, desperate sob could be heard from the other side of the door, and then the corridor fell silent once more.

"There now girls, you see? We're safe in here. Why don't we prepare some...," Mirabelle said, but she was interrupted when the deck suddenly shook under their feet, throwing Kaylee roughly to the floor. A distant clanking sound was heard, and her body lifted from the deck. The other girls' hair floated above their heads like grass in water, and orbs of tea slipped from their mugs in shimmering globes. The ship's artificial gravity had failed.

Fighting the nausea that threatened to overtake her, Kaylee stretched out her hand and caught hold of a low-sitting table in the middle of the lounge in order to stop her momentum. She stared at the girls around her, their faces a mixture of despair, and acceptance of their fate. No matter what happened out there in the passageways, Kaylee would not wait for another like Akiyama to come for her.

Flipping her legs so that she was standing on the table, she squatted down and then launched herself toward the lounge's exit. Mirabelle grabbed her just as she left the table however, and dragged her back.

"Child, do you have any idea what's going on out there? What'll happen to you?" Mirabelle hissed into her ear. The madam had found an overhead handhold, and the other girls watched the pair with a mixture of fear and curiosity. "I can't keep you safe if you leave here. I can't keep any of us safe if the crew knows we're still alive."

Kaylee gazed back at the lounge. "I'd rather die free than live in this prison," she said determinedly.

Mirabelle's eyes slipped shut. The wall she had built against the *Ichikari*'s unending sadness was, threatening to burst, but only a single tear escaped, trickling slowly down her white-painted cheek.

"Then take this," she said, handing Kaylee the knife she pulled from her obi. Once the knife had been handed over, she pushed against the ceiling and floated back to where the other girls watched with stricken eyes. Kaylee turned away from them, unable to bear their expressions, and after resetting herself on the table, she launched forward toward the hatch once more.

"Wait!" Mirabelle called just before Kaylee reached the door. Kaylee turned to see her madam floating in the zero-G, her shimmering white robes swirling like clouds that any man on board, under normal circumstances, would have mistaken for a vision from heaven.

"I have to go. Please try to understand," Kaylee practically pleaded.

"I know child, but please...take Rika and Atsuko with you," Mirabelle urged. Kaylee's friends had already risen from the lounge and were pushing awkwardly toward her. Taking on an air of formality, she continued, "And if you find food, or survivors who might still be able to help the girls, please think of us."

"I will. Listen...I just wanna say thanks. I mean, for everything," she said sincerely. Mirabelle knew exactly what she meant, and nodded her acknowledgement.

As soon as Rika and Atsuko floated over and grabbed a hold of her robes, Kaylee turned and released the seal on the hatch. As soon as it was open, she grabbed a rail and pulled herself out into the flickering passageway, with Rika and Atsuko in tow.

Rika screamed as her foot brushed against the body of a dead crewmen that was just barely floating off of the deck. The body bounced off the deck and then floated up a bit as it moved along with them. Kaylee threw her hand over Rika's mouth and gave her a look that said in no uncertain terms that she was not to scream again. Their only chance of survival was to be able to move silently, and undetected.

Rika nodded that she understood, so Kaylee pulled her hand back and grabbed another rail that was attached to the far wall. Looking both ways, she turned them to the left and then pushed with as much strength as she possibly could. They were now free on a ship with no gravity, and with a crew that had lost its collective mind. Unfortunately for her, terror had just begun.

"You came to me," he sobbed as he wrapped his arms around her tightly.

"Leave me alone!" Rika cried. She struggled, but the man was too strong for her.

"I'm coming, Rika!" Kaylee called to her. The man looked up and smiled as the girl hurtled toward them.

"Oh, another one," he said, leering at her lustfully. He held out a bloodstained palm while Rika twisted under his opposite arm. "Come to me girls. We'll talk to the voices together."

Kaylee pulled her feet in front of her and drove them into the man's chest, trying to knock him backward, but the officer seized her calf and her momentum sent the three of them tumbling against the far bulkhead. Rika bit into the man's thick forearm after the impact, trying to get herself free, but he didn't seem to notice the pain, even in the slightest. The man pulled Kaylee closer and closer until she floated mere inches from his face. She tried to kick loose from his grip, but he only laughed with demented glee, spraying warm spittle across her face.

"We're all bound together," he slurred. "Did you know that?"

"What's wrong with you?" Kaylee demanded as she struggled.

At this, the man's face quivered. Behind his wisped beard and swollen nose, she saw a strange reflection in his eyes, as if two sets of pupils were glaring at her.

"Everything," he muttered, and suddenly his mouth opened in an unhinged scream. A white blade of flame burst through Hotaka's chest. His eyes bulged and he released Rika and Kaylee to beat at the blinding heat that cut through him. The plasma torch sliced off his fingers, carving up from his sternum as his scream faded to a pained gasp. Finally, the torch withdrew. The man shuddered and froze before them. Kaylee found a handrail, anchored herself, and kicked at the dead man to push him away down the corridor.

As the corpse slipped away, she gasped. Atsuko was floating behind him, holding the plasma torch that had been clamped to the dead officer's belt.

"Oh my god, thank you so much!" Rika whispered.

"We need to hurry," Kaylee insisted. "Someone else is bound to have heard all that noise."

Instead of turning to follow the yellow arrows to the life pods, Atsuko blinked and shuddered. Kaylee's eyes widened as the girl's face twisted toward her, and she recognized the same manic look that had consumed Akiyama and the other officer.

"No, Atsuko...please...no," she moaned in despair.

"*We should not have seen, but we did*," Atsuko's strained voice intoned. The torch in her hand blurred to life once more, spitting out a foot-long spike of plasma. She lunged forward, trying to slash at them wildly. Rika screamed, scrambling backward along the wall. "*We're not worthy of seeing. We're not worthy of anything.*"

Kaylee gathered her legs under her as Atsuko drew parallel to her in the corridor, then rocketed forward. She tackled Atsuko, driving the girl's skull into the bulkhead, leaving her dazed and floating freely in an uncontrolled manner. Her eyes fluttered for just an instant, and then closed as the plasma cutter slipped from her hand.

Kaylee seized Rika's arm, turned them both around, and pulled as hard as she could in the direction of the life pods. Behind her, Atsuko's torch spun into the hull, slicing through the metal as it ripped opened seams into the black void of space. Alarms squalled, and Kaylee pulled them faster and faster along the handrails as the whistling scream of the air escaping through the hull filled her ears.

"What's happening Kaylee?" Rika sobbed. "What happened to Atsuko?"

Kaylee turned the corner, halting just long enough to slam down the control that sealed the pressure doors behind her. As the passageway closed, her last glimpse of Atsuko was of her friend dying from the depressurization. She'd regained consciousness, and was struggling as her stricken eyes pleaded with Kaylee for release from whatever had overtaken to her. Her death would be her freedom, and it terrified Kaylee to think that death may end up being their only escape as well.

* * *

The corridor widened and split off at two distinct angles, with lifeboat arrows pointing the way past the large windows on each side. Behind the windows was the engineering station, the only obstacle that lay between them and the life pods that were just beyond. Inside the engineering control room, a dozen men and women were tearing frantically at the ship's controls.

"Why are they hurting the ship?" Rika whispered.

"I don't know," Kaylee whispered breathily into Rika's ear. "Come on. We need to be careful."

Kaylee pulled herself along beneath the handrail until she was nearly crawling along the deck, with Rika following along behind her in a similar fashion. From this angle, they were shielded from view of the crew in the engineering room, so they moved forward as quickly and silently as they could down the left-hand passage, both of them breathing in shallow, silent breaths, as though it would help to conceal their passing.

"Will not work!" a muffled voice cried from the other side of the windows.

"Make go faster!" another voice shouted. It was almost as if something was controlling the minds of the crew.

Kaylee tensed at each scream and crash above her, and her mind suddenly flashed to Mirabelle and the other girls. She hoped they'd survive this whole ordeal, but she knew better. No one would be able to live through whatever madness had struck the *Ichikari*. The only hope was escape.

Once they'd cleared the engineering room's windows, she kicked hard against the bulkhead to propel herself toward the life pods. She could just see the bays glimmering in front of her, but when she glanced back to check on Rika's progress, a sudden chill ran down her spine. The girl had gone off at an awkward angle, and was pressing her hands against her head as she fumbled through the air.

"Rika!" Kaylee whispered.

"Kaylee, my head hurts," Rika cried in a strained voice.

Kaylee grabbed a hold of a rail once she'd reached the life pod station, and then she reached out to help Rika, who'd finally managed to catch up with her after righting herself. Her stomach twisted at the sight of sweat crawling down Rika's terrified forehead. The same thing that had happened to the crew was coming for each of them.

"It's okay Rika," Kaylee sighed with relief. "We made it. I'm gonna get you outta here."

Tears bubbled in the corners of Rika's eyes. "No...," she murmured. "No, they're all gone."

"What? Who's gone?" Kaylee asked. She looked deep into Rika's eyes, and saw that her pupils were already starting to dilate, just as Atsuko's had before whatever this thing was took over her mind.

She turned away and pounded her fist against the bulkhead wall, letting out the sob she'd been holding since she'd first seen Akiyama. Red indicator lights were flashing next to every pod. The launchers were all empty.

"I don't want to end up like Atsuko," Rika said. She was trying to sound brave, but nothing could hide the fear that had taken over.

"I won't let that happen. There are more pods on the other side. Come on!"

With Rika's sweating hand in hers, Kaylee pushed back toward the engineering station, but she attempted to move too quickly and misjudged her trajectory. They floated past the distorted faces of the engineering crew, who snarled at the sight of the two girls on the other side of the glass.

"Hurry!" Rika cried as she squirmed out of Kaylee's grasp. Both girls pulled themselves along the handrails as fast as their arms could move, flying past the entrance of the engineering bay just as the wailing, deranged crew were about to come piling out through the door after them.

The engineers didn't even try to control their momentum in their wild dash toward the girls, so they ended up slamming into the far wall, opposite the door. The ones at the back of the pile scrambled off quickly, reaching for anything they could grab to regain control of their movement, so they could chase after the girls. They were nothing more than animals at this point. Puppets whose strings were being pulled by whatever power had seized their minds.

Kaylee breathed a sigh of relief when they reached the other bay and saw that several of the ship's life pods remained in their docks, each bathed in a welcoming green light. Quickly, she aimed herself and pushed free of the wall.

"Kaylee!" Rika screamed beside her.

One pod was big enough to fit them both, and now the key to their freedom lay just a few meters away.

"Rika?" Kaylee said as she glanced back to look at her friend.

"It's happening," Rika groaned.

"Ensign Purcell, begin the initial test of the security array," Aric ordered.

Bryon turned to him, stunned at what he'd just heard.

"Ummm...sir?" the weapons officer asked.

"Yes Ensign?"

"Sir, uhhh...Danny's still out there."

"Is Lieutenant Xiao in the line of fire for any of the lasers?" Aric asked.

"Uh, no sir, but the radiation could kill him!"

"Hey, Aric," Danny's voice sounded in Aric's ear. "Aric, what are you doin'?"

"It's *Captain Keith* to you Danny. You'd best remember that. Byron, begin the test."

Bryon swallowed hard, and then tapped his console obediently.

On the holoscreens, a brilliant blue beam of supercharged plasma shot from the corvette's underbelly to the first mirror in front of the ship. The vast distances between the mirrors meant that Aric could track the beam's progress on the holoscreens with his naked eye. The laser bounced to the second mirror in geostationary orbit above Gertie, then the third above Judgment, and onward until a shimmering arc hung in space between the nebula and the Sword Belt. As the laser turned at the last gas giant in the system and began its home-stretch toward The Gate, Aric stood from his chair, and the elation he was feeling at what he was seeing quickly wiped away the anger he'd been feeling toward Danny.

"Oh my god, it's gonna work! It's really gonna work!" he exclaimed.

But as the beam struck the final mirror that Danny had been working on, the one that would close the loop's circuit and render the array's power supply self-sustaining, it knocked the final mirror out of alignment. The plasma beam fractured into hundreds of comet streaks, and the sensor ring fell dark. The test was a catastrophic failure.

Aric watched the sudden debacle, and the anger he'd been feeling quickly returned tenfold. "Oh my God, I swear I'm gonna kill him!" Aric growled, his hands shaking with rage as he headed for the airlock.

* * *

"What the hell were you tryin' to do out there?" Danny barked as he pulled off his helmet. Sweat plastered Danny's black hair across his wide forehead. He threw his helmet at Aric as he emerged from the airlock. "You could have gotten me killed!"

"What did you do to the mirror Danny?" Aric asked pointedly.

"I didn't do anything!"

"I personally checked that mirror's orientation and diagnostics this morning. This is the fifth time the array has failed and each time you've been working on the satellites. Now answer me. What the hell did you do to that mirror?"

"Check the video logs," Danny said as he tried to push his suited shoulder past Aric and into the ready room, but Aric held his ground, preventing Danny from passing. "I didn't do anything. It was probably your terrible array design that screwed the whole thing up."

"I'm the captain of this ship; a promotion for which you were passed over, whether you like it or not," Aric said through gritted teeth. "If you insult me one more time..."

"I don't really care who you think you are, or what you think I am," Danny said flatly.

"Tell me what you were doing on the satellite!"

"I don't have to listen to this," Danny said as he tried to push past once more. "I'm the one who keeps this piece-of-junk boat running. Who else would spend their time tracking down parts for the quantum vacuum, or carbyne patches to fix up the hull when it gets damaged?"

Aric pushed him back, and his back stiffened as he met Aric's steady gaze.

"You don't want to be touchin' me, Aric," Danny warned, "Believe me, you really don't, especially after you tried to kill me out there."

"You know Danny, when I figure out what you're doin' and what your game is, I'm gonna put you in deep freeze. That's a promise."

"So is this," Danny said as his gloved fist smashed into Aric's eye. The acting captain stumbled back into the corridor, tripping on the hatch's threshold as he fell down hard onto the deck. Still sheathed in a suit that was impervious to everything but meteorite impacts and fusion lasers, Danny loomed over his captain.

"Who got passed over now, bitch?" he sneered, raising his fist again.

"Hey!" Pandith called as he pounded down the corridor and tried to step between the two.

"Don't you have some piss to turn into wine Pandith?" Danny sneered as he pushed the specialist out of his way. From where he lay on the deck, Aric drew his fusion pistol and held it on his supply officer. Danny lowered his fists, but the snarl remained on his face while Aric accepted Pandith's help and got to his feet.

"I don't know what the hell you've been up to Danny but you've just struck a superior officer. Effective immediately, I'm placing you under arrest. Pandith, get the sedatives," Aric ordered as he held his sleeve against his split eyebrow with his free hand.

Fear rippled across Danny's face. *Sedatives.* The recognition of what he'd just done began to strike home.

"Come on Aric, you gotta be kidding! No! No, wait Aric! Wait! I'm sorry!"

"Save it for your new neighbors on Judgment," Aric snapped. "Now, let's go."

* * *

SSC Messenger Vessel Mosquito
Entering orbit around Gertie

Falconi felt the claustrophobia that had been squeezing his chest fall away. No matter how many times he watched the Alcubierre drive's warp bubble replace the stars with its uniform gray dimness, the crawling sensation of faster-than-light travel never felt entirely natural.

His latest trip had quickly grown doubly uncomfortable, thanks to the brooding man who'd shared his cramped bridge and living quarters for a week without speaking so much as five sentences to him. As his boat decelerated back into normal space, all he wanted to do was reach Gertie so Captain Atlas Carter could be dropped off as quickly as possible.

The bigger man sat beside the young Falconi like a clenched fist. His skin was a smooth brown against the blackness of space, and he wore the dark blue of a Sol Space Command officer like a shroud. The broad bones of the new captain's cheeks and nose could have been made of pounded iron, branded with a web of scars that shone under the ship's light. He would have been handsome if he had allowed himself. Falconi had asked the captain whether he'd been a boxer, a rumor he'd picked up on Earth, but Carter had just turned his broad back and kept writing in the log tablet he carried. He would fit in well out here. For a time, Falconi had given up on speaking to Carter at all, but in his relief at surviving the jump, Falconi couldn't stop his normal, youthful garrulousness.

"That's as far as we go," Falconi said, gesturing out the bridge's viewport toward the Orion Nebula's riot of gases as his courier ship slid into orbit around Gertie. "Sol's put everything on the other side of the nebula off-limits. Too much risk of running into the Bwain out there, or something worse. Those wildcat miners and the pirates don't seem to be too awful bothered by it, but for the rest of us, it's off limits."

As usual, the captain said nothing. The view window's dim reflection showed the same sad look tinged with anger Carter had carried ever since he stepped foot on the ship. The man was wrestling with something, but Falconi knew that the only ones who found fulfillment out here were the criminals.

"Sol Space Command thinks the Bwain don't come through because of something in the nebula. Maybe the radiation, since it seems to mess with their telepathy. I mean, nobody really knows. Trying to talk to them is like...well, like trying to talk to you I guess," Falconi quipped.

Carter twisted his head to face Falconi, and Gertie's faint green glimmer reflected in his bright green eyes.

"What's that about The Gate?" he asked.

"The Gate? Oh, didn't they brief you on that? If you look about seventeen degrees off to starboard, you'll see a wedge where the nebula looks sorta pinched. The radiation dips there for whatever reason. I mean, I guess the Bwain could pass through there. *We've* got ships that can get through there, but with the aliens' lower tech, I'm not sure they could make it. Then again, I'm no expert on what they've got technology-wise."

"What ships do we have that can get through there?" Carter asked.

"Well, there's a lot of proplyds out there in the nebula, and the miners have hardened ships because of because of what they do. Even though its illegal, they go after the metals in the protoplanets. It's easier to extract from them because the crusts are still forming. I don't read the messages from Earth, but the orders that Administrator Tannin gives me to send back are always askin' for more help and more resources. Seems like it's gettin' pretty bad out here."

Carter's rigid silence disturbed him. Whatever passion and humanity the captain carried, he had pushed it so deep inside himself he could have been one of the experimental androids that they'd often talk about on the news.

"I mean, you had to have known what's going on out here, right?" Falconi continued. "I hate to be the bearer of bad news and all, but…"

"I know that the *Fate's Winds* needs a captain. Anything else beyond that doesn't matter."

Falconi swallowed hard as the friction from Gertie's atmosphere blurred his view screens with red heat.

"With all due respect, I don't know if your orders are gonna mean all that much out here. You're not back on Earth anymore ya know."

"Really?" he asked as he looked around sarcastically. "Who the hell are you? I've been Shangaied! Help! Help!"

"Very funny," Falconi said indignantly. "Look, I'm just tryin' to clue you in on what's goin' on out here. If you're not interested, that's fine with me."

"Whatever's out here, I'll deal with it as it comes. My only concern right now is getting to my new ship so I can take command and get settled in."

"All right, fine. Don't say I didn't try to warn you though."

"I wouldn't dream of it," Carter said dryly as he went back to staring blankly at the viewport.

* * *

Gertie
The planet's surface

Administrator Tannin skimmed the updates that Falconi brought with him from Sol, flipping faster and faster through each holographic talking head, or block of text that sprung from the tablet.

Since Falconi had last seen the man, Tannin had aged severely. The thick curls of his hair ran gray, with a yellow-white flecking his beard. He was solidly built, but seemed to be sort of locked into a permanent hunch, and his eyed seemed to be filming, as if filled by cataracts.

Regardless of whatever physical problems he might be experiencing, he still seemed to enjoy Gertie's weather. The windows of his residence were wide open, and a pleasant breeze filled each of the rooms. Falconi found the sunlight, and the fresh, cool air quite a pleasant change from the stuffy confines of his ship. He would have even smiled if Carter hadn't been standing at stiff attention right there beside him.

Once he'd finished going through all the updates, Tannin tossed the holotablet onto his desk, got to his feet, and then turned to face the window behind him. Outside, golden stalks of genetically modified wheat struggled up from Gertie's native soil, and clouds tinged with the nebula's light billowed a gauzy pink. Falconi had seen the administrator throw offended tantrums upon receiving instructions from Sol on more than one occasion, so he braced himself for yet another such outburst.

"You know Carter, they just don't seem to get it. It's like they're trying to get blood from a stone here," Tannin said flatly.

"How so?" Carter asked.

"How so?" he asked, turning back around to face the captain. "I'm asked to prepare shipments of fresh foods and metals for system G-1290. That colony was founded seventy-five years before us, and I am ordered to offer them assistance. With what exactly?"

"I believe 1290 is having trouble with its nanofactories," Carter recalled from the reports he'd read. "Their industrial capacity is severely inhibited."

"And so because of one incompetent engineer, I'm supposed to put all the progress we've been making here on hold? We have two habitable worlds here, at least one of which is rich with a variety of metals, plenty of water, and a biosphere that tolerates our staple crops without terraforming. Systems like the Sword Belt are a one-in-a-million find in the galaxy, and what aid does Sol send me?"

"Sir, I…," Falconi started, but Tannin quickly cut him off.

"Criminals!" Tannin bellowed. "Sol is happy to send shiploads of prisoners to Judgment, but they leave no space in their cargo holds for a fusion reactor, or even a desperately needed nanoreplication factory. We need industry here, and perhaps more importantly, we need ships. Have you been informed about the recent pirate activities?"

"I've read your reports," Carter replied.

"Have you?" the administrator asked with a surprised look. He licked his lips, and a strange smile spread across his face. "I wonder what you did back on Earth to have been shipped all the way out here, because you certainly don't strike me as the sort of a man who'd be dumb enough to have volunteered for an assignment like this."

From the corner of his eye, Falconi saw Carter swallow. The bigger man's shoulders remained ramrod straight, but the silence stretched out between the two men.

"You may ask my superiors, sir," Carter finally answered. The man's voice had flattened, as if he'd purposely suppressed any and all emotion from his answer. "My service record will be made available to you."

 Tannin strolled closer, tilting his head in interest.

"There are no choir boys out here my dear Captain. Nor is there room for weakness. Pirates destroyed your sister ship not a week ago, and if you're not on your toes out there, they'll do the same to you. I expect you to follow my orders precisely if you want to keep your crew alive."

"What *are* your orders, sir?" Carter asked.

A smile broke through the gray tangles of the administrator's beard. He seemed quite taken with his new officer's obedient brevity.

"Take command of the *Fate's Winds*," Tannin said. "Bring order to my system. Throttle the pirates. Assess the conditions on the other planets. Help me make this colony into a true stepping stone for the human race."

"And what reply am I to send to Sol?" Falconi asked. Tannin's face darkened once more as he glanced over at him.

"Tell your masters that I will be happy to personally present them with a list of grievances and needs at their earliest convenience."

"Grievances? But, Administrator, you're only…"

"I do not need to be reminded of my status, Falconi!" the administrator barked. Then, noticing Carter still standing there at attention, his face softened. "You, Captain, will at least have enough antimatter for an Alcubierre jump back to Earth. I, it seems, am destined to be an administrator here for the rest of my life, which I'm sure Sol hopes will be a short one. Dismissed, Mr. Carter."

Carter gave the administrator a slight nod, and then shot Falconi a silent glance, and nodded to him as well, which was probably about as much of a tanks as he could expect for flying him all the way out to Gertie.

"What do you know of him?" Administrator Tannin asked after Carter had left. The messenger boy was young, barely a year out of the SSC Academy, and with youth came the pliability that set secrets loose between the stars.

"To be honest, not very much," Falconi said. "I wouldn't call him a conversationalist. Or even friendly for that matter."

"So, a man of few words, then. That's good. You know, there are those in the service who only seek to do only what they're told. If our new captain is one of those, then that'll a great help to me. Tell me, is he loyal to Sol?" Tannin asked as he studied Falconi's face.

"I think you can be sure about that. The only thing he wanted to know was your orders."

"And what if I have to bend him a little? Say, if he had trouble seeing my position out here?" Tannin asked. Falconi swallowed nervously before he answered.

"I guess I'd say, good luck to anyone who thinks they can push that man anywhere he doesn't wanna go."

"Yes well, I suppose we'll have to see how things play out. Anyway, you're dismissed. I'm sure you're eager to get back to your ship."

"Yes sir," Falconi replied. With a quick nod, he turned and headed for the door.

"Oh, and Falconi..."

"Yes sir?" he asked, turning back around to look at the administrator.

"Don't forget to deliver my message to those intransigent bean counters back on Earth."

"I will sir, but..."

"Just do it. Off with you now," Tannin said. Without another word, Falconi resumed his previous course. Tannin watched him go, replaying his meeting with Captain Carter over once again in his head, and a smile played at the corner of his mouth as he sat back down at his desk.

Chapter Four

The Fate's Winds
In orbit above Gertie

Danielle Hoff watched the editable packaging surrounding her lunch swell and bubble in the galley's warmer. Even the smallest SSC ships grew live fruits and vegetables in their day rooms, but their proteins and carbohydrates were synthesized and rehydrated by the meal printers in the ship's galley. Today she'd be eating the printer's interpretation of chicken and wild rice. It wasn't fine dining, but it kept them alive.

"You shouldn't have acted like that with Aric," a voice said from behind her.

She turned to see who it was just as Communications Ensign Julie Ford entered the galley. Julie struck her as the nervous type for whatever reason. She was the newest member of the crew, and always seemed to be struggling to fit in. She wore a damp sweat suit, and pawed at hair that had grown stringy and brittle. Hair loss was an aftereffect of the diet pills that Danny had been smuggling in for her, but now that Danny had been court-martialed and she was running out of her medication, she'd grown rather irritable and unsure of herself.

"Why not?" Danielle asked. "It's not like he's doing a better job than any of us could have done if we'd have been given the chance."

"But he's the *captain*. Imagine what would have happened on another ship."

"I wish I *were* on another ship," Danielle grumbled.

"Really? Why would you want that? There's no way I'd wanna be on another ship," Bryon said as he came in to join them. "I mean, where else could you find yourself fighting pirates one day, and aliens the next? Hell, sign me up for the SSC and the Sword Belt any day!"

"Hmmmph," Julie said as the weapons officer slung his arm around her shoulder and pulled her close.

"What do you say we get you out of those workout clothes? You know, out here on the razor's edge, it can get pretty lonely for a marine. Know what I'm sayin'?"

"Get off me Bryon!" she snapped as she shoved him away.

"Hey, I thought we were friends!" he protested.

"You don't have any friends," Danielle answered as she pierced her lunch's wrapping with a fork. Wisps of steam wafted up, smelling like a mixture of hot plastic and butter.

"Now come on Danielle, you know that's not true. Aric likes me," Byron countered. "He'd probably like me even better if you'd stop distracting him all the time."

"She shouldn't be flirting like that," Julie said as she hungrily watched Danielle raise her fork to her mouth. When Danielle noticed the look on Julie's face, she put on her best fake smile and held out the food.

"Want some?" she asked.

"No, I just ate. Thanks though," Julie said, though in truth she could have eaten Danielle's lunch, and at least two others as well. With the diet medications wearing off, her hunger was returning with a vengeance, so she had to be extra vigilant about trying to control her impulses.

"You shouldn't worry so much about our illustrious acting captain. At some point here in the next few weeks we'll have our new captain, and then Aric's gonna find himself back down in engineering, so you'll never have to see him again."

Julie's drooped face seemed to sag even farther. Would she be sad to see less of Aric? Danielle flirted because it helped her establish her place in the crew's pecking order outside of their respective ranks. Her own feelings toward Aric seemed to run much deeper than mere flirtation, though she hadn't really thought about it all that much until she saw Danielle flirting with him. Now she wasn't sure what she was feeling. She just knew that seeing Danielle flirting with him made her feel uneasy. Was it jealousy? Again, she wasn't sure, but now wasn't the time to think about it.

"No, not a few weeks," Bryon said through a mouthful of apple. "Our new captain's gonna be here in a few hours."

"A few hours???" Danielle asked as both she and Julie shot him a surprised look. Before he could answer, Aric's voice erupted through the ship's intercom system.

"All bridge crew to your stations. We're receiving a transmission."

Danielle swallowed one last bite, and then handed the rest of her meal to Julie as she left the galley.

"Let's go see what our fearless leader needs now," she said as she stepped out into the corridor.

* * *

Personal Logbook: Captain Atlas Carter
Entry 7 - Gertie

Pirates...Narcos...they're all the same. They see only what they can take.

The administrator wants me to clean up his system, Aida. He has no idea how good of a man he picked for the job. I know how these people think. When Cazador and I sparred so many years ago, he'd throw jab after jab at me, but I'd just circle around him, waiting for an opening.

"Are you afraid?" he'd ask me. He asked me that same question when he first offered me cocaine too. It was the night he told me the *Narcos* were

planning to take Belize. Criminals think in terms of brute strength, not subtlety. In the boxing ring, I'd wait for Cazador to tire himself out before I'd close in on him. He had an older fighter's stamina because of the muscle he'd built up over the years. It weighed him down and drained his energy. I held my own against him, but in his mind he always won, just because he thought I wasn't aggressive enough.

I wonder if Cazador asked you there on the rooftop if you were afraid. Did you even know why he dragged you up there? I keep wondering if he told you that I was sitting out there watching, and that you were the insurance policy that would keep me away. God, I'm so sorry Aida. I'm so damned sorry. I don't know what I could have done, but I should have at least tried to do something to save you. If only I could go back...

* * *

Gertie
Outside Landfall

Hal stumbled into the orbital supply crate he'd repurposed as his living quarters. His empty glass clattered into the small sink that had been one of the first tests of his printing factories' abilities, and he belched as he leaned against the fixture's cool metal. Sweeping his long black hair from his face, Hal squinted into the mirror. A broad red nose stretched over his face, and inflamed capillaries webbed his cheeks. His eyes had reddened so much that he couldn't make out the brown of his irises, and that powerful chest, a relic from his teenaged construction work on the reservation, had collapsed over a fat ball of stomach.

A cool breeze swept over the hills and into his crate. After approving the latest printing designs, Victor had forgotten to close the door when he'd left. Shivering, Hal staggered to the threshold. The agriculture minister had disappeared into the half-kilometer that led to Landfall, but Hal could still admire the checkerboard of clean, waste-free factories under Gertie's permanent twilight. The nanos would have foundations assembled for two more printing stations next week, and it would only be another week until they were online. It was slow progress, but at least he was *building* something here. Leaning against the doorway, he smiled to himself. Even with Tannin and Danny both besieging him with requests for a fleet's worth of equipment, he'd managed to come a long way from that hopeless wreck of a life he used to have, trying to hide the whiskey on his breath while holding on to both a job *and* a wife back in Oklahoma.

Six rows in front of him, one of his factories flashed red.

Inventory nearing depletion, warned the monitoring system that had been implanted into his skull before he'd left Earth.

"Damn it," Hal slurred to himself. Fumbling at the side of the door, he knocked over his umbrella and coat before finally digging out his antique fusion pistol. With the pistol in hand, he staggered his way out toward the factory under a half-lit sky. "I'm gonna get you this time you bastards! You damned pirates are messin' with the wrong Indian, believe you me!"

This wasn't the first time he'd been raided, but it made him wish he didn't have so much nightcrawler flowing through his veins.

The factory they'd broken into was number ten, the farthest north in the valley. He'd been begging Tannin for militia support to protect the factories from the pirates. Even a security fence, but Tannin hadn't come through with any of it, and in the end he was left taking matters into his own hands.

The heavy grass whipsawed against his shins, and the insects that roamed the plains buzzed against his face. The heat of the glowing factories washed over him, causing him to sweat as he passed the two-meter-tall sheds.

As he got closer, he started hearing voices up ahead of him. As quickly as he could manage, he ducked over and took cover behind factory six.

He couldn't tell exactly how many pirates were crouched next to the hovercart when he peeked at them around the building, largely because he was still quite drunk, and his vision wasn't exactly what it should be.

They'd cracked open the factory's entrance and were loading sheets of carbyne steel onto the vehicle as quickly as they could. He raised his pistol, closed one blurred eye to try and steady his aim, and squeezed the trigger. Instantly, a bolt of electric-blue flame angled high up over the valley, hitting absolutely nothing.

A flurry of blurred bolts started firing back in his direction, so he ducked back behind the factory, the liquor sloshing around in his stomach as he tried to force himself to focus.

Printing station six is offline, his computerized assistant warned in his ear.

"Damn it you bastards!" he bellowed. "I swear, I'm gonna scalp every last one of ya!"

The magnetic thump of the hovercart's engine strained as the pirates climbed aboard and tried to make off with their prize, firing random shots in Hal's direction in an effort to keep him pinned down until they could get away.

Hal staggered to his feet and with a quick motion, he spun around the edge of the building and aimed at the center of the three carts he saw in his blurred vision. Steadying his pistol with both hands, he ignored the shots that were flying past him, and unleashed a shot of his own. This time he hit something, but it wasn't exactly what he'd been aiming at. Rather than hitting the cart, like he'd intended, he hit factory ten.

Printing stations six and ten are offline, the computer's voice spoke pleasantly in his ear.

"Oh shut up!" Hal yelled as the pirates fled into the deepening twilight. His stomach bounced against his belt as he gave chase, but the pirates only laughed and taunted him. They slowed just enough to keep him in view for a few hundred feet as their cart climbed the low hills, which only angered him more.

"Hey Yellowknife, Mephista sends her thanks!" one of them called before the cart accelerated up onto the plateau and disappeared from sight.

Hal threw his pistol down into the dirt, puffing for breath with his hands on his knees.

Sometime later, as he trudged back to his crate, the streak of their drop-ship scrawled into orbit high overhead. He stared at it for a long moment, shielding his eyes against the glare that caused tears to form at the sides of his eyes.

The factories were all he had, and he'd be damned if he let those rotten, thieving bastards bleed him dry.

* * *

The next morning, Hal followed the thin outline of a trail up into the foothills that overlooked his factories. The land was rockier here, and the pirates' hovercart had left behind some slight, linear marks where it had zoomed over the bare earth. Wracking his hung-over brain as he studied the plateau's endless fields, he finally started off toward the northwest, on roughly the same course he remembered from his last encounter with them.

He sipped from his canteen as he walked, trying to wet a mouth that still felt dry thanks to the copious amounts of nightcrawler he'd consumed the previous day.

After he'd clipped the canteen back onto his belt, he checked to make sure his pistol was still secure, and then he scanned the horizon for signs of the pirates.

As much as he hated to admit it, Mephista's men were smart. They wouldn't have just landed and gone after his steel. They'd have reconnoitered, assessed the security situation, and then made their move.

"They must have some kind of base of operations nearby," he muttered to himself, as he pulled the canteen from his belt and took another sip.

He clapped binoculars to his aching eyes and scanned the plain. No trees had evolved on Gertie yet, so its biosphere was limited to grasslands, low shrubs and ferns, and insects. Victor and his biologists said that the planet was like Earth in the Permian period. All that meant to Hal was that he could see for kilometers in any direction, but he had no idea where to go.

He wasn't even sure what he'd do if he found the pirates. There couldn't be more than a handful of them. Maybe he'd sneak up on them, kill them all, and then that would be the end of it. As personal as his fight with them was though, he wanted to know what they were doing up there. Had the fight with the *Mercy* damaged their ship, or were they building something?

His binoculars showed a black smudge on a low hill about two kilometers distant. Zooming in, he knew he'd found his target and set off at a brisk walk that helped clear his head. He drew the pistol as he approached and thought maybe he should call the administrator's office, or even Vartan, on Gertie. But they'd never sent help before, so he put the thought aside.

The pirates had chosen a flat piece of land for their rudimentary launch pad, and the burn pattern bore the distinctive double ring trace of an orbiter's two-stage booster. The grass and ferns here had been trampled by a number of boots and crates, but what he saw didn't quite make sense. The pirates never would have camped in the open. For a group that always seemed to be one step ahead of the militia, a security mistake *that* big was totally out of character. So where had they come from?

Squatting in the charred sourness of the burnt vegetation, Hal tried to follow the tracks through the grass. The hovercart would have likely broken the stems of the grass with its magnetic pressure, but he didn't find any pattern he could trace.

Getting back to his feet, he stood and circled the launch point once again.

Had this been simply a rendezvous point? Was their camp elsewhere?
He cocked his head, trying to see any trails that ran over the hills above
him.

Before he knew what was happening, he suddenly felt the ground beneath
his feet give way. He roared in surprise as he desperately fumbled at the
lip of the chasm, trying to find anything he could possibly grab a hold of
to stop himself from falling. Unfortunately, all he was able to grab a hold
of was a half grown bit of shrubbery, which quickly tore away from its
roots and sent him freefalling into the all-consuming darkness below.

* * *

Orbiter from Fate's Winds
Entering orbit above Gertie

Gertie's purple sky fell away from the orbiter's view screen, replaced by
the deeper black of space. Pandith eased the space plane above the green
planet, tilting its attitude until it was in line to intersect with the *Fate's
Winds*. Carter could see the small dot of Landfall below them.

"We're excited to have you join us, Captain," Pandith said in a soft voice.

"Thanks," Carter said flatly. Pandith expected more of a response from
him, but when none seemed to be forthcoming, he simply continued on.

"The past week...or to be perfectly honest, this whole mission so far hasn't
exactly been easy for any of us."

Carter tensed as they escaped from Gertie's atmosphere. For a moment
he closed his eyes and felt the storm winds battering his helicopter over
Belize, thousands of light years distant. It seemed like a lifetime ago, but
in truth he had barely had enough time to deal with the grief he felt over
the loss of his wife.

"Tell me about the pirates," Carter asked, as much for a distraction as he
did for information. "What do they want?"

"Honestly, I have no idea. The raids began two years ago, and since then they've become systematically more intense. We believe they have a base somewhere out there in the nebula, but we've never had the ships to go out and search for 'em. Their destruction of the *Mercy* really hit everyone hard."

"How'd the crew take the loss?"

Pandith set the autopilot and released his restraints. Carter watched him consider his response as he floated free above his holocontrols.

"I'm sorry Captain, I'm not sure I know how to answer that," he said, a bit of anxiousness creeping into his voice.

"If there's one thing I'm going to demand from my crew, Mr. Pandith, it's absolute honesty. Now, speak your mind," Carter said firmly as the engineer glanced over and looked him straight in the eyes.

"Sir, I've been cross-trained in both medicine and psychology, so I don't say this lightly, but the crew just isn't functional. With Lieutenant Xiao's court-martial, and..."

"I'm sorry? Court-martial? What happened there?" Carter asked.

The engineer shrank from him, as if embarrassed that he'd even mentioned it.

"I think Lieutenant Keith should probably be the one to provide you with the details on that whole thing, but the long and the short of it is, there was an incident on a recent test of the array."

"Where is Mr. Xiao now?" Carter asked.

"He was sentenced and sent to Judgement," Pandith said awkwardly.

Carter stared at Gertie's sea of endless green rolling slowly above him. The settlement of Landfall had slipped away under the planet's rotation.

The orbiter was now approaching the terminus, and the glow coming from the sunset that was creeping down over the horizon reminded him of flames washing over the land back on Earth.

In his mind, just for a moment, he was walking among the smoking ruins of his city. The smell of burnt flesh and the screams of agony from the people he thought he was protecting was almost more than he could bear. He squeezed his acceleration chair's armrests until his fingers burned in protest. He then used that pain to channel his anger just as Cazador had taught him in the boxing ring.

"Will there be any further action taken?" Pandith asked.

Carter breathed through his nose and exhaled through his mouth, falling into a cycle of breathing that he'd honed in his fights as a teenager. He thought of the endless distance around him, the fragile planet below, and everything that Tannin had said about building this system. He should have been told more about the status of operations. Much more. These were just kids, trying to win a game they barely knew how to play. He'd become numb during the long trip here, and now, for the first time in months, he felt a desire to get involved. A desire to find out what was going on. A desire to help.

"There will be action, Mr. Pandith. You can count on it."

* * *

The Fate's Winds
In orbit above Gertie

"The pirates took our Sol-blasted wheat stock!" the prisoner's voice whined over the *Fate's Winds'* radio. "What the hell are we gonna eat next season?"

Aric swallowed, and the starched fabric of his dress uniform scratched at his throat. Julie inched closer to him, her arm brushing his as if she wanted to help just with her presence, but he stepped away from her to try and clear his head. On top of having to maroon his supply officer on Judgment, now Mephista's pirates were raiding the Sword Belt again. He'd have to deal with the communications ensign's inappropriate interest later.

"I understand your concern, but at the moment we're under orders to remain in orbit around Gertie. We're..."

"Is that what the administrator says?" the man's English accent bellowed through the radio, cutting him off before he could finish his explanation. "Is he letting this happen? That bastard has no right to leave us to die over here just because we're prisoners!"

"You're speaking to the captain of this ship, and I'm following the orders I was given by Sol Space Command. If you have an issue with those orders, then you can take it up with the appropriate authorities," Aric said, his patience for the conversation waning quickly.

"You sound awfully important up there, Mr. Captain. You drop off one of your own crew and leave us to starve while you sit up there all high and mighty. I bet you sleep real well at night, while we aren't even allowed to have weapons to defend ourselves," the man grumbled. "I'll tell you one thing right now. Your little ship up there, and Gertie for that matter...we don't need *either* of you. The next time any one of you comes down to Judgment, we'll string you up nice and tight so you can starve with the rest of us."

The connection dropped, and Aric closed his eyes to block out the painful brightness of the holocontrols.

"Mephista's never tried so many raids before," Julie noted.

"Ensign Ford is right," Granger said from behind him. "Her attacks are getting more frequent all the time. What do you think could be behind it?"

"We're just a flyswatter out here," Aric grumbled as he turned back toward his station. "There's nothing one ship can do to stop any of it."

He trailed off as he caught sight of Bryon and Danielle pressed closed together, stealing a moment when his back had been turned. Danielle's eyes lingered on Aric for a second before she pulled her lips away from Bryon. When the weapons officer opened his eyes, he flushed and spun back to his station.

"Ensigns, is that the behavior your new captain will expect?" Aric barked.

"Jealous?" Danielle said, throwing him a quick wink before she drifted back to her station.

"Ensign Purcell, is your station in full working order?"

"No sir," Bryon responded. "I've got a malfunction with missile bay door two. Danny said the nanos can't handle it. It's a part that we need from Gertie."

"What the hell's the matter with you Bryon? We have a weapons malfunction and you don't even bother to tell me?" Aric asked, his already inflamed temper threatening to boil over at any minute.

"Well, it's not like we're going out to fight anyone," Bryon shot back. "I mean, that farmer was right. We're just sittin' around here doin' a whole lotta nothin'."

"WE'RE NOT JUST SITTING AROUND!" Aric shouted at the top of his lungs.

The crew, stunned by his sudden outburst, said nothing. Aric's heart was pounding in his chest, and his muscles all tensed because of the adrenaline fueled rage.

"What the hell do you think the new captain's gonna say when he sees all this? There's food packets and water bulbs stuffed in the corners of every station, shorted out holoscreens waiting for replacement parts, Bryon and

Granger both unshaven and in wrinkled uniforms...," he said as his voice lowered somewhat. He knew he was the one who was responsible for the state things were in, but he wasn't ready for the responsibilities of being the caption. It had all been too much for him

"And I want to tell you another thing you son-of-a-bitch," the transmission from Judgment crackled again through the tension on the bridge.

"Julie, just shut the damn thing off," Aric instructed.

"You don't know what it's like to be stuck out here, to know you're never gonna see home again. You know what my crime was?   Political dissent. They shipped me out here to die because I was a member of the Pragmatist Party, and I..."

"ENSIGN, THAT IS AN ORDER," Aric barked at the top of his lungs.

"You won't even help, will you?" the prisoner continued. "You're afraid. You're like a scared little girl up there, and you're all we've got standing between us and..."

Julie cut the transmission with a swipe of her hand, while Aric stood there in the silence, absolutely mortified. The crew didn't even try to hide their looks of disgust, but what had they ever done for him, other than make each day worse than the last?

The silence was broken when bridge's hatch coughed, and then swung open.

"Attention on deck!" Pandith's normally soft voice cried as forcefully as Aric had ever heard it.

Aric pulled his cap from the armrest of the captain's chair, slapped it on his head, and snapped an angry salute at the hulking man who stepped onto the bridge. The man Pandith escorted had polished the boots and brass star of his captain's rank to a high sheen. His dress uniform seemed barely able to contain the rigid tenseness that radiated from him. A snarl of disgust lifted the man's lip as his hard eyes swept across the bridge, and Aric's heart sank even lower.

"Was that a request for assistance from a planet in this system?" the captain asked.

"Yes sir," Aric answered. "The pirate attacks are increasing in frequency, and they were requesting…"

"And you ordered their transmission terminated?"

"Yes sir. The administrator ordered me to remain on station pending your arrival, so we were unavailable to provide the requested assistance."

"Well I've arrived now Mr. Keith," Carter said, his voice rising in a way that fixed each member of the crew in place. "Effective immediately, I am taking command of this ship in accordance with Sol Space Command order 937562, and my first action will be to find those pirates and kill them."

*   *   *

The Fate's Winds
In orbit around Judgment

Alarms squalled on the bridge of the *Fate's Winds*. Carter's holoscreens showed a large cruiser-class ship in high orbit above Judgment. It looked as if it could have been a military vessel, with thick lines designed for everything from low-orbit combat operations to years of patrolling out in interstellar space.

"Jesus, that's the pirates' ship?" Bryon blurted. "She's gonna pack a lot bigger punch than we are, Captain."

"Your orders sir?" Carter replied.

"Sir?"

"Those are the next words I want to hear out of your mouth," Carter said in a tone that made it clear to everyone that he would only teach this once. Bryon looked completely cowed as the eyes of the rest of the bridge crew fell upon him.

"Your orders sir?" he asked timidly.

Carter enlarged the holodisplay until he found what he was looking for. He then highlighted a small orbiter working to boost itself up from the planet to dock with the pirate ship.

"I want you to target our main laser on that orbiter," he instructed. "We can't stand toe-to-toe with a cruiser the size of the *Tranquility*, so if we have to engage the cruiser we'll fire missiles at their orbiter, and then withdraw so that they follow right into our volley. Be prepared to work very quickly Mr. Purcell."

"Roger that, Captain," Bryon called as his hands weaved through his holocontrols.

"You can't be thinking of fighting that thing," Aric commented nervously.

"Ms. Ford," Carter ordered calmly, ignoring Aric's comment. "Send the following message to the pirate's ship. Attention, unauthorized vessel, this is Captain Atlas Carter of the Sol Space Command corvette, Fate's Winds. You are ordered to stand down while we halt the illegal transfer of colonist property. Should you take any action to protect or harbor the orbiter on approach to your vessel, we will consider you hostile and will act as necessary."

"If that's Mephista, she's not the surrendering type," Bryon informed him.

"Sir, they're responding," Ensign Ford said.

"Put it through to the bridge."

A woman's laughter bubbled over the speakers. He would have expected a deep, mocking laugh, but her voice was strangely light given the situation.

"Welcome to the system Captain," the pirate said. "You're new to the Sword Belt, so I think you'll find it's a little different out here than it is back home. I'm wondering if you're aware of recent events?"

She sounded casual, like an adolescent making conversation. He wondered what kind of woman, who sounded like she had the authority of a kitten, could command a group of hardened criminals at the edge of known space.

"The ship is holding station," Danielle called, "I'm showing its quantum vacuum powering up and its lasers charging."

"Ensign Purcell, are you targeted?" Carter asked.

"Yes sir."

"Captain?" the pirate asked. "I'm a reasonable woman, up until the point when I'm not. Whatever happens next is your choice."

"You may fire when ready Mr. Purcell," Carter stated flatly.

"But sir, their orbiter is unarmed and contains only food stolen from the colony," Julie said as she turned to face their new captain.

"No, it's a choice...and a message," Carter replied calmly as blue fury lanced out from the *Fate's Winds* and carved through the pirate's orbiter.

*   *   *

The Tranquility
Bridge

Mephista chewed her cuticles as she watched the holoscreen count down the minutes until her orbiter reached the *Tranquility* and the cargo could be secured. She both loved and hated the massive distance of space. It served as a reminder of their smallness and fragility, and that in turn drove every decision that she made. On both Sol and Gertie, they called her a criminal...a deserter, but out here on the edge of human space, she had a chance to rebuild her life. It was more than she could say for the rabble that had been shipped off to Judgment to die. If anything, taking their food was a mercy, for it would only speed up the inevitable.

"Captain, the *Fate's Winds* is charging its laser!" her sensor officer said. Mephista floated to join him with her numb, useless legs tucked under her in a well-practiced zero-G lotus. As soon as she arrived at his station, she grabbed him by the shoulder and leaned forward a bit so she could study his holoscreens.

"Nanos and mirrors are ready Captain," her weapons officer called.

"So this is the way Green's replacement wants to play it," Mephista whispered to herself. She watched the sleek needle of the *Fate's Winds* magnified a thousand times on the main viewscreen, and wondered to herself just how much spine this new captain had. She'd hoped that they could avoid any more confrontations with help from the administrator's office, but if Tannin wanted his entire fleet destroyed, then so be it.

"Deploy chaff," she ordered. "Ready the missiles."

"Firing!" her tactical officer called back to her.

"Helmets on and locked," Mephista ordered. Flight suits around her hissed as her bridge crew sealed themselves against any depressurization. Alone among them, she floated back to her station, free of any special protection. After the Bwain had forced her to taste the vacuum once, she no longer feared its return. There were far more terrifying things in this universe than the vacuum of space.

As soon as she settled back in at her station, she looked at the viewscreen once again and her eyes widened slightly as a frown played at the corners of her mouth. She'd expected to see the *Fate's Winds*' blinding plasma torch scattering against her countermeasures, but instead she watched silently as its fury tore through her orbiter instead. The small craft disappeared into a cloud of super-heated molecules, almost as though it were nothing more than a mockery of the nebula beyond. Furious, Mephista slammed her fist down on the arm of her command chair.

 "It seems as though we need to teach Tannin a lesson," Mephista said in a low growl. "All hands, remain at your battle stations!"

* * *

The Fate's Winds
Bridge

"Their missile bays are opening," Danielle called out anxiously. On the holoscreens, the destroyed orbiter's debris scattered against the pirate vessel's hull. Triggered by Danielle's mental interface, her holoscreens showed dozens of telemetry scenarios that she could call upon as needed. Either ship could run, fight, or do something entirely unpredictable, and she needed to be ready for whatever their new captain wanted. She'd never been in a fight before, and never had to call on this part of her training outside simulations. She tried to push the panic from her mind, but she was finding it difficult. All the horror stories she'd heard about space combat and what had happened to the *Mercy* sent a chill down her spine, and opened up a hollowness in her stomach.

"Hot damn! Now this is what I signed up for!" Bryon said enthusiastically beside her.

"Ms. Hoff, bring the ship to a stop," Captain Carter ordered.

"Bring us to a stop? But Captain, won't we…," she started to ask, but he quickly interrupted her.

"Momentum and inertia are your enemy in a fight," Carter said loud enough for the whole bridge crew to hear. "The moment you become predictable, you die. Now, full stop Ms. Hoff. I will not explain myself again. Mr. Purcell, what's your charge level?"

"Fifty-six percent, and climbing!"

A sparkle of red flashes emerged from the pirate's hull.

"They've launched missiles Captain!" Danielle shouted.

"Smart or dumb?" he asked.

"I'm...not really sure," she replied hesitantly.

"How much propellant do they have?" Bryon asked from beside her.

"Mr. Purcell, make ready to fire," the captain ordered.

"Judging by their mass," Danielle said as she tried to make sense of the flood of data, both on her holoscreens and in her mind. "I think...or at least the computer thinks they're dumb."

"Looks like the missiles have already finished their burn Captain," Bryon called from beside her.

"Then it's an unfair fight," the captain observed. "Mr. Purcell, target the ship and fire. Ms. Hoff, take us to ninety-degrees positive declination, full thrust. We're gonna do as much damage as we can to her before we run."

From the corner of her eye, Danielle saw Bryon's fingers flashing effortlessly through his controls, but she couldn't react. The stream of data, the missiles charging toward her...it was all too much. Suddenly a powerful hand gripped her shoulder from behind.

"Ms. Hoff," Carter said sternly. "I will remove you from your station unless you start attending to your duties."

For a second Danielle could only nod, but then she exhaled, swept the controls that engaged their plasma thrusters, bringing the ship straight up and out of the missiles' path. It was a simple maneuver that brought the ship out of danger, but it had frozen her. She stood at her station, trembling nervously as the *Fate's Winds'* laser crackled toward the pirate ship.

The beam exploded into a thousand pieces, flickering out before reaching the other ship's hull.

"It's chaff Captain," Bryon called. "They were ready for it."

A flashing light caught Danielle's attention.

"They're turning Captain," she exclaimed in surprise. "Looks like they're heading toward the nebula."

"Mr. Purcell," Carter ordered, "Lock on the propulsion missiles and fire."

"Ummm, I'm sorry sir. I can't do that," he responded.

Danielle glanced behind her just long enough to see anger tighten the captain's face.

"You have five seconds to complete that order, or I will put you in the brig," Carter growled.

"I'm sorry captain, but the missile bay door is inoperable. It's down for maintenance," he said apologetically.

Tense silence filled the bridge. Danielle watched the pirate ship slip into the irradiated protection of the nebula until it disappeared from her trackers. A last, warbling communication floated from the ship before she lost its signal completely.

"Captain, I have a transmission," Julie said.

"Put it on," he said. Julie tapped her control screen, and suddenly they heard Mephista's voice.

"Your point is well taken Captain, but you'd better pray for your sake that we never meet again," she said, just before the interference from the nebula killed the signal completely.

Part Two:
Uncommon Alliances

Chapter Five

Judgment
The planet's surface

Threed stepped out from the shade of his mud brick hovel, hunting for the sound of the fight. Judgment's heat bored into him, steaming up from the paths of beaten dirt between the survivors' hovels as he jogged toward the shouting and yelling. The swollen sun blinded him as he climbed up to the small plain where the prisoner colony did its farming, and for a moment he could only hear hoarse screams and the sound of fists pounding against flesh.

The work gang that had been digging the latest irrigation trench from the river had thrown down its tools and formed a circle around two brawling men. One was Bear, a hulking, bare-chested prisoner who'd been sent all the way from Earth for the murder of an SSC officer. Here he had his chance to face another one in Lieutenant Xiao, the wiry boy who'd been dumped here by his colleagues from the *Fate's Winds* without a word of explanation.

Bear stomped back and forth in the swirling dust, snorting and wiping his face. As soon as he planted his feet and bent his knees, Danny recognized what was about to happen, and he danced out of the way just as the bigger man lunged at him.

"Who started this?" Threed asked the crowd as he stepped over the discarded shovels and pickaxes to join the spectators.

"Xiao did. He asked for the radio again," the man next to him said. "Bear told him that, as your official representative, he had to go through him."

"Did he now?" Threed asked.

Sweating in his flight suit, Danny's face betrayed no emotion. This was the boy's fourth fight in just the few days since he'd become a prisoner, and though he carried the ugly puckers of bruises all over his body, the only scrap he'd lost had been to Threed himself. The river stones which served as currency were changing hands as bets lined up, and the action was heavily on Bear to get the win, but Danny had other plans.

Bear lunged for him again, only instead of ducking away the boy stood his ground and threw everything he had into a punch that was magnified by the larger man's momentum. The sickening crack of Bear's nose breaking got a roar from the crowd, and as his opponent's blood poured out into the dirt, fistfuls of stones were paid to some lucky winners. First blood was always a popular wager on Judgment, and today was no exception.

Bear snorted hard, and was trying to get his eyes to focus just as Danny struck again. He kicked at the side of the man's knee, snapping into the joint with all his force. The big man howled in rage and swung wildly as he staggered. This time, Danny wasn't as nimble. Bear caught the boy with a thick fist, pulling him down with him as he fell. Danny struggled to escape, but Bear was able to wrap his massive arms around the boy's throat.

The crowd closed in, eager to see the final demise of an officer who'd carried so many of them to Judgment. Threed watched the calm in the boy's eyes, saw Danny's boots scissor out to pull the handle of a pickaxe up to his free hand. While Bear puffed with the effort of strangling the officer, Danny swung the ax high into the air and brought it down with an appalling crack against Bear's skull.

Silence fell. Danny threw off Bear's limp arms and rolled himself up onto all fours, shuddering as he tried to fill his air-deprived lungs.

When he finally got back to his feet, he scanned the crowd and quickly found where Threed was standing among them. Reaching down, he pulled the pickaxe from Bear's eye socket.

"The radio," Danny growled.

* * *

"Where are you from, back on Earth?" Threed asked Danny as they made their way back toward his hut.

"China."

"I heard that China executes its criminals."

Danny said nothing, in response as he limped along beside him. When his family decided to move from Earth to a colony on the outskirts, he had thought things couldn't get worse. Then the Bwain attacked, and he thought the same thing again, but now he knew the truth. Things could always get worse, and no one cared in the slightest. He had nothing left to lose except the most important thing to him, but in order to keep her alive, he had to get back to work. That was all that mattered.

"Looks like you might have a broken rib there, judging by the way you're walkin'. Threed observed. "Better have your doctor look at it next time he comes around."

"He won't," Danny said. "We have orders not to associate with prisoners."

"You must have done somethin' pretty special for 'em to have dumped you down here with us. Figure you're probably innocent. Most of us are to some degree or another. Certainly ain't as guilty as they'd have you believe anyway. Some of us were just...inconvenient I guess you'd have to said. So what's the deal here? You want the radio so you can tell somebody you didn't do it?" he asked. The boy's glare was more calculating than angry.

"What I did doesn't matter," Danny replied.   "It's what I can do for you that you should be interested in."

"So you're gonna call your ship back?" Threed asked incredulously. "You gonna get 'em to pick us all up and take us off this rock?"

"I could use a pardon," one of the survivors called from his hovel.

"I could use a drink!" added another.

There was a harshness to their laughter that rang sour in Threed's ears. These men and women were hard enough to survive life on an inhospitable world, but without their grain reserves, and without enough irrigated cropland to grow more, they were all finished. As their mayor, Threed would only last for as long as they considered him their best chance of survival.

"I'm a friend of the administrator. I can talk to him," Xiao offered. Threed spat on the ground in front of him in disgust.

"That bastard Tannin ain't no friend of ours," he growled angrily. "We were promised we could work for our freedom, that we'd have all the tools we'd need to build a colony. But just look at this place! It's a total hell hole thanks to him and his broken promises."

Around him the village shimmered in mirage. The incongruous, green wedge of cropland, clinging to the banks of a river which sank into the canyons, had all but disappeared behind them.

"Tannin is no one's friend," Danny agreed, "but at least he'll answer when I call."

Threed drew to a halt outside his hut. He seized the grimed scrap of Danny's collar and pulled the boy close. Hoots and growls rose from the prisoners clumped in the shade. Jolina stepped out from Threed's hovel with the colony's only weapon, an ancient pistol Threed himself had smuggled in when he arrived.

"By this summer we're gonna get awfully low on food. We might even need to find a new source of protein. So if whatever you're planning to do here doesn't work out for us, you're gonna find yourself in a whole lotta trouble."

Xiao had a hardness to him. The boy didn't whimper or grovel like so many others when they came face to face with Threed. Instead, he seemed calm as he weighed his options.

"I can give you a chance at least," Danny said, apparently not fazed at all by the not-so-subtle threat. "Let me see if I can make a deal."

* * *

The Fate's Winds
In orbit above Judgment

"They would have killed us," Danielle said, her voice weak and trembling as she stood with Bryon in the airlock ready room, helping him into his EVO suit.

"They almost did," the weapons officer responded. "Why did you hesitate instead of initiating evasive maneuvers?"

"I don't know," she said meekly. He could tell by the look on her face that she was deeply troubled by the whole incident. "I mean, I've done thousands of simulations, but…"

"A sim isn't the real thing," he finished for her as he stepped into the legs of his space suit.

"No, it's not."

The EVO suits were a semi-rigid combination of an exterior carbyne steel mesh and a heavy interior pressure lining that housed the life support machinery. As he drew the magnetic seal up his chest to his neck, the suit's nanos glowed with life and swarmed him, causing the computer-controlled induction thrusters to glimmer at each of his joints. Danielle always thought the suits gave the impression of a heavyset scuba diver, shimmering with some sort of a bioluminescence.

"Though, I gotta say, our new captain sure treated those pirates like it was the real thing," Bryon added.

Danielle handed Bryon his helmet, and then leaned forward to press her lips gently against his cheek. He pulled back and gave her a look that was both awkward and apologetic.

"I think we need to cool it for a while Dani. I don't want either of us to end up on Judgment. We need to feel out what this new captain is like before we go on with this, just in case he's a hard ass about the regs."

"Is there a problem here?" Aric asked from behind them. He'd slipped through the ready room hatch without either of them noticing, and in spite of herself, Danielle turned away from Bryon with her response to his statement left unspoken.

"Oh shut your hole Aric. Just leave us alone," Bryon grumbled.

"Carter put me on EVO with you," Aric said. "After all, I *am* the ship's engineer if you remember."

Danielle wanted to say something to Aric. In her mind, what he'd done to Danny had been cruel. A demotion would have been a much more fitting punishment, but something in Aric's pinched face made her hold her tongue. She nodded to Bryon as she left the men to prepare for their spacewalk, and as she walked toward her cabin wrapped deep in thought, she was bothered by the sense that things were about to change.

* * *

Gertie
Landfall

In the first of the morning light that poured into the compound, Gertie's rolling hills were like waves of shadow coming to wash over Administrator Tannin. His staff had opened the windows to let in the cool night air, and the planet's native four-winged moths fluttered and battered against the corridor lights in mindless ecstasy. Tannin swatted at the annoying creatures as he passed. One clung to his palm and he held it for a moment, feeling the light brush of its wings, before crushing it in his fist and tossing the small body behind him.

The weak made way for the strong. It was the way of all life, human or alien, and the arrogant governors on Sol would realize this before the end. Their pandering messages promising to look into what could be done to better his situation showed that they had no idea of the kind of man Tannin was, or the power he'd discovered, and that power was close now. Achingly close.

The militiamen guarding Tannin's private chamber drew open the doors and snapped to tired attention as he passed them. He'd ordered his bedroom to be built without windows; it prevented distraction and hid the planet's infuriating backwater from his view. Inside was a large bed, his wardrobe and nightstand, and a holoscreen showing a shining image of Earth. It was a constant reminder of his goal.

After he'd slammed the bedroom doors shut, he activated his holoscreen by waving a hand in front of it. A three-dimensional keypad appeared, which he tapped a few times to bring up a private, off-planet channel. Danny Xiao's face showed on the flickering holoscreen, battered and dirty.

"I don't normally take calls from the condemned, but your presence on Judgment intrigues me," Tannin said, cocking his eyebrow slightly at the younger man.

"Aric court-martialed me and sent me here," Danny said, getting right to the point. "You gotta help me Tannin."

Tannin sat back, looking rather stunned. "So it wasn't Carter who sent you there?"

"Who's Carter?" Danny asked.

Studying the boy, Tannin tried to assess his own vulnerability. Danny knew little of where Hal's production runs had been going. The only thing he knew was that Tannin had been submitting the orders. He'd been careful to keep all of his conversations with Danny private, so that even if he were to turn on him at some point, there wouldn't be any evidence that could link the supply officer's activities back to him. It would be Danny's word against his, and now that Danny had been convicted and sent to Judgement, that left him in an even more favorable position.

A second man muscled into view beside Danny on the holoscreen. This one had a deep-tanned face and a shaved head. The prison overalls he wore had been patched repeatedly by hand.

"My friend here says you can help us," the prisoner interjected, "He says you two are pals."

"And who's this?" Tannin asked.

"Threed," the man replied without formality. "I'm the mayor here."

Tannin's eyebrow arched, and he had to fight to keep a smile from his face at the idea of a criminal mayor. It wouldn't do to show a lack of sympathy for Danny's plight. He still needed the boy, so he needed to make sure he stayed loyal.

"Danny, our situation has changed. The last orders were just picked up from the factories. I'm afraid I can't help just now, but as soon as things are settled, I'll see what I can do."

"Tannin, you can't just leave me out here!" Danny said.

"He promised us food!" Threed growled. Anger knotted the man's forehead, and his snarl showed a missing incisor.

"I can't speak to Danny's promises Mr. Mayor, but I will give you my assurance that we are working on your problem with the limited resources at our disposal."

"We're all gonna die here if you don't help us! The damn pirates stole most of our food!" Danny shouted.

For the first time, Tannin saw emotion in the boy as a combination of anger and fear flashed across his face.

"Danny, I'm sorry," the administrator replied without emotion as he wiped the moth's gore from his palm with a rag. "I need you to be strong during this time while I work with your new captain to see what can be done."

"So that's it then? I'm just supposed to sit on my damn thumbs here while you're gonna be doin'…what? You gonna cut a deal with him and leave me out in the cold?" Danny growled.

"I will do what I can, when I can. That's all I can tell you for right now. You'll just have to be patient. Now, if there's nothing more," Tannin said as he reached out to tap the control pad once more. Threed started to shout something at him just as the channel closed, but he was cut off before he could even get a word out. A grin played at the corner of Tannin's mouth as he examined his hand to make sure it was clean, and then headed over to lay down on the bed.

*   *   *

The Fate's Winds
In orbit above Judgment

Aric released his EVO suit's magnets, pushed off from the airlock's handhold, and then skimmed along the *Fate's Winds'* hull. Up close, the ship's carbyne glimmered with the golden flecks of trillions of nanobots that swarmed its surface, each tasked with patching up whatever holes were created by bits of space debris, as well as making sure its instruments were kept clear of dust and ice particle buildup. Powered by photonic energy from the surrounding stars, the nanos were an incredible technology, but unfortunately, they were a technology without any specific skills when it came to more complex repairs. When it came to failed missile bay door motors, a human still needed to climb into an EVO suit and suit and go for a walk outside.

Slowly he coasted over toward where Bryon knelt next to the damaged missile bay, blinking his left eye twice every few seconds to show his destination to the suit's computer, so it could adjust his inducers accordingly. He could rotate his limbs and waist if he wanted to fly manually, but being an engineer, Aric trusted his machines implicitly, and soon he was able to grab a hold of a handle alongside the weapons officer. Bryon had set an electromagnetic ring around the bay to keep the nanos from trying to clean their EVO suits from the hull. In training, Aric had seen a nanoswarm break down an EVO suit into its component molecules in forty-five seconds. It would be a nasty business if they were to do that to someone in a real life situation.

He glanced up at the deep black of space, and the nebula's pulsing orange clouds. What would it feel like to be torn into molecules and spread among the stars he wondered to himself as he triggered his suit magnets, so that his momentum wouldn't carry him farther down the hull.

Bryon had already managed to remove the bay door and held the part up to Aric once the engineer was settled onto the hull beside him.

"It's broken all right. Take a look," the weapons officer said as Aric carefully took the part from his grasp.

Bending to dip his head into the bay, Aric peered at the rows of red-tipped missiles marching away into the bay's darkness. They could be programmed to seek out a range of signatures or materials. The *Fate's Winds* even carried fusion nukes that would have done considerable damage to the *Tranquility* if the system had been working properly, but like everything else had done since he'd taken command, the bay door had failed.

"What kind of warranty do you think we've got on this thing?" Bryon asked as Aric bent to examine the lift mechanism. It was easy to see what had happened. The motor assembly mounted to the hull ended at a lever that slid into a groove in the bay door, but the lever had somehow snapped and jammed itself into the motor's gears. Aric pulled an autowrench from his tool belt and went to work loosening the mounting bolts.

"Do you think we could have beaten that pirate?" Bryon asked.

Instead of answering, Aric concentrated on steadying himself against the autowrench's force. Working in zero gravity was much more tiring than the same task on the inside the ship, where he'd be anchored down by the ship's magnetic gravity. Every motion had to be counterbalanced, and the effort of pushing against the wrench's torque strained his back and shoulders.

"Hey man, are you gonna say anything?"

Lying on his stomach and reaching into the bay, Aric pulled the motor free. He scanned the serial number with his helmet's camera, and inventory information flashed on his HUD.

"No spares," Aric noted brusquely. "We're gonna have to repair it."

Bryon's helmet swung back and forth as he searched the bay door for a dent or impact that would have driven the hatch into its own motor. With the sandy glow of Judgment reflected in Bryon's visor, it was hard for Aric to see the ensign's expression.

"What do you think happened to it?" Bryon asked.

"The same thing that always happens in this damn system," Aric said. "It just fell apart. I should have been monitoring things. I should have done a better job."

"Is that why you sent Danny down there?" the weapons officer asked. "You thought he was sabotaging things?"

He didn't respond right away. He needed proof. Captain Green suspected something was rotten was going on, and then he'd been blasted to oblivion. Aric remembered seeing the *Mercy*'s debris on the scans as they'd orbited Judgment. In a few weeks, all that would be left of the other corvette would be a lot of barely visible shooting stars, streaming down through the atmosphere.

"Look Bryon, I did what I had to do."

"You could have at least talked to him," Bryon said.

"You heard him on the comms that day. He was grossly insubordinate," Aric said. Bryon's face shield twisted toward him.

"He was one of us Aric. He was just a screw-up like everyone else out here. This mission is a joke, and everyone knows it. We can't make anything any better with just one ship to take care of a whole system. Whatever Danny was doin', maybe it was just his way of...jeez, I dunno. Maybe it was just his way of dealing with that feeling of uselessness."

The weapons officer didn't wait for a response. He simply released his magnets, and then jetted back toward the airlock, leaving Aric to reseal the missile bay's hatch. The panel wouldn't fit cleanly back into the opening however, so it took him quite some time before he finally managed to slip it back into place., and for a long time he tried to maneuver the covering until it slipped into place. When he finally got the job finished and turned back for the airlock, the sunset's red flame had started to slice over Judgment like a knife drawn across its throat.

What was he supposed to have done? What could anyone do in this godforsaken place where the only choices available seemed to be bad ones? Sometimes it felt like a no-win situation all around.

*   *   *

Personal Logbook: Captain Atlas Carter
Entry 11 - In orbit above Judgment

The crew's afraid of me, Aida. My methods are foreign to them, but I don't really have time to explain everything. The pirates surprised me by running, but they could be back at any minute, and something else is wrong in this system. The Administrator ordered the *Fate's Winds* not to aid Judgment. The acting captain court-martialed the supply officer, but from what I've seen on board it could just as easily have been anyone else among the bridge crew. They have no morale, and apparently not much respect for each other either. To be honest, it would be the perfect ship for me, if I didn't have so many memories weighing me down.

I stood by and watched death once before, and it cost you your life. I won't do it again. My crew has a job to do, and I expect them to do it.

* * *

The Fate's Winds

"This one is finished," Pandith said.

He set the completed Majorana probe on the workbench next to where Granger was examining a holoimage, trying to make sense of their experiment's data. The science officer pulled his hands apart, zooming in on the representation until it showed a section of space a few AUs on the other side of The Gate.

"Pandith, will you take a look at this?" Granger asked.

Their dozen homemade probes had cut ragged lines through the Orion Nebula as they recorded their data. This fed into the computer's realization, which was an overlaid geometric rendering of the twelve-dimensional amplituhedronal space called for in Granger's theory. With each component dimension pinched and curled back on another, the image resembled a rose. Pandith often wondered how many things of beauty were out there that that human eye could not perceive. Things like these stunning, coincidental patterns right there in the middle of space.

"The probes are still getting readings," Granger said. "We're seeing string oscillations that sure look like they'd be caused by another dimension. According to our model, those vibrations should be constant if we've found evidence of one of the dimensions. Except that they're clustered right here."

Granger's finger circled a large blob of yellow that indicated a logarithmic increase in the Majorana particles at the edge of their first probe's range.

"So what is that?" he asked.

Pandith blinked at the swollen indicators. The data was spotty in sections, obscured by the nebula's dust and radiation, and the anomaly lurked at the edge of their explored range.

"I don't think I can tell exactly," Pandith answered. "We're gonna need to send out more probes to cover the area beyond where the current ones are, and then maybe we'll get a better picture of what's goin' on out there."

"I knew that's what you'd say, and that's good methodology," Granger said as he continued to stare at data that was coming in. "If we found somethin' out there, then we need to be sure. Part of me is glad that Danny kept us from gettin' too carried away. If we'd have gone to Aric with the data we had at the time, he'd have probably just blown us off. Now at least we've got a better picture of what we're dealing with."

Boots stomped down the gangway, coming toward them from the port side airlock. They both looked up just as Bryon came into view, but the ensign brushed past them quickly, without making eye contact.

"I wonder what that was about?" Pandith muttered.

"Who knows? I really can't figure out some of the people in this crew," Granger said. "I mean, I don't have any problem at all talking to you, but everyone else is so caught up in their feelings and what not that it makes it pretty tough. We're here to do a job after all, and I think we should just do it. The situation with the pirates, and with Danny..."

"Granger...," Pandith said uneasily as his eyes seemed to shift up a bit.

"Well, we have to talk about it, don't we? You're a psychologist. You know it's not healthy to keep stuff like that inside. I mean, Aric sent him down there, and I know it doesn't make sense, but I keep having this nagging fear that I'm gonna end up doing something wrong and getting my ass sent down there too. What are the rules out here exactly? We haven't been authorized to use official SSC parts for our little hobby here, so does that mean we're gonna be the next ones to get thrown out of the airlock if we're caught?"

"Oh, I don't think so Granger," Carter's voice said from behind him.

Granger spun around quickly, a look of both shock and embarrassment on his face. He leapt up out of his chair in an attempt to salute and come to attention, but all he really managed to do was to knock Pandith's finished probe off of the workbench. The softball-sized sphere clunked and rolled on the deck, snapping two of the delicate antennas.

"I'm sorry Captain. I didn't mean to...," the engineer said, but then he fell silent as he stood there stiffly, trying to maintain a perfect *at attention* posture. In the bright glow of the holoscreen, his eyes flashed with uncertainty as Carter stood there staring at him. Pandith squirmed a bit amid the awkwardness.

"Anything we can do for you Captain?" he asked sheepishly.

Carter glanced over at him. It was obvious that if he ever needed a calming presence to help control a situation, Pandith would be the one to call.

"I'm on my way to see Mr. Keith. I'd like to speak to him before we leave orbit," he said as his eyes shifted back to the science officer. "At ease Granger. You're gonna constipate yourself if you keep standing there like that."

"Yes sir! Thank you sir!" he said formally, snapping the captain a quick salute before he allowed himself to relax once again. Carter returned the salute, and then without another word he continued on and disappeared through the opposite door.

"Oh my god, why didn't you tell me he was standing there?" Granger asked after he'd taken a deep breath and let it out slowly, his shoulders sagging in relief.

"What was I supposed to say? He just sort of appeared," Pandith said calmly as he bent over to pick up his probe. "Look what you did. I'll have to fix this now."

"Just be glad we're not gonna have to fix it down on Judgment," Granger said as he sat back down and leaned back in his chair, closing his eyes as he took another deep, cleansing breath.

Chapter Six

The Tranquility
Captain Mephista commanding
Inside the Greater Orion Nebula

"What could it be?" Mephista mouthed quietly, her eyes locked intensely on the holoimage that was was sliced into shards and fragments by the nebula's interference. *Something* was out here among the clouds with her, but because of all the interference, there was no way of telling what it was exactly.

"It's got squared edges," her science officer reported. "Spectrometer readings are showing iron, carbon, and traces of helium that could be from active fusion. I don't believe it's natural."

Mephista zoomed and rotated the computer's reconstruction, focusing on what could have been a bow, or what might have been a heat sink glowing a faint red color, but the holoimage disappeared as the *Tranquility* lost contact with its ghostly target.

"How far was it from us?" she asked.

"Two point three AUs, Captain. From the data we did manage to get from the object, I've been able to extrapolate a course that appears to be parallel to ours, but I couldn't track its speed," the science officer said.

"That's close enough for radio contact. Open a narrow band laser channel directed at your best guess for the target's location," she ordered.

"But, Captain..."

"If that's a miner or another pirate vessel out there, then we've just found ourselves a bonus, but if it's a Bwain ship trying to sneak through the nebula, then I'll be damned if we're gonna let 'em get close enough to surprise us. Put the channel on speaker."

Twisting static flooded the bridge as the signal laser bored through the dust and gas of stars that had been dead for millions upon millions of years. Mephista closed her eyes and waited silently. If what they'd seen on their sensor readings was a Bwain vessel, they'd make no reply at all. The aliens' ships didn't need radios when their minds served the same function. If it was a human vessel, part of her hoped that its captain would have the good sense to ignore her. She'd spent many restless nights with Captain Green's final words repeating over and over in her troubled mind. She'd hoped that sparing the *Fate's Winds* would have eased her conscience, but as she hid in the nebula's shroud waiting for a response, the weight of her past continued to grow heavy on her.

"One minute now, and no response," her communications officer called.

"Keep the channel open. We still don't know exactly what's out th...," she said, but she was interrupted when a sudden screaming ripped through the bridge. Both she and her crew slammed their hands over their ears, trying to dull what sounded like a soul being tortured beyond sanity. Mephista tried to maintain enough focus to make some sense of what they were hearing. She thought she could recognize the sound of clanging metal, and other throats moaning in the background.

"Captain, please...let me shut down the comm link," her communications officer begged with a pained look.

Mephista waved her hand for silence so she could focus on what she was hearing. The screamer drew a ragged breath, panted hard for a few moments, and then stopped suddenly as they shuffled away from whatever microphone they'd used.

Calling up the previous holoimage, Mephista enhanced it and zoomed in on a black shadow that was just slightly brighter than the emptiness of space. Was that a shuttle bay bulging from a hull? Was the gray streak beside it the hiss of atmosphere leaking from a rupture?

"Your orders, ma'am?" the navigational officer asked.

"Take us back to the Sword Belt," she ordered. "Full thrust."

"But ma'am..."

"If we're gonna fight what's coming for us, we don't have much hope of winning if we can't see the damn thing, now do we?"

"Captain, what did we hear?" the communications officer asked.

"A human being...or what used to be one anyway," she replied. "Unfortunately, I know exactly what happened to him. The last time I saw it happen, I still had the use of my legs. Now, get us out of here."

* * *

Gertie
The Planet's Surface

Hal landed hard on the packed earth floor, sprawling on his hip and coughing as the dirt and grass showered over him. Once his vision had cleared, he saw that his weight had triggered a disguised trap door some three meters overhead. He struggled to his feet in a panic, ignoring his throbbing hip as he scrambled around, desperately trying to locate his pistol. After a bit of searching, he finally spotted its glow coming from beneath a large clod of dirt a short distance away.

After he checked over the pistol to make sure it was still in working over, his eyes swept back and forth around his new surroundings, and once he was sure he was alone, he finally allowed himself to relax a little. This had apparently been one of the pirates' hideouts at one point, and the area he was in currently looked to be some sort of a giant, underground storeroom.

They'd reinforced the chamber every few feet with posts and crossbars made from some of the carbyne steel that they'd looted, and they'd cut shelves into the walls. Judging by the size, it must have taken them months to construct it all.

He ran his palm against the cool metal of one of the girders. How many batches of these had he labored to produce for the colony, only for them to end up being used by the pirates instead?

Lacking a flashlight, he charged his pistol until its blue-white glow illuminated an area that extended just a few feet ahead of him. It wasn't much, but at least he could see where he was going as he made his way deeper into the underground warehouse.

The boot prints crisscrossing the earth in front of him caught his eye, so he knelt down to examine them for a moment, and noticed that each of the prints also bore a symbol that was well indented and preserved in the damp earth. The symbol consisted of eight rings around the letters *SSC*. It was the Sol Space Command emblem, but what was it doing here? It made no sense.

Passing beyond the hovercarts, he found empty crates and discharged plasma cells that must have been used for both heat and light, but he found little else until he reached the far wall. There, he stretched his pistol as high as he could over his head, and watched as the shadows twisted against the machine in front of him.

Its buckets and treads still clogged with dirt from digging out the chamber, the excavator had been driven into the earth and left by the pirates. He remembered each lever and button on the machine's control panel. He'd helped load this piece of equipment on the colony ship back on Earth. He'd even used it to level the ground for his printing factories, but Victor had told him that this excavator was on the south continent.

Hal swept his pistol behind him, making sure he was alone in the chamber, and then, grimacing at the pain in his hip, he made his way back to the dim column of light falling through the trap door. There were no stairs, but he saw a rope ladder dangling in the near corner. He holstered his pistol and climbed, gritting his teeth with each passing rung. Finally, he reached another disguised entrance. Carefully he wrapped one arm around the top rung and used his other hand to push open the camouflaged disk of earth and grass. As the sunlight filtered in through the entrance, a sudden feeling of freedom washed through him. He relished that feeling, and it filled him with the strength he needed to complete his climb.

For a moment, he could only lie there in the grass next to the entrance, panting hard while his hung-over mind tried to put together the pieces of what he'd found. The pirates probably could have stolen the boots since they were standard issue pretty much anywhere in the galaxy, but the excavator? If it too had been stolen, then why would Victor have lied to him?

Slowly, he pulled himself to his feet. Pressing his hand against his aching hip, he scanned the grassland in search of any other silhouettes on the horizon. He saw nothing, his body ached, and he'd lost whatever ambition he otherwise might have had to continue, so he turned and slowly started limping his way back home.

The situation on Gertie was much worse than he'd thought. Victor, Tannin, and hell, maybe even the whole Colony Council had been lying to him about resources, shipments, and their plans for the future of this place. What else had they been lying to him about? Had any of them ever told him the truth about anything, and where did this knowledge leave him now that he knew? He had a lot to think about, but all really wanted to do right now was to get back home so he could rest...and perhaps self-medicate. After all, he needed something to kill the pain he was feeling.

* * *

Hal drowned the evening hours with a bottle of nightcrawler. He didn't even bother changing out of his muddy, grass-stained clothes before he reached for the bottle, but even the numb fog that filled Hal's mind couldn't erase what he'd seen, and he still had a decision to make about what he was going to do with that information. Hopefully the nightcrawler would grease the wheels so to speak, and help him to figure out his next move.

"What happened to you?" a voice called from the threshold of his crate.

Hal squinted into the twilight, but remained silent.

"Jeez Hal, are you that far in the bag?" Victor asked.

"Nah, I'm all right," Hal slurred. "Come on in and have a drink."

Victor propped his foot on the stool next to Hal. Gertie tended to get cool at night, so he was wearing long pants and a heavy sweater in order to keep himself warm. Two militiamen accompanied him, laden with field packs and fusion rifles.

"Thanks, but not tonight. We're headed out on some official business I'm afraid," Victor informed him.

"Gonna do some berry picking in the moonlight are ya?" Hal asked.

The militiamen behind him chuckled, and as the sun dropped on the horizon, the shadows from Hal's factories crept across the shuddering hills.

"Nah, nothing so pleasant. I'm doin' another survey for the administrator," Victor said. "Lots of flora out there to be catalogued. You know how it is. It's just part of the job."

"He keeps you out there most nights it seems," Hal noted.

"Botany is one of our illustrious administrator's passions, which means my passion for sleep comes second again tonight," Victor sighed.

"So, it's Tannin then, is it?"

"I'm not sure what you mean."

Hal tilted his glass to his lips, numbly sucking down the last of the liquor. Then he sat back against the cold metal of his crate and closed his eyes.

"I didn't mean anything Vic," Hal said. He heard Victor's boot slip off the edge of the stool, and the militiamen head off through the grass outside.

"You get some rest, and for Christ's sake, take a damn bath once in a while," Victor said, grinning to himself.

Hal nodded, trying to force himself asleep so the thoughts that roiled in him wouldn't betray what he knew, but suddenly his eyes flew open, and the words were out of his mouth before he knew it.

"Vic...about these *surveys* you've been doin'. Your quote unquote botany expeditions. Why is it that you're always comin' back with bags full of *mushrooms*?"

Victor cocked an eyebrow at him, and seemed to consider his answer carefully before he opened his mouth to reply.

"You know how it is Hal. When you're stuck out here in a place like this that's so far away from home, entertainment's where you find it."

Hal stared at him for a moment, and then nodded slightly. Victor smiled at him a bit awkwardly, and then headed back out to join the two militiamen who were already making their way down through the rows of factories.

*   *   *

The Fate's Winds
In orbit around Judgment

Aric pulled all the ration packets from the ready room locker, stuffed them into his flight bag, and then headed toward the weapons locker.

"Are you worried we won't be coming back, Mr. Keith?" Carter asked from behind him.

"It's a penal planet Captain," Aric said flatly.

"Yes, I'm well aware of that, as I believe are you."

Aric felt Carter's constant supervision like a stifling blanket, and a part of him wondered if he wouldn't end up starving to death in a sweaty mud hut on Judgment, just like Danny Xiao. He began to tap the weapons locker's code, but Carter stayed his hand.

"We're not bringing any weapons," the captain said.

"Sir, with all due respect, that would be suicide," Aric warned.

"You're not thinking strategically Mr. Keith. Now, I said no weapons. That's an order."

Aric turned and stared into the eyes of his captain for a moment. They were the eyes of a real captain. They were decisive and stolid, and in that moment he knew that it'd be useless to argue any further. Without another word, he slung his bag over his shoulder and then entered the airlock that led to the cargo bay. Carter watched him go, narrowing his eyes slightly as Aric stepped through the other side of the airlock and disappeared around the corner.

After all the damning comments that Captain Carter had received from the rest of the crew about his command capabilities, Aric felt that sooner or later he'd probably end up being court-martialed, which was fair enough. To be honest, he'd rather just get it over with quickly and be done with it. Maybe he deserved to be judged for overreacting with Danny the way he did. Those acts of sabotage, and he was sure that was what they were, should have been tried in a court. Instead, he was tried for attacking his captain. Wasn't it standard procedure though to discipline someone who attacked their captain? He'd heard of the SSC executing people for less. Things out in this part of space may lack order, but if he'd have allowed discipline to break down, then they truly would have descended into a state of unworkable anarchy.

The slender, aerodynamic orbiter hung in its magnetic dock above the bay doors, with Danny's empty station near the bay's manual controls.

Squeezing inside the narrow hatch, Aric passed through the hold and dropped into the pilot's station. The captain was somewhere behind him, no doubt angry with him over his insubordinate behavior, but Aric was beyond caring at this point.

Drawing the restraining straps tight against his shoulders, he tapped the holocontrols to bring the shuttle to life. A camera above the hatch entrance showed that Carter was just now stepping onto the orbiter. Aric sealed the hatch quickly behind him once he was inside, and then he began the launch sequence.

Normally, he'd feel right at home piloting a shuttle. Technology always comforted him, because he understood it. There was an order to it that one could always count on, and in the event of a malfunction, there was an orderly way of processing the repairs. The uncertainty of his fate, however, was making him feel quite ill at ease.

"Sir…," Aric began.

"Yes?" Carter asked as he strapped himself into the chair next to him.

"I'd like to know what your intentions are regarding myself and Lieutenant Xiao."

Carter looked over the holocontrols in front of him as they flashed green. As soon as all of the shuttle's systems and sub-systems were active, he reached out and tapped the launch button.

"My intention, Mr. Keith, is to find out if your disciplinary action had any effect on him," Carter replied as the magnetic locks clanged open. In moments they entered Gertie's atmosphere, and Aric's stomach twisted as the orange-green haze burned around him.

* * *

Through some trick of its formation, a ring of mountains trapped nearly all of Judgment's water and precipitation in a crown at its frigid northern pole. A single river trickled down from the mountains and wove its way through the planet's vast deserts until it died of evaporation a few hundred miles from its source. That river had been running for millennia, and had carved a canyon so deep into the surface rock that it left very little in the way of arable land other than the small wedge near the prisoners' settlement. Survival was measured in single seasons for those condemned to serve their sentence on Judgment, and no one was ever paroled.

The orbiter's engines blasted grit and stone against a cluster of haphazard mud brick buildings that studded the riverbank as they touched down. Men and women appeared in the doorways, shielding their faces as Carter and Aric stepped out into Judgment's baking heat. The sun-blistered prisoners wore stained SSC coveralls, most of which had been torn and repaired in dozens of places. They carried with them shovels, pickaxes, and adzes. To a man they looked lean and hungry, like the packs of stray dogs that had roamed Belize City looking for corpses to devour after the *Narcos* came.

"And who might you be?" a man called out to them as the prisoners circled the orbiter. Ragged stubble crowned his head, and he'd fixed a lieutenant's stripes to the threadbare shoulders of his coveralls.

"You're British?" Carter asked.

A woman beside him snorted. She wore a rivet driven through her nose, and her hair was swept back in dirty curls.

"No countries here, space boy," the Brit replied. "No spaceships either, but I'm guessing you're the one I talked to on the radio the other day — and it looks like you've brought us a nice ship that can get us all the hell off this rock."

"I believe Mr. Keith here is the one you spoke with," Carter said. "You should know that the orbiter only flies if one of *us* does the flying. The controls are keyed to our genetic signatures."

The man and woman in charge of the settlement exchanged calculating glances. "There are two of you," the British man said.

The sun was a brutal thing, bloated and high overhead. It reminded Carter of the jungle heat from his training runs in Belize long ago.

"What's your name?" Carter asked the man.

"Threed. What's yours?"

"Carter. I'm in command of the *Fate's Winds* now."

"Congratulations on the promotion, I guess" Threed snorted. "So why are you here, Carter?"

"Is the officer Mr. Keith brought here earlier still alive?" Carter asked.

The woman cackled, twisting a mattock in her hands, but she still had not spoken. Carter wondered if she was even able to.

"That depends what he's worth to you," Threed responded vaguely, but his meaning was clear.

Carter's eyes swept over the hundred-odd prisoners who'd surrounded the orbiter. These people wouldn't hesitate to overcome two officers and keep them alive just long enough to escape to the *Fate's Winds*. Then they would take over the ship in a savage mutiny. He'd seen the same plotting look on Cazador's face, back in Belize, and he had recognized it all too late. Years of experience had taught him that, when facing a larger number of opponents, you needed to keep them off balance.

Carter dropped a heavy hand onto Aric's shoulder and squeezed the engineer's muscle in a painful clench.

"I'm wondering if we can arrange a trade," Carter proposed to the Brit.

* * *

Threed's men frog-marched Aric to a thick-walled hut that had its entrance blocked with a heavy stone. Four of them heaved the boulder aside, then shoved Aric into the dark room. Just before the stone rolled back into place, he had time to see ropes and chains fixed to the hut's walls, the desperate scratch marks in the baked clay from dozens of fingernails, and a small pit fouled with the waste of who-knew-how-many prisoners.

Then the daylight disappeared, leaving only Danny's laughter.

"Well, look who's here. You know, I've turned into a pretty good fighter down here Aric," the supply officer said from somewhere on the hovel's floor. "I'd kill you myself, but I think it'd be more fun to watch them torture you."

The supply officer sounded as if something was wrong with his mouth. In the dimness sifting from the cracked ceiling, Aric could just make out Danny's swollen profile. Aric's heart pounded in his chest, and the stench of his wounded shipmate filled his senses.

"Not gonna say anything?" Danny asked. "That's all right, I don't have anything to say to you either."

The silence in the muted acoustics of this sullen, despairing place was terrible.

"Danny, I'm sorry," Aric said, his voice trembling nervously.

"Oh, you're sorry are you? Well, I guess that makes everything ok then," Danny replied bitterly.

"Look, I know you were stealing parts and making false orders. Carter ordered an inventory when he arrived. Nothing you ordered was on the ship."

The supply officer's laughter sounded like the snap of a wet cloth.

"If you did your job so well Aric, then why are you here?" he asked.

"It's not like that, Danny. I don't think that…"

"I don't care what the hell you think, Aric! I don't care what anyone thinks! That's what you never understood about me."

Aric backed against the doorway, feeling for any gap where the stone met the brick, but there was nothing. He was just as trapped as Danny and slid down to face the supply officer's dim shape. Honesty was hard in the Sword Belt, and maybe for Danny it was even impossible. Regardless of what each one of them had done however, their fates had now been tied together.

"I know," Aric conceded. "I misjudged you. Misunderstood you. I'm truly sorry."

"You have no idea how sorry you're gonna be, Aric. No idea at all," Danny said. He would have smiled mirthlessly, if his battered face had allowed it. Instead, he closed his eyes and leaned back against the thick wall of his prison. There wasn't anything left to say. At least, not for the moment.

*　*　*

"Why would you make a deal like this?" Threed asked. Carter squatted next to the mayor like a boulder sparkling in the sun, studying the river's pale waters dozens of meters below. Thin rows of wheat and corn straggled to a stop where the ground dried to desert, and a hot wind whispered through the brittle crops.

Carter ignored the question. "What do you call your village?" the captain asked instead.

"Place is called Last Chance," Threed answered. "Seemed appropriate, given the circumstances."

Carter lifted a stone from the ground and turned it over in his palm. Its sandy soil clung to his perspiration. "What did you do before this, Mr. Threed?"

"It's best not to ask that question around here, Captain."

"I'd like to know," Carter continued.

Threed studied the captain for a moment, then stood and walked to the edge of the river. When Carter joined him, the man seemed to be standing straighter, the roughness of his demeanor replaced with a fuller humanity.

"That's Suicide Leap," Threed noted, pointing to a ledge overlooking the river's canyon a mile from them. "Most of us go that way. It's better than starving to death. I was gonna give Xiao the chance to jump. Boy fought hard, so he earned that much at least."

"Sounds honorable."

"The point is, he was responsible for sending a lot of us here in the first place, so you're gonna have to be a little more convincing if you want me to let him go."

Carter sighed, squinting off into the distance as he carefully considered what he was about to say.

"You know, I used to be a Major in Sol's planetary defense forces, but I was corrupt. I let the *Narcos* take my city without lifting a finger. I lost everyone and everything I loved. I thought I was helping to create a better place, but in truth I was just used and lied to. Still, in the end, it was my choice to go along with it. That's how I ended up getting reassigned out here. I'm lucky I wasn't executed, but someone else ended up taking the fall."

Threed listened, staring down into the river. It wasn't often that an officer, much less a captain, revealed so much about himself.

"So why are you tellin' me all this?" Threed asked.

"I'm telling you this because promised myself that I'd never again make the mistake of standing idle while people suffered," Carter said as he turned to look at the big man. Threed's eyes flashed with a sudden and unexpected glimmer of empathy, and he nodded slowly.

"I was a politician. I was an MP in London actually. I spoke out against forced colonies, if you can believe that," Threed said, and then he spat into the dust irritably. "How ironic is it that I'm now gonna end up dying in one?"

"Very ironic I'd say," Carter said as he tossed the stone he was holding in his hand, and then flicked it toward the water. "Have the pirates been coming here more frequently of late?"

"You know what the worst part is? They actually used to help us. They'd bring us food and equipment. Basically, all the stuff the administrator wouldn't give us, but lately they just take. There's a lot of us here who'd rather die fighting than to just sit around here starving to death. At least the pirates never use force when they come here. They show up at night sometimes, or when we're out workin' in the fields," Threed explained as his gaze returned to the gently flowing river below.

 "What do you think they want?" Carter asked.

"What everyone here wants I suppose. They wanna get the hell outta here so they can head back home and never have to think of this Sol-blasted system ever again."

"So why would they steal food, or metal for that matter? How does that help them exactly if all they really need is antimatter fuel for their Alcubierre drive?" Carter asked.

"I wish I knew. To be honest, I've been wonderin' that myself. No one else around here thinks much of it, but I do. It just doesn't make sense."

"Look, you people need help, and you've got something I need, so let's just lay our cards on the table here. Can we cut a deal, or not?" Carter asked.

"You've got years' worth of supplies up there on your ship, and we've got a whole bunch of starvin' people down here, so if I'm gonna let you go, then I'll need somethin' in return. What is it you're offerin' exactly?" Threed asked as he pretended to study the river nonchalantly. The tension in his shoulders made it obvious that he was trying desperately to conceal how much this new opportunity meant to him.

"First things first. I need to find out who holds the real power in this system, but I'll make a promise to you right now. I'll treat you and your people like human beings, rather than criminals, and I'll do what I can to help you, including sending you down some food."

Threed listened carefully to the captain's words. He'd been lied to enough in his life to know when someone wasn't being honest with him. Carter wasn't lying, and for the first time in a very long time he actually dared to imagine a very different kind of future for himself and his people. Suddenly, he spat in his palm, and then extended it toward the captain.

"All right Captain Carter, we've got ourselves a deal," he said as Carter gripped his hand and shook it firmly.

*　*　*

The Fate's Winds
Bridge

Danielle studied Judgment's sandy surface on her holoscreens, wondering if Danny was still alive. Part of her still couldn't believe how quickly it'd all happened. The destruction of the *Mercy*, the arrival of a new captain, and then the first real combat situation of her admittedly short career. Everything seemed to be changing, and it left her with a constant feeling of uncertainty.

"Have you heard anything from 'em yet?" she asked Julie again.

"No, nothing yet. The orbiter's still powered down," Julie answered.

Arms slid around Danielle's waist, and suddenly she felt Bryon's lips tickle her ear.

"Hey there gorgeous. I changed my mind. The captain won't be back for ages, so what do you say we go back to my cabin and make a little contact of our own?"

Frowning, she grabbed Bryon's arms and pushed them back off of her. She was far too anxious at the moment to deal with his advances.

"Oh come on, don't you love me anymore?" he asked playfully, but when he saw the look on her face, his expression suddenly turned to one of concern. "You're not thinking about Aric, are you?"

Danielle pulled her attention away from the holoscreen just long enough to glare at him for a moment.

"Or is it Carter you're worried about?" Bryon persisted. "Those scars he's got are sure somethin'. I'll bet he's seen more than his share of fights over the years. Is that what you want Dani? You want a bad boy?"

"Bryon, cut it out," Julie snapped impatiently.

"Oh come on you two, I'm just tryin' to lighten the mood around here. You're both so uptight today."

"Officer on deck!" a voice called from the bridge's entrance.

Bryon turned and snapped to attention, but in his surprise, he nearly broke discipline.

"Pandith?" he asked. "What's this all about?"

"Mr. Pandith is the ranking officer on the ship right now, and you will address him as such," Granger said firmly.

"Oh...sorry," Bryon responded as he stiffened once again, and then snapped a salute that Pandith returned in kind.

"At ease," the environmental engineer said as he headed purposely over to Bryon's station. His voice was still soft, but something was different about him.

"What's going on?" Bryon asked as he walked over to join Pandith at his station.

"Before he left for Judgment, Captain Carter asked me to carry out his instructions. This may come as a shock to you, but it will be for a good cause. Ensign Purcell, please begin your preparations for a laser burn of this duration and intensity," he said as he tapped a code into Bryon's holodisplay that brought up a firing pattern with all the necessary power calculations.

Bryon glanced at Pandith in shock for a moment, and then he turned his eyes back to the holoscreen.

"Are you sure this'll work?" he asked.

"We've calculated it down to the atomic radius," Granger confirmed. "It'll work."

"What's goin' on?" Danielle asked. "What are we gonna be doing?"

"First Mate Hoff, I'm sure Captain Carter will be happy to answer any and all questions, but for the moment, he's simply asked that we carry out his orders without contacting him. Do I make myself clear?" Pandith asked.

"Yes sir," she said sheepishly.

"Good. Now all that's left to do is to wait for his signal," Pandith said as he walked over to the captain's chair and sat himself down in it. Granger looked over at him approvingly, and shot him a little grin. Pandith didn't notice however. He brought up the tactical display on his own holoscreen, just to make sure that everything would be ready when the time came to put the plan into action.

*　*　*

Judgment
Last Chance

The boulder ground away from the hovel's entrance, and Aric was suddenly blinded by the evening sunlight. He'd braced himself for his fate, after having had long hours to come to terms with it. If Captain Carter chose to court-martial him, then he'd accept his punishment like the man he'd always wanted to be.

To his surprise however, no one came in to get him. Instead of fists or farm implements looming at the entrance, Threed's much-pierced woman stuck her head around the corner and beckoned to the prisoners.

"Both of you, follow me," she called out to them.

In the light, Aric finally got a good look at Danny's face. The supply officer was a battered mess. Bruises filled his cheeks, and salt ringed his split lips. Threed's companion tossed over a wet rag that landed between Danny's legs. For a moment he did nothing with the cloth, but then slowly he picked it up, lifted it to his lips, and sucked the moisture from it.

"Can you walk?" Aric asked Danny.

"I don't know."

Squatting down, Aric worked his arm around Danny's torso and hauled him unsteadily to his feet. Putting one foot in front of the other, he helped Danny to limp out into the into the heat, and then followed the woman as she led them through the center of the village. Aric expected to see malevolent glares from every hut, but there were no other prisoners to be seen. The woman led them above the village toward where Carter stood on a large stone overlooking the river. This was where the prisoners had all gathered, and as Aric and Danny approached, the crowd parted to allow the officers through.

When they reached the Captain, Carter nodded to both Aric and Danny. Wind sputtered around him, knocking dust and tumbleweeds across the landscape, but when Carter turned to face the prisoners, his voice rang out as clear as day.

"I don't care why you're here," the captain called to them. "Fact is, no one else does either. So what does that make us?"

The prisoners all grumbled and spoke to one another in hushed tones, trying to figure out what this whole thing was all about.

"I'll tell you what that makes us. We're the garbage that Sol would rather not think about, but as long as we're all stuck out here together, I think we should start helping each other," Carter said as he tapped his jaw to activate the transmitter in his implant. "Pandith, this is Carter. Execute my orders."

"What's he doing?" Danny asked nervously. Carter's arrival had given him hope of a reprieve, but now he wasn't really sure what was going on.

"I don't know," Aric whispered back to him. Carter's eyes fell on both of his officers as he continued.

"We've all made mistakes, but I'm here to give you a message," the captain said grimly. His hands rose skyward, and he nearly shouted his final lines. "It's a new day in this system, and it's about time we all started acting like human beings again!"

Threed's woman suddenly screamed as she looked up at the sky and pointed at a blur of blinding light that lanced down with incredible speed.

"That's coming from the ship," Aric said, astonished at what he was seeing. "It's gotta be."

The laser struck the bank of the river a quarter mile upstream, and then carved a steaming path off to the west. Aric shielded his eyes as the beam followed a steady pattern, and when it finally stopped nearly three minutes later, he had to blink and look away for a long moment before he could see what the captain had done. Where seconds ago there had been nothing but desert, the sloshing river now flowed into a shallow basin that formed a perfect lake. Smaller pulses had cut irrigation trenches north and south of the lake, and Aric watched the prisoners' mouths fall open as the soil darkened at their feet.

Threed pushed past them, tears rolling down his face as he fell to his kneels before the captain and took his hand. "Thank you! My god, thank you!" he said over and over again.

Carter wanted to smile, but he restrained himself. The mayor had gone from being the tough and jaded leader of the people here, to a giddy little farm boy in the space of just a few minutes. Hell, there might even be a celebration tonight, perhaps for the first time ever on Judgment

"There, you have a chance now," Carter said as he slipped off the rock. "I hope you'll all make good use of it."

The captain left the hill and walked toward the orbiter as criminals slapped him on the back, thanked him, wrapped him in sweaty hugs. Carter paused in the middle of the throng, looking back at Aric and Danny with the same inscrutable expression.

"Well?" he called to them above the grateful tumult. "Are you coming?"

The pair looked at each other in confusion for a moment, and then Aric wrapped his arm around Danny's back once again so he could help him over to the shuttle.

Chapter Seven

Gertie
Landfall

"This had better be good," Administrator Tannin said to the assembled Colony Council.

Victor Sheddick, Vartan, Hal Yellowknife, and the rest of the members of the Colony Council all crowded around the Council chamber's oval conference table, their faces lit by the glowing holoscreen. They were studying Captain Carter's storied face, curious as to how the man would react to his first official dressing down. Hal reached for the pitcher in the center of the table and poured himself a glass. He was two days sober, and his insides were giving him absolute hell.

"Am I to understand, Captain, that you initiated a major infrastructure action without my, or my Agriculture Department's knowledge or approval?" Tannin shouted at the holoscreen.

Hal slumped at the table with his head down, trying to control his trembling fingers. The meeting had already run late into the evening, and from the look of withering anger on the Administrator's face, he wasn't in any mood to let Captain Carter's affront go unpunished. In fact, Hal couldn't remember the last time anyone had challenged the administrator and come out of it unscathed. He was starting to wonder if there was more of a reason for Tannin's anger than just a simple bad temper.

"I was not aware that I was exceeding my authority," Captain Carter responded calmly. "You have my deepest apology."

"Your apology?" Tannin fumed. "Captain, your ship is the most valuable resource we have in this system. I expect you to keep me informed of every action you take. To waste your efforts on condemned prisoners is…"

"In that case, sir," Carter interrupted. "I need to report that we engaged and destroyed a pirate orbiter around Judgment yesterday and chased its mother ship into the nebula."

"You…*engaged* the pirates?" Tannin asked, his voice suddenly becoming incredibly tight.

Hal straightened in his chair. Vartan suddenly looked rather uncomfortable, and Victor looked absolutely pale.

"Yes sir, we did. A malfunction prevented us from pressing the engagement, but for a first action, the results were satisfactory."

"That was…uhhh…very brave of you, Captain," Tannin stammered as he choked back his anger. "Please send the Council's commendations to your crew."

"It would be my pleasure, sir."

"There remains, however, the matter of addressing your actions on Judgment. Remember that you are under civilian jurisdiction, Captain. That means that you answer to me."

"Understood, sir."

"Our most pressing priority is the intelligence array. It will be critical in ensuring the security of the area," Tannin announced. "I'd like you get it up and running as soon as possible."

"Yes, sir," Carter said.

"I also understand that two of your crewmembers have, in your view, received sufficient punishment on Judgment, and will now be reunited with their crewmates. Is that the case Captain?" Tannin asked.

"Yes, that's correct sir. Mr. Keith and Mr. Xiao are both back aboard."

"Excellent," Tannin said, trying to hide the rising glee he felt at the reinstatement of his tireless mole.

"Is there anything else, sir?" Carter asked. As reprimands went, he knew this one had been a cakewalk.

"No, there's nothing else Captain. That will be all. Safe journey to you and your crew," Tannin said as he swiped the connection closed and then turned to glare at the Council.

"Well I'll be Sol-blasted. He went after 'em, didn't he?" Hal observed, breaking the silence with a voice that was filled with both wonder and hope.

Tannin's eyes flashed. Evening shadows tangled the administrator's thick hair and beard, making it seem as if only half of him was in the room. Victor had told Hal that the administrator had once been considered handsome enough to go into politics back on Earth, but neither of them had any idea how he ended up on Gertie with the rest of the unlucky sods. Now Hal was starting to put the pieces together.

"Out of respect for our captain's reputation, I'd been hoping to keep this private, but Captain Carter was in command of the SSC detachment guarding Belize City in 2132," Tannin remarked slyly, hoping he sounded at least *somewhat* sincere.

"The *Narco* revolution? Carter was the idiot who was asleep at the switch?" Hal asked, his eyes widening in surprise.

"Asleep?" Tannin asked, unable to keep the mocking tone from his voice. "Or paid off?"

Murmurs rippled around the table where the Council members were seated.

"Quiet gentlemen, please," Tannin said to the assemblage. "Now, we need to ask ourselves how much we can trust Captain Carter, and just what we'll do if he goes astray."

As the group discussed the matter amongst themselves, Hal remained silent. He'd had high hopes for their new captain, but now he didn't know what to think. Could he be corrupt, like Tannin suggested? If so, why would he attack the pirates, and then help the people on Judgment? Something didn't add up, but he was suffering far too much at the moment to figure out what it was.

* * *

The Fate's Winds
En Route to The Gate

Danny left Captain Carter's quarters next to the bridge, and rounded the upper deck's horseshoe-shaped passageway until he reached the entrance of the day room. Sol's naval psychologists had recognized that the best relief for human beings cramped in close quarters was to give them a sense of open space. Danny hoped that the large chamber's engineered grass and trees would help to take his mind off the heavy weight of a truth that he could never tell, even to the man who'd saved his life. Yet, as he strolled through the carefully cultivated vegetable gardens and miniature fruit groves, the dark cloud in his mind only thickened.

"You're still limping," Julie commented.

She was sitting on a rock near the stream that bubbled from the top of the room and then sloped downward to gather in a shallow pool.

"Pandith says I'll heal up eventually," Danny said in a rather subdued tone. "He offered to give me some pain killers, but I don't want 'em."

"Yeah, you never take any kind of drugs like that, do you?" she asked.

The sight of Julie shocked him. He'd been on Judgment for only a few days, and in that time she'd lost so much weight from the pills he'd smuggled from Earth that her cheeks had become unhealthy caverns, and he could see her collarbone jutting out from her flight suit. There had been a time when he'd been attracted to her, and now he saw what the drugs had done to someone he could have cared about, and a sudden sense of guilt made him feel hollow inside.

"Julie, things are different now. I can't help you anymore."

"I don't know what you mean," she said as she glanced away at the vegetable plot with a flip of her thin ponytail.

"I mean what we were doing before I got court martialed. I shouldn't have done it. I'm not gonna get you any more of that drug. It's bad for you," he said. He truly hoped that she'd be okay, and that she'd be able to get back to her old self once the meds had finally worked their way out of her system. The medication he'd supplied her with could be addictive, and the last thing he wanted was to be the cause of anyone else's suffering, ever again.

He started toward the rear of the day room, headed for the cargo deck so he could lay down in his cabin to think about things, but she jogged in front of him and blocked his way to the airlock.

"Tannin called for you, right after the captain talked to him. Now, why would he do that?" she asked.

"I have no idea," Danny said, but his stomach churned nervously at her words. This was the call that he knew would be coming sooner or later, and the administrator's reaction to what he had to say worried him.

"I'll put it through to your cabin, and I won't tell the captain that you're talking to...well, *you know who*. Just let me have the rest of the pills."

Sweat shone in her stringy hair, and cloudiness swam in her eyes.

"When you make a mistake, the worst thing you can do is keep making it

over and over again. Don't let that happen, Lieutenant."

The captain's words echoed in Danny's mind as he stared at the strung out girl in front of him.

"Thanks for putting the call through, but I'm not giving you any more of those meds. You can go ahead and tell Captain Carter anything you want," Danny said as he slipped around her, opened the bulkhead, and made his way down the ladder to the cargo deck.

"Danny, you can't do this! I need those meds!" she called out to him desperately as she quickly moved to the bulkhead and looked down at him.

"I'm sorry Julie. I really am," he called back to her, hoping that she wouldn't try to follow him down to his quarters. Fortunately, she didn't, but her quiet sobs reverberated down to him, tearing at his conscience with each passing rung.

*   *   *

"You've certainly looked better," Tannin's voice announced from Danny's holoscreen.

"You were just gonna leave me to die out there on Judgment, weren't you? You didn't lift a finger to do a damn thing about it," Danny muttered bitterly.

"Neither will you when the lives of your crew are at risk," the administrator said, pausing for a moment to let those words sink in. "That is, unless you'd prefer to cancel our arrangement?"

Danny looked down at where his sister's laughing face shone from his wristband. She'd been thirteen when the photo was taken, just a year younger than him. Her eyes shone like stars, and were filled with the innocence and wonder of youth. There was really nothing else for him to say.

"That's what I thought," Tannin sneered. "Are you en route to The Gate?"

"Yeah, that's where we're headed. The captain left right after you spoke to him," Danny said. "I'll take care of the array, just like before."

"That's good. That's very good. And you'll inform me if he does anything like this again?"

"Of course."

"Excellent! It's nice to know we're still on the same team. Your sister's treatments will continue, by the way. I'll be sending a double payment with Falconi next time."

"Is that supposed to be an apology?" Danny asked.

"No, not an apology. Just consider it a salary, and I expect you to remember who you work for," Tannin said, and then he ended the transmission abruptly before Danny could respond.

He stared at the screen for a moment, and then he laid down in his bunk, replaying the conversation over and over in his head. He'd grown to really despise Tannin, but working with him was the only chance he had to keep his sister alive, and to hopefully get her back someday. His hands were dirty, and he was growing weary of it all. Unfortunately, he had no other options.

*　*　*

Julie reached out and caught herself against the bulkhead to avoid falling. Hunger twisted through her abdomen, and the lightheadedness it caused made her somewhat unsteady as she pushed herself further along the corridor toward their new captain's cabin. If Danny wouldn't give her the pills she needed, then he shouldn't be on the ship. She was going to tell Carter about Danny's conversations with the administrator and get the supply officer sent right back to Judgment where he belonged.

"Captain Carter, can I speak to you a moment?" she asked when she'd reached the door of his stateroom.

Her jawbone implant sensed her proximity to the captain's door and transmitted her request to his cochlear implant, but she received no response. She swayed in front of the stateroom for a moment longer, saliva filling her mouth while she daydreamed of Danielle's latest meal in the galley. She shouldn't even be hungry right now, and she wouldn't be if Danny had just given her the pills.

SSC communications officers carried override codes for all access levels of the ship. She focused her blurry vision as she typed the code into the holocontrols outside of Carter's door, and the portal slipped open.

Immediately in front of her, a desk and holostation sat underneath a bunk bed. A few tablets along with some odds and ends filled the shelves on either side of the living area, while the captain's still-packed duffel bag lay on the floor. Carter wasn't there, so she staggered over to the adjoining room. This space had been set up for meetings or meals, with a circular desk that could seat six in the center of the room. This room was vacant as well, but the captain had left the table littered with scraps of paper.

She picked one up, squinting at the profile of a woman's face. The portrait's subject had a beautiful rounded nose and strong forehead, and the pencil shading of her skin was a rich mahogany. A red scrawl slashed through the woman's throat over and over, devolving into angry strokes that had ripped through the page.

Julie felt nauseous and let the drawing slip from her hand.

"Can I help you, Ms. Ford?" a voice asked from behind her.

Captain Carter had emerged from the washroom. She couldn't be sure, but his eyes looked rather red and puffy, and his face seemed drawn by some intense sadness. He still wore the same dusty uniform from his trip to Judgment.

"Yes sir. I need to tell you that Danny...," she said, but then her legs buckled. She tried to catch herself on the stateroom's table but grasped the drawings instead.

"Mr. Pandith, get to my stateroom immediately! We have a medical emergency!" she heard the captain say. Seconds later she was on the floor, staring upward as the captain's drawings sifted over her like fluttering confetti.

"Are you all right?" Carter asked as he leaned over her.

"It's not so bad," she responded with a strange smile. "I can't feel anything."

"You can't feel anything? What do you mean?" he asked anxiously, not really knowing what he could do to help her.

"Maybe it's better this way," she said weakly, and then she closed her eyes and fell silent for a while.

The captain reached down and pressed two fingers against the side of her neck. Her pulse was erratic, and her breathing had become shallow and irregular.

"You just hold on now. He'll be here soon, and then we'll get you all fixed up," he said as he gently brushed the hair away from her face.

* * *

The Tranquility
Inside the Great Orion Nebula

In the few hours she spent in her cabin each night, Mephista seldom slept. The stem cell pills she still stubbornly took after all these years kept her in constant pain as the long-severed nerves in her lower back struggled to reconnect themselves. Even worse than that, however, were the memories that flooded her mind whenever she closed her eyes.

The *Shift* had been a small patrol boat, and her first command. She should have realized that her ship was being offered up as bait when her orders put her so many AUs from the support fleet. She'd been young and unscarred by experience at the time, so when she was told to keep her defenses down, she dutifully did as she was ordered. Unfortunately, both she and her ship had paid a steep price for her obedience.

She lay in her bunk, remembering how the shot from the fusion pistol had torn through her EVO suit as she floated through space, and how flecks of blood floated up and smeared across her helmet's faceplate. The shot had come from one of her own crew. The telepathic influence of the Bwain was strong, and as she closed her eyes, her mind filled with images of her fellow crewmen, screaming and tearing at themselves as the strange aliens captured their minds, as well as their ship.

The call to battle stations boomed in her ear and snapped her back to the present. She knew what was coming, and her thirst for revenge burned far hotter than whatever physical pain she was currently experiencing.

Calling up her cabin's tactical visuals, she immediately spotted the small, ugly Bwain ship that was cruising about four AUs from her stern. It appeared to be a first generation Bwain patrol ship, which generally looked like a swollen bubble of glassy igneous rock that was studded with pathetic weaponry.

She couldn't confirm her suspicion, but every Bwain vessel she'd seen appeared to be hand built. For beings that supposedly shared thought across vast distances, they had surprisingly limited technical capabilities. That said, the ship had somehow gotten into the *Tranquility's* range without being detected, so at least on a tactical level, the Bwain seemed to be improving.

"Bring us to within firing range and eliminate that ship," Mephista ordered as she flung herself into the corridor. A junior officer standing watch outside her cabin handed her a canister of compressed air, and she used the oxygen as a thruster to push herself quickly to the bridge while her implant relayed her order to the crew.

By the time she arrived on the bridge, the *Tranquility* had closed in on the Bwain's ship, and its missiles were arcing in red streaks toward the alien craft. The Bwain tried to execute an evasive maneuver, but they didn't have time to initiate their faster than light engines, and their thrusters couldn't generate enough delta-V to avoid the missiles. Since they lacked the ability to generate any protective countermeasures against the attack, the projectiles made a direct hit on the ship's bow. The depleted uranium cores melted through its hull before they detonated, turning the Bwain ship into an expanding, molten cloud that quickly faded against the background of the nebula.

"Target destroyed," the sensor officer announced with a broad smile.

It was indeed a victory, but in truth it was only an opening shot. She had her doubts about whether they would even notice the destruction of a lone scout ship. The thing about the Bwain was that they always traveled in swarms. The fact that they'd just encountered one of their scout ships meant that there were likely more ships on the way, and it was a safe bet that they weren't too far behind.

"The Bwain are coming," Mephista called out to the crew as she entered the bridge. "I want everyone on full alert. It's time to get some revenge on those bastards."

*   *   *

Personal Logbook: Captain Atlas Carter
Entry 14 – En route to The Gate

I'm sorry Aida, but your picture's torn. I'll make you another one...a better one.

Julie's in the medical bay with Pandith watching over her. She was severely malnourished, a victim of a diet medication overdose. Danny was her supplier, but he refused to give her any more after he returned to the ship. Is that progress? I don't know, but it sure seems like it.

Atlas' Last Stand

My instinct here is to try to help people. I brought Danny back, and I
helped all those prisoners down on Judgment, but it seems like
everything I do to help is the wrong move, at least in the eyes of the
administrator.

You know, I don't sleep much, and in the quiet times at night I wonder if
it'd just be better for everyone if I were to join you and all the others who
died that day.

When Julie first spoke, for some stupid reason I thought it was you. I let
myself truly cry for the first time after that. What surprises me more is
that I'm actually writing about it. Did you ever see me cry? No, I don't
think you ever did. Sometimes I guess I wish that you had, just so you'd
know that I was capable of it.

I'll have more time for drawings after we finish building Administrator
Tannin's array. You know, it's good actually. Focusing on my duties
takes my mind away from all those other thoughts that I just can't seem
to control.

Cazador once found me sketching instead of training, and he asked me
why I took time to make art when I could be out there living instead. I
told him the truth. I told him that I needed my art, because it kept me
human. What I didn't say out loud however was that it kept me from
turning into a conniving animal like him. I don't think he'd have
appreciated that too awful much.

We're all searching for something out here. I guess for me, I'm trying to
find some sort of redemption. My soul is so broken right now. I just hope
that these logs will someday find their way to yours, and that when they
do, you'll know that I'm finally coming home.

* * *

The Fate's Winds
Outside The Gate

At first, the faint distress beacon barely registered in Danielle's conscious mind. She was so focused on keeping the array mirrors aligned with the ship for their latest test that it took her a moment to understand what she was seeing.

"Ensign Purcell, charge level?" Captain Carter asked.

"Seventy-five percent and rising," Bryon answered.

"Excellent. Mr. Xiao, is there anything I should know about that laser array?" Carter inquired of his supply officer.

"No sir," came Danny's reply from the cargo hold.

Danielle squinted, zooming in on the flashing green dot that had emerged from the nebula.

"Very well, then. Mr. Purcell, you may…"

"Captain!" Danielle cried out, interrupting his order.

"What is it Ms. Hoff?" Carter asked as he directed his attention to Danielle, who was staring intently at the display before her.

"Captain, I'm getting something on the sensors," she said as she tapped the readout in front of her and sent it to the main holoscreen at the front of the bridge.

"It's transmitting," Julie called from her station. She still looked rather frail, but Pandith had managed to get her back on her feet, and back to her duties fairly quickly. Unfortunately, it would take some time for her to truly recover from the damage the diet medication had done to her body.

"Let's hear it," the captain said. Suddenly, a stream of what sounded like Japanese blurred through the bridge, swiftly changing to the slightly robotic sound of the English translation.

"This is life pod 785 from the mining freighter Ichikari. I have one survivor on board. This is life pod 785..."

For a few brief moments they all listened carefully to the pod's tinny plea for attention, and then without the slightest hesitation, the captain snapped into action, calling out several orders in rapid succession.

"Ms. Hoff, plot a course to the life pod, and plot a reverse trajectory on it. I wanna know where it came from. There might be others out there as well. Mr. Pandith, please head to Airlock 2 with a medical kit. Mr. Xiao, join me at Airlock 2 and suit up for a spacewalk. The rest of you, we're standing down from our test of the array until further notice. Maintain your stations and await further orders."

"Captain," Danielle called as the computer extrapolated the pod's trajectory. "That pod out there. It came through The Gate."

"What?" he asked, narrowing his eyes at her as he tried to process what she'd just said.

"Reverse trajectory indicates that the life pod traveled *through* The Gate," she repeated.

"All right. Ms. Ford, keep trying to hail them. I doubt you'll get a response other than that automated signal, but keep trying anyway," he ordered.

"Yes sir," she replied as he turned and left the bridge.

Chapter Eight

The Fate's Winds
Outside The Gate

Carter stepped into the snug grip of his EVO suit, ran his arms through the chemically cooled padding, and then drew the magnetic seal up his chest. He then slipped the opened helmet over his head, reached up to pull down the face shield, and then locked the helmet into place by twisting the handles on either side of his head. The HUD flashed across his visor as the suit powered up, and the nanos marched over his limbs in a gold shimmer.

Danny flickered onto Carter's display as the supply officer sealed himself up and activated his own suit. The captain got to his feet, and immediately felt the additional weight of the carbyne mesh that now covered his body. He spent a few moments getting accustomed to the feel of the suit, and then he hefted the induction thruster from the floor. The thruster's heavy Casimir plates used the quantum properties of space itself to generate thrust, and operated in the exact same way as his suit's own inducers. With more surface area however, the thruster was able to generate a much stronger acceleration, which in turn would allow them to slow down the mysterious life pod.

"Captain, you need to hurry. At the speed the life pod is traveling you've only got a small window of opportunity before it passes us," Danielle's voice said through his implant.

"Copy that," Carter acknowledged as he followed Danny into the airlock's cramped funnel.

"You know, Aric and Granger are more qualified for this than I am," Danny said.

"Maybe, but I chose you," Carter stated flatly as he set down the inducer and then turned to seal the airlock's inner door.

As soon as the panel flashed green, he turned his attention back to Danny and scanned him using the sensors that were built into his suit. If there were any spots on Danny's suit that hadn't sealed properly, they'd show up on the HUD display.

"You don't need to do that ya know. I'm showing all green," Danny said.

"There was a time when I thought I didn't *need* to do a lot of things. Atmosphere exchange in ten," Carter noted as he returned his focus to the task at hand. Danny's sigh whispered over their intercom as both men tethered themselves to the handrails.

"Depressurization in five seconds," the ship's computer warned them. *"Four...three...two...one. Depressurizing."*

A whistling outside Carter's helmet quickly faded to nothing as the ship withdrew the airlock's atmosphere. His HUD flashed yellow for just a brief moment, and then red to indicate exterior vacuum.

"Opening exterior hatch," Danny intoned as he tapped the airlock's control.

The hatch's ring spun, and as soon as the door had opened, Danny stepped out into the vacuum of space. Carter followed, and instantly found himself having to push past the stomach-churning sensation of moving from the ship's magnetic gravity field, out into the weightlessness of space.

Stars suddenly filled his field of vision, like billions of pinpricks in the night. The nebula's frothed rainbow gradually swallowed them until it dominated the space in front of the ship. As far as he could see both above and below him, the remains of the long-dead star hung there in space like the end of the world.

Danny waited next to a handrail just outside of the airlock, floating against the nebula's background. This was his last test. Even knowing that Aric had most likely told him about the faulty mirrors, Danny had chosen to lie about the array's operational readiness. What Carter needed to know was *why* Danny was trying to sabotage the array, why he'd been sending the fake orders to Gertie, and what he'd been talking about in those encrypted messages to administrator Tannin. It was clear that the supply officer was the key to cracking the mystery of what was happening in this system, but so far Danny had chosen to remain silent on the matter, just as he himself had done once when he'd been afraid.

Tannin had been quick to dispatch the *Fate's Winds* far from Gertie after they'd helped Judgment. In spite of the pirate raids, Tannin's orders to Captain Green had kept both ships far from the Sword Belt's planets for the duration of their mission. Why? What was Tannin trying to accomplish?

Carter triggered his inducers to float along the *Fate's Winds'* shimmering hull, and Danny followed a moment later. The nebula's gasses billowed in red, pink. and purple cushions of dead stars that once might have held whole civilizations, but were now nothing more than a raw wound that seeped over the shimmering blackness of their suits.

"I'm showing your intercept point at coordinates 123 mark 492 mark 75," Danielle advised them through their implants.

"Copy that," Carter called. When they reached a flat point of the hull, the captain triggered his thrusters to bring himself and the outboard inducer he was carrying to a halt. "We'll hold here."

"Captain, do you really think there could be someone still alive in there?" Danny asked as Carter unclipped his tether and tossed it to him. The buckle drifted through space and bounced against chest. He looked down at it, using the sensors in his visor to examine the metal.

"I doubt it, but if there's even a chance, then we have to try to help them before it's too late."

"Captain...I don't...," Danny started to say, but Carter interrupted him before he could finish.

"Listen to me. You're a part of this crew Mr. Xiao, whether you want to be or not. Right now we've got a job to do, and we're running out of time, so let's go get this done," Carter said, his voice steady as he looked pointedly at the supply officer.

Danny took the carabineer in his glove and clipped the buckle to his waist. As soon as it was secured, Carter tapped the spider steel with an electrified finger, sending a molecular signal down the material that hardened it into a rigid support that would keep both of them locked together.

"Prepare for thrust in three...two...one...engage," Carter said. He activated the inducers in his suit, and from the corner of his eye he watched as the supply officer followed him away from the hull.

Danny activated his own thrusters, which caused his suit to glow from each of its joints. The suits needed no fuel or oxygen, using only the particles spontaneously produced by quantum vacuum fluctuations. These were converted into plasma which, in turn generated acceleration, and in this way, the suits could theoretically serve indefinitely; their only limitations were the bodies inside them.

The life pod glowed a distant green on Carter's HUD, but he could not yet see the craft with his naked eye. Suddenly a warning light started to flash. They were drifting out of the optimal flight path because Danny was pushing his inducers too hard.

"Mr. Xiao, please correct your thrust," Carter ordered. "We're getting off course."

The supply officer slowed, his induction rings a blur of blue-white streaks as fire bled from his joints. They only had a few more minutes to wait before the pod would be upon them.

"Captain, can I ask you a question?"

"What is it Mr. Xiao?" Carter asked.

"Why did you come back for me?" Danny asked as they floated there.

"*Fate's Winds*, intercom only," Carter instructed. The command cut the transmission relay that ran back to the ship, so that they could speak privately.

"Why did you lie to me about the array, Lieutenant?" Carter asked.

The golden glass of Danny's visor turned away, streaks of reflected plasma where his eyes would have been. Carter's suit shifted as his navigational computer executed a course correction.

"There are some answers I don't think you'd really wanna hear," Danny said in a subdued tone.

"We're not broadcasting," Carter said. "It's just you and me out here."

The first glimmer of the life pod appeared as a white streak against the star field. He had no idea who or what they'd find, but he needed his crew to be united. More importantly, if he was going to end the threat to the Sword Belt, he needed to know where it came from.

Danny drifted next to him, and they both watched in silence as the pod grew closer with each passing minute.

"I should have died on Judgment," Danny said, breaking the silence all of a sudden. Carter couldn't tell if the comment was meant for him, or if he was simply thinking out loud.

"If anyone on my crew dies Mr. Xiao, it'll be because they died in the course of performing their duties, not because they were left to rot on some desolate planet. I would advise you to remember that," Carter said. Danny didn't answer. He just continued to stare silently at the approaching vessel.

* * *

"Twenty meters out," the captain reported after he'd removed the restrictions on their communications channel.

"Roger that," Danielle's voice spoke from his ear. "We have you on the halos."

"The pod looks undamaged, but it's older tech, so there's no nanos on it," Danny observed. "I can't believe it's in as good a shape as it is."

As the craft's course brought it closer to them, Carter saw that frost and scorch marks covered the life pod's bullet-shaped hull.

"It may not be in as good a shape as you think Mr. Xiao. Hopefully the environmental systems, or the hull itself haven't been compromised," Carter said. "Ten meters now. Are you ready?"

"Yeah, I'm ready. Let's do it," Danny said.

Both his and Carter's suit inducers fired in unison, pressing their bodies against the impact gel that lined the inside of their EVO suits. Their momentum brought them parallel to the life pod as it floated past. Once they were in position, the ship's computer took over. It adjusted their thrust to match the pod's exact orientation and velocity.

As they inched closer to the life pod, Carter saw that its single porthole was caked with frost. If there was in fact someone alive in there, he was going to have an awful lot of questions for them, starting with what the *Ichikari* had been doing *outside* of The Gate.

"Five meters now," Carter called. "Course and speed are matched, and we're closing in. Mr. Granger, can you give me some background on the *Ichikari*?"

"Will do. Let me dig around and see what we've got," the science officer replied through his implant.

Carter's inducers fired, nudging him closer and closer to the pod's handrails. He loosened the spider steel that tethered him to Danny, allowing them both to resume their own independent motion, and then he reached out and seized a cold handrail above him. Inducers fired from every joint, working to match the pod's trajectory while keeping his arm in its socket as the tether suddenly pulled taut and the supply officer was jerked forward.

"Contact," Carter announced. "Securing the pod now."

"Acknowledged," Danielle's voice called back to him.

Carter tethered himself to the life pod, then released the inducer and floated it toward Danny. Lieutenant Xiao's suit fired to counter the heavy object's movement, and then he pushed forward past the captain, and around to the nose of the craft.

Carter ran the line of spider steel through several of the handrails to make create a towing loop. Hopefully, they wouldn't need to bring the pod in manually, but it never hurt to be prepared.

"Activating inducer magnets," Danny said. "Magnets are engaged. We've got a good seal on the pod's exterior, and the inducer is hot."

"Copy that. Brace for course correction," Carter replied. Just then, Granger's voice crackled in his ear.

"Captain, I've got that info you wanted."

"Ok, let's hear it."

"The *Ichikari* was assembled in Martian orbit in 2218 under the Japanese flag. Its last flight plan had it traveling to the Sigma Orionis cluster on a survey mission more than seventy years ago."

"So it's been off the books all this time? I'm guessing it was being used for illegal mining operations then," Carter replied.

"That would be my guess too. Any clues from the pod as to what happened?" Granger asked.

Carter studied his watery reflection in the ice crystals that had built up on the pod's porthole. Danny joined him a few moments later. He clipped his tether to the handrail, and then held onto the metal as tightly as he could.

"I'm hoping we'll be aboard shortly with the answer to that question. Initiate course correction now Ms. Hoff," Carter ordered.

"Initiating course correction in three...two...one," Danielle said. The heavy inducer fired hard, both slowing the pod, and adjusting its course so that it was now headed toward the ship.

The sudden deceleration would have thrown both men flying off into the darkness of space if they hadn't been tethered securely to the craft. Even tethered, they both held on for dear life as their momentum changed both suddenly and drastically.

"You guys ok out there?" Granger asked through their implants.

"I think I just crapped in my suit, but I'm all right I guess," Danny replied in a strained voice.

"Eh, don't worry about it. The nanos will clean it up for ya," Granger said with a laugh. "You ok Captain?"

"Just fine Mr. Granger, and thankfully I'm still in full control of my excretory system," Carter said.

"Hey, I am too," Danny said defensively. "I was just kiddin' about that."

"Uh huh...," Carter said as Danny let out an indignant huff.

*　*　*

Gertie
Landfall

Hal pushed his hovercart quickly through Landfall's streets, eager to escape the glares of Vartan's militia. He worried constantly that in one of his drunken rants he'd let slip his suspicions about the truth behind the pirate raids, and in Tannin's resulting arrests. His fears had turned his weekly supply trip into town into an ordeal. The shivering weakness in his muscles and the desperate longing for a drink he kept feeling didn't help either.

He could see the farmer's market up ahead. It was his last stop of the day, which was a massive relief. The sooner he could get away from the tension that gripped Landfall, the happier he'd be.

Lisa ran the market that sold all the fresh fruits and vegetables that Victor's people could coax into growing on Gertie. The colony still had plenty of nutrient powder that could be printed into meals, but there was nothing Hal liked better than fresh food. Well, nothing aside from nightcrawler anyway. He was salivating for a crisp carrot or an apple when he turned in to the tent, but instead of the usual welcoming smiles that usually greeted him, he found that he'd just walked in on a rather tense scene.

A table of stores had been knocked over, and Lisa's husband Dax was picking them up and putting them back into their containers.

"We know you've been working with the pirates!" a militiaman growled, hauling the tall farmer back to his feet. Hal paused at the doorway, wary of this unexpected confrontation.

"Tell the truth now, and it'll go a lot easier on you," his comrade added.

"I don't even know what you're talking about!" Lisa shouted at them, tears streaming down her face as she glanced nervously at her husband. Half of her blond hair had slipped from its bun, and her ruddy face was pale with fear. "All we do is collect the produce from the farms! We don't have any dealings at all with pirates!"

"That's not what we've heard," the first soldier said. "We've heard you've been talkin' to the farmers about what's goin' on."

"Of course we have!" Dax admitted. "We're all scared! It's not safe out there anymore, but instead of doin' your damn jobs and goin' after the pirates like you're supposed to, you two jerks are standin' here harassing us!"

"I'd watch what I was saying if I were you," the militiaman warned as his hand dropped to his pistol. Lisa's husband raised his thick hands defensively, showing all the calluses he'd built up from years of working in the soil.

"What's goin' on here?" Hal demanded.

The two militiamen turned, their sneers fading as they recognized the Colonial Council badge that Hal wore on his chest. "We're conducting an investigation into the recent pirate activity, sir."

"What's happened now?" Hal asked.

"We're not hitting the food quotas," Lisa explained. "Tannin thinks that someone's been siphoning food to the pirates."

"Well that's something I can bring up with Victor Sheddick and the rest of the Council," Hal said. "Now, you don't need to be harassing these good people. It only makes the whole damn colony afraid of you. Go back to Vartan and tell him that I'll vouch for these two."

The militiamen glanced at each other for a moment, and then stormed off. Hal watched until they'd both turned the corner, and then knelt to help Dax pick up the remaining berries that had scattered around the floor.

"Oh my god, thank you *so* much Hal. We sure do appreciate it," Dax said he rose back up and sighed with relief.

Lisa stooped to pick up the last errant piece of fruit, and then wrapped her arms around Hal, practically crying into his shoulder.

"I don't know what we would have done if you hadn't have shown up. They won't listen to reason. I don't know what's happened to them. They used to be good people that did their best to help everyone."

"I know darlin'. Everyone's worried about what's been goin' on around here," Hal acknowledged as he stepped back and tried to flash her a reassuring smile, that mostly just ended up looking rather awkward and uncertain. Every day spent without nightcrawler made his mind more and more clear. He remembered more things, was able to put more pieces together from not only the Council meetings, but from Victor's offhand comments over the gin bottle as well.

"What did those men mean about *talking to the farmers*?" Hal asked.

The couple exchanged a glance, weighing how much they could trust a drunken Indian on the Council. Finally, Lisa offered a subtle nod. Dax faced Hal and studied his face for a moment before he spoke.

"People aren't just scared, Hal. They're fed up. If Tannin can't protect us, then we might just need to take matters into our own hands. We could sure use a friend on the Council," he added, almost as an afterthought.

Hal stared at him for a moment as he processed what he'd just heard, and he found himself caught between his suspicions and his caution. Going against Tannin was foolhardy to be sure, but like him, Dax and Lisa were just colonists who were trying to make things better. If Tannin and Vartan had turned to terrorizing innocent families, farmers, and merchants, then how much longer did he have? His membership on the council would only buy him so much leeway.

While his thoughts raced, Lisa rested a bag of apples on the top of Hal's cart. Dax offered him a sack of potatoes and two pints of strawberries as well.

"Oh come on you two, I can't eat all that!" Hal protested.

"It's on us," Lisa answered, "Consider it our thanks for helping us."

"Yeah well, I'll do whatever I can to help. I think before we can really do anything though, we need to figure out just what exactly is goin' on with this whole thing," Hal said as he shook each of their hands solemnly. "You two have any more trouble with them, you let me know."

"Thanks again," Dax said as he placed his hand on Hal's shoulder and walked him out to his cart.

Once Hal had mounted up and was headed back out of town, the gears in his head started turning for what felt like the first time in weeks. If only he could put it all together.

*   *   *

When Hal pulled up in front of his home, he found Victor sitting there on a stool, waiting for him at the entrance.

"You must be gettin' old Hal," he called. "Normally the trip into town takes you a half an hour."

"How'd you know I went to town?"

"The Council has its ways," Victor said in mock seriousness, tapping the side of his nose knowingly.

Hal steered his trolley up against his trailer, palmed open the door, and pushed the food inside while Victor followed him in.

"That's a lot of food!" Sheddick observed. Been doing some favors for Dax and Lisa?"

"I guess you could say that," Hal muttered.

"You got time for an afternoon repast with an old friend?" Victor asked as he picked up two glasses and clinked them together.

Hal licked his lips, his hand shooting out before his friend even finished pouring. His grip tightened around the glass, and he looked back at the rest of the food that was still sitting on the top of his cart.

"Let's go outside, Vic," he suggested.

They sat in Gertie's pleasant sunshine and watched as the factories hummed away, pumping out the last of the mysterious supplies that were destined for the *Fate's Winds*. The warm sun and Victor's company helped to calm the fear that had been rising in Hal. The drink remained in his hand, but he hadn't yet touched a drop of it.

"What do you make of our new captain?" Victor asked after a long swig.

"It's hard to tell really, but it seems to me like we might finally have someone who can do some real good. Went after them pirates and chased 'em right out of orbit. I thought Tannin was a little harsh with him over that whole thing."

"He still hasn't fixed the security array," Victor said.

"That's true, but then again, he just got here. I think we need to give the poor guy a chance."

"Uh-huh," Victor murmured doubtfully as he sipped his nightcrawler. Glancing over, he saw that Hal hadn't made any progress with his drink. "Too early for you?"

Hal looked down at his glass, pretending to be startled. The sickly sweet odor wafted into his nose, and his body was filled with urges that he was desperately trying to fight.

"No, I'm just thinking about what we're gonna do," he said as he forced himself to look away from the tempting drink in his hand.

"Well, you can give Carter a chance if you like, but I'm worried about him," Victor continued. "What if he goes off and does something stupid? I mean, if the *Fate's Winds* is gone, then we're toast. The pirates will be able to do anything they want with us."

"Carter doesn't seem like the stupid type to me."

"Maybe not, but do you know how many people died in Belize City...on *his* watch? The *Narcos* wanted to make an example of the place, and he just sat back and let them."

Hal whistled as though he were surprised, but something about the whole conversation seemed off to him.

"Tell me somethin' Vic. Where did the pirates come from?" he asked.

"Well, we don't really know anything about 'em, do we? It's not like we ever catch any of 'em."

"I guess what I mean is, why would they come all the way out here? Sure we've got minerals and soil and what not, but you don't get rich stealin' food and metal. We're decades away from havin' any kind of wealth in this system, so why come here?"

"How am I supposed to know what a pirate thinks? Maybe they're just out here because we're an easy target," Vic suggested.

"I don't think Carter's gonna be all that easy," Hal countered. Victor frowned as he looked down at his drink.

"Hal, were you even listening to me? That man is negligent. Maybe even a criminal, or at worst a traitor."

Hal found himself nodding, though he didn't believe a word of what

Victor had said.

"It's just that things are getting' bad. The militia were harassing Lisa and Dax when I got there this afternoon. I put a stop to it, but the Council shouldn't be inciting fear like that. People need to know that we're on their side."

Victor got to his feet, tipped his glass, and drained the last of the liquid down his throat.

"I'll look into what you said, Hal. If we've got unrest between the militia and the people, the Council's gonna have to take action," Victor said. Hal set down his full glass and shook his friend's hand. "It's good to see you're almost finished with the last shipments."

"Just doin' my part for the cause," Hal answered. "See you next time."

Victor nodded, and then turned and headed off down the path, away from Hal and the factories. Hal forced himself to spill his drink out on the grass, and as he closed his eyes to avoid watching the spillage, a thought suddenly occurred to him. "Hey, Vic! How'd you know I was in town?"

"I already told you, Hal. Think about it," Victor said as he turned and flashed him a half-smile while he tapped the side of his head. A quick second later, he turned back around and continued on his way. Hal watched him go, the gears in his head grinding harder than ever.

"Now what the hell did he mean by that?" Hal muttered to himself as he turned and headed back inside.

* * *

Hal pushed the last hovercart into the warehouse that he'd erected on the eastern side of his factories, and then unloaded the newly-printed microprocessors into a cargo bin. The chips had a universal bus that could be plugged into virtually any component, after which it would be flashed nearly instantaneously with whatever code was required for its operation. There were thousands of them, and for a while he'd wondered how the *Fate's Winds* was using so many of the damn things, but Victor's visit had just confirmed what he'd already suspected. They weren't for the ship at all. Someone on the Council…definitely Victor, and maybe even Tannin himself was working with the pirates. There was no other explanation for what was happening in town, the ridiculous production demands, or for Victor's veiled threat.

Reversing the cart, Hal pushed it out over the grass toward Printing Factory 12. He pressed his palm to the control, waited for the entry door to slide back, then slid the cart inside. The factory's interior smelled of polymer, silicone, and heated metal. Rows of half-printed chips lined the walls, waiting to be finalized by the machine's molecular jets before they were nudged down the conveyor belts and into the waiting cart.

Hal locked the hovercart in place, checked that the nanos had resupplied the station with copper and silicon, and then resealed the factory.

"Printing Factory 12 online," his monitor confirmed. The soft whir of the printers resumed as they began conjuring electronics from the elements once more.

Instead of returning to his trailer, Hal went for a stroll through the rows of factories while he considered his options.

In a typical colony, a colony's construction engineer would take both a family, *and* an apprentice. The ultimate goal was to build a guild of makers that helped the colony grow, but Hal was still married to a woman back on Earth, and in spite of the fact that he'd never see or speak to her again, it just didn't feel right to take another wife on Gertie. For a long time, he'd preferred to be alone with his nightcrawler, rather than think too awful hard about anything in particular. He'd become far too out of touch with what was going on in the colony, which was why he hadn't noticed what was happening until it was too late to do much of anything about it. Still, there had to be *something* he could do to help people like Lisa and Dax. They shouldn't have to suffer because of the corruption of others.

He stopped at factory three, one of his large-format printers, and stepped inside. A haze of ultrafine carbyne dust hung in the air, so he quickly pulled a respirator over his face in an effort to avoid inhaling any of the powdered carbon and steel. This five-by-five-meter factory churned out sheets of carbyne steel that could be nanoformed into whatever shape was required.

The factory was currently producing a panel that would be used for a space ship hull. He stared at it for a moment, and then he knelt down and ran his hand over the still-warm, half-finished product.

"Just what the hell are you up to Tannin?" Hal wondered aloud.

Suddenly, all the anger that Tannin had directed at Captain Carter finally clicked into place. As Hal's theory solidified, a furtive hope filled him. He hurried back to his crate, not even bothering to remove the respirator until he reached his design computer.

"New CAD/CAM session," he gasped at his monitor.

"Design library?" the computer queried as Hal tossed the respirator onto his desk.

"Weapons."

Chapter Nine

The Fate's Winds
Medical Bay

"I don't know what's wrong with her," Pandith sighed as he tossed his examination gloves into a disposal cabinet. The young girl that Carter had carried in from the life pod lay unconscious in the medical bay's examination chair, pale and chilled from her time in space. She was Asian in descent, and her long dark hair flowed around a beautifully smooth face that still bore traces of heavily stylized makeup. Danny had helped Pandith clean the dried blood from her face and arms, while a still-recovering Julie had changed the girl out of her soiled kimono and into a flight suit that was too big for her, but it was the smallest size they had. Through it all, the girl had never once regained consciousness. Even now, as her eyes fluttered under their almond lids, and tension creased her beautiful, young face, the girl would not awaken.

"Her heart rate's elevated," Pandith noted. "Her synapses are showing unusually high activity, and she's sweating quite a bit. It's almost as if she has some kind of fever, but her blood tests are normal. She's in some form of a coma, but not due to any disease or injury that I've been able to find."

Carter brushed a hand over the girl's hair, feeling the warmth from her forehead. Her slight body barely left a ripple under the bed sheet. It was nothing short of a miracle that she'd survived, but what was the point of surviving if they couldn't bring her out of this coma that she seemed to be stuck in?

"Do you have children, Captain?" Julie asked.

His hand stilled, and he pulled it back to his side without answering.

"I'm sorry. I didn't mean to pry," she said awkwardly.

"Captain, we've downloaded the pod's telemetry," Danielle's voice crackled over the med bay's intercom. "The girl's pod went active three weeks ago."

"There was no distress call from the *Ichikari*?" he asked.

"There's no way of knowing. If there was, the nebula would have blocked it," she responded.

"The only way we're gonna know what happened on that ship is if she tells us," Carter said as he stared thoughtfully at the girl's young face, and the dark hair that feathered out behind her head.

"She won't be saying anything," Danny commented.

Carter had dismissed the supply officer after they'd brought the pod through the airlock, but Danny had stayed to help Pandith. The captain didn't know if this was a positive development or not, but whatever Danny was wrestling with was starting to show as strain on the young officer's face.

"And why is that exactly?" Pandith asked.

"Do you know what girls like this are used for on a smuggler's ship?" Danny asked. Pandith looked away, embarrassed. "She's not gonna want to tell you anything. It would be shameful in her culture."

"And in ours?" Carter asked.

The supply officer looked at Carter, his face a mixture of sadness and determination as he shook his head. Just then, the girl suddenly shot bolt upright. She seized Danny's arm, and jerked him toward her with a frenzied strength. Her eyes had rolled up in her head, and her mouth fell open into a silent scream. Then a moaning string of Japanese escaped her, and the girl lapsed back into unconsciousness.

"What the hell did she just say?" Carter demanded. "Computer, replay."

"There's no need," Danny said. "I speak Japanese."

"You understood her?" Julie asked.

"She said that the old ones are coming"

"The *old ones*?" Carter repeated, a slight look of puzzlement furrowing his brow.

"It's how the Japanese refer to the Bwain. Captain, I think it's a pretty safe bet that the Bwain killed the crew of the *Ichikari* - everyone except for her," Danny said, frowning with concern as he glanced down at the girl once again.

* * *

Aric climbed the ladder to the upper deck, following both Granger and Danny up to the bridge. The whole crew had been summoned, and this was the first time he'd left engineering since Danny had returned from Judgment. None of the others said a word as they jogged along the horseshoe that ringed the day room. Even that in itself was a change; when Aric had been in command, there would have been sniping and slacking the whole way. Captain Carter had instilled a sense of discipline in the crew that they hadn't known before.

He had no idea what the captain was going to say, but his feelings toward his new captain were changing. In spite of the guilt and shame he still felt over the mess he'd made of his command, he and the rest of the crew also felt something that none of them had felt in a very long time. They felt hope.

Danny opened the hatch, and the three of them joined the rest of the crew on the bridge. The only absentees were Pandith, and the captain himself. Julie and Danielle looked up from a whispered conversation, but their eyes quickly left Aric. Whatever interest Danielle had shown in Aric had cooled after he'd chosen to maroon Danny. For his part, the supply officer stood away from the others, refusing to meet anyone's gaze. Aric watched him for a moment, and then made the decision to go stand next to him. Danny didn't say anything, but he didn't move away either. It felt like the right thing to do.

Carter stepped onto the bridge and the crew snapped to attention. He drew himself to his full height and snapped a salute.

"At ease," he called. The captain's face betrayed little, and to Aric it seemed Atlas Carter was even more closed off than Danny was. Not that it mattered though. Whatever it was that drove the man, the crew was responding to it.

"I'm not gonna mince words here. The survivor from the *Ichikari* has given us reason to believe that the Bwain are active near this system. From this point forward, this ship will be on battle footing at all times, and we'll exist under the assumption that we're operating in hostile territory."

Aric's heart sank as the crew murmured in surprise. Granger of all people seemed the most nervous. The captain paused for a moment to let his words sink in before it continued.

"Thanks to the fine work of Ms. Hoff, we know that the survivor left the *Ichikari* three weeks ago, and that their ship was most likely headed toward The Gate from the other side of the nebula. So if the Bwain were chasing that ship, they'll be here quite soon. Ms. Ford, I want you to put out a warning to the entire system, and keep that message transmitting. I consider it our duty to warn any other ship out there of the threat, even if they're pirates or illegals. As for us, we will withdraw to Gertie and make preparations to defend the population center. Are there any questions?"

"How many of them are we up against?" Bryon asked.

"We can't know that yet. Until Mr. Pandith can get our survivor conscious and lucid, we'll be operating mostly on assumptions. We still don't know exactly what happened to the *Ichikari*, but I intend to take every possible precaution in the meantime."

"They swarm," Danny said in a rather subdued tone from beside Aric.

"Mr. Xiao?" Carter said as everyone glanced over at the supply officer.

"The Bwain attack in swarms," Danny clarified. "They're like birds. I've – I've seen it once before...when I was younger."

"That's good intelligence, Lieutenant. It matches what I've been able to study on their tactics. Anyone else?" Carter asked as he glanced around at the rest of his crew.

"Captain," Bryon piped up. "I'll fight those birds anywhere, any time. You put me up against them with my lasers and magna-cannons, and we'll be eatin' fried chicken for the rest of this tour."

In spite of himself, Aric chuckled. Danielle's eyes widened, but she couldn't hide her smile either, and laughter at Bryon's joke filled the bridge for the first time since Aric could remember.

"Thank you, Ensign Purcell," Carter acknowledged. Aric couldn't be sure, but it seemed that the captain's clenched fist had loosened just a bit as well.

After the meeting, Granger requested a quiet word with his captain while the others returned to their duties.

"Um, sir...," the tall science officer began. He looked as nervous and unsure as Carter had ever seen him, and for a moment it seemed as if he'd forgotten what he was going to say.

"Yes Mr. Granger?"

"I think I have something you need to see."

* * *

"Pandith and I think it's a theoretical breakthrough," Granger said as the main bridge holoscreen filled with the strange flowered representation he'd been studying for days at his science station. "Most scientists accept the amplituhedronal model of the universe, which states that reality is composed of twelve dimensions; but no one has ever been able to observe any of the characteristics of these other dimensions. At least, not until Pandith and I sent out our probes," he said, flushing slightly as he glanced over at the captain.

"Go on Mr. Granger," was Carter's only reaction. Bryon stood a few meters away, watching it all closely and trying to absorb what he could, but he didn't really understand what Granger was talking about, or why it was so important.

"Majorana particle theory states that there is no matter or antimatter, at least, not as we know it. Rather, the particles extend into the other dimensions that exist outside of our observable, physical universe. Out here on this mission, I've had a lot of time to think about it, and I realized that neutrinos would be the key to tracking these particles since they're nonresponsive. If we could make a probe that..."

"Can you skip to a part that we'll actually understand?" Bryon interrupted.

"Errr, yeah. Sorry. Ok, the first thing we did was to study each other in the lab to make sure the probes work. It was actually Pandith who found out that the human brain gives off and absorbs Majorana particles, so that got me thinking. What if the fifth dimension is actually thought? A connected, universal consciousness? If we could figure out a way to interpret these Majorana particle readings, we could identify intelligent life pretty much anywhere in the galaxy. We might even be able to read minds! Anyway, we built the probes, and when we sent 'em out, this is what we found."

Carter frowned while the rest of the crew studied the swollen blob of data points that were floating just outside The Gate.

"Granger, can I talk this through with you?" Julie asked.

"Of course."

"The Bwain are telepathic. They can see each other's thoughts instantaneously, even hundreds of light years away. It's a unique form of communication called the *Bwainsong*."

"Yeah, that's actually one of the things that led to my theory," Granger said.

"It's not like their minds have an Alcubierre drive or whatever, so if I'm understanding you here, you're basically saying that their thoughts are traveling within what you're calling the fifth dimension, and they have a thought-sense that humans never evolved?" Julie said, and then she paused for a moment to make sure she was on the right track.

"Exactly. We've only evolved to perceive physical reality," Granger agreed.

"So humans are giving off Majorana vibrations as well, even though we can't sense it?" Julie continued. Granger scratched at his head, shifting his feet. He was impatient now, eager to explain more.

"Yes. Now, if you'll just look..."

"The vibrations should be constant, shouldn't they?" Julie asked, "And the pattern should be small and compact. I mean, the Bwainsong, and our thoughts, and those of whatever other conscious organisms exist. It's not as though millions more would just suddenly evolve."

"Well, no," the science officer said. "I suppose you're right."

"So what could make such a large signature?" she asked.

Granger squinted at the shining bulge hurtling through the nebula toward The Gate on the holoscreen.

"Pandith pointed out that anomaly a few days ago," he said. "I believe it's...oh, my god."

"That's not thought out there, or anything else that's coming from the fifth dimension. That's a swarm, and it's only about a day away from The Gate," Carter concluded as a sense of dread suddenly filled them all.

* * *

Gertie
Landfall

"You're taking a very big risk calling me like this," Tannin chided irritably.

"I'm aware of our arrangement, but you need to hear this," Mephista answered, the seriousness in her voice struck him. The pirate captain seemed to have aged years since he last saw her, as if the hold that her wasted body kept on life was slowly weakening. It would be a pity to lose her. She'd served her purpose well.

A recorded announcement issued forth from his holoscreen: *"Attention all spacecraft in and around planetary system G-1726 and the Great Orion Nebula. This is Atlas Carter, Captain of the Sol Space Command vessel, Fate's Winds. We have received a credible report of hostile Bwain activities against human spacecraft on the other side of The Gate. We believe further hostilities are imminent and urge you to enter orbit around Gertie to assist in preparing a defense. Whatever has brought you to this system, I will grant amnesty until this threat has passed. It appears to be a Bwain swarm, so we'll have a far better chance of survival if we stand together. Good luck to you all, and Godspeed."*

Tannin looked away from the holoscreen. His frown deepened into a scowl as the shaking rush of angry adrenaline flooded him.

Mephista's image filled his holoscreen. "He makes a persuasive argument Tannin. Earlier today we destroyed a Bwain scout ship. It seems that the aliens have finally gotten curious."

"Is the *Sanctuary* ready?" Tannin asked.

"Every bolt and screw is in place. It needs some finishing touches, but it'll fly," she confirmed.

"Then I suggest you meet our good captain in orbit," he said. Mephista cocked her head curiously.

"You want us to bring both ships? But if we do that, then he'll find out about *Sanctuary*. If you'll remember, that's why I had to eliminate the *Mercy*. You wanted the *Sanctuary's* existence kept a secret."

"No captain, I want you to bring your own ship. Leave *Sanctuary* behind in the nebula," he said.

"Leave it behind? That ship is our only shot at leaving this godforsaken system," Mephista argued. "It's too big of a risk to leave it sitting where it could be captured by those things."

"I'll have the *Fate's Winds'* antimatter soon," Tannin said. "We won't lose any time."

"You still trust that *boy*?" Mephista asked skeptically.

"As much as I trust you," he said flippantly.

"All right, I'll set a course for Gertie, but I'm bringing *Sanctuary* with me. If we're gonna strand Carter out here anyway, then I guess it doesn't really matter what he sees."

"NO!" Tannin cried in a rage. "You will follow my orders or I'll have Carter fire on you the moment you arrive."

Mephista's image flickered and reconstituted. At times he had trouble deciding which of her disfigurements were from her wounds, and which came from simple interference on the channel. All he knew was that he hated looking at her, and hoped this would be the last time he'd have to.

"Just remember who can inform Sol Space Command of the current location of a hundred and twenty deserters, a treasonous captain, and a former ship of the line," Tannin threatened.

"Of course…Administrator. After all, it's your system," Mephista said after a brief moment of silence. Tannin reached for the transmission controls, but the captain stopped him.

"If there's nothing more…," he said.

"Tannin?"

"Yes?"

"When you take the *Sanctuary* back to Earth, the *Tranquility* goes too. That was our deal."

"Of course my dear captain. I don't know what I'd do without you," he said, his voice dripping with insincerity as he tapped the button to end the transmission.

*　*　*

The Tranquility
Inside the Greater Orion Nebula

Floating at the rear of her ship, Mephista studied her crew's tense faces as they attended to their duties. They were putting their systems through a thorough diagnostic scan, rehearsing drills which would bring the ship quickly to a battle ready stance, and making sure that any and all loose equipment was secured. Every one of them had watched Sol's incompetence cost the lives of their friends and colleagues during that first, deadly Bwain attack. The humans had been unprepared for the threat they'd be facing. This time around, every last one of them was ready for what they knew was coming.

She passed the top deck's weapons bays, its airlocks, and then the officers' quarters and mess. She finally slowed to a stop when she reached the aft observation room. It was a small compartment, big enough for only ten crewmen at a time, but the electroglass ceiling that looked out onto the vastness of space made the room feel infinite.

Mephista twisted onto her back, studying the enormous sphere that her engineers had magnetically tethered to the *Tranquility*. No one would mistake *Sanctuary* for a finely crafted ship built in an Earth-orbiting construction yard, but the habitat was still a sight to behold. Two years of cobbling together black market parts, stolen carbyne steel, and spare inventory from trading ships she'd raided throughout the system had created a vessel big enough to hold five-hundred of the administrator's supporters. Yet it was still small enough for *Tranquility* to fit within its warp bubble once the *Fate's Winds'* antimatter fuel was on board and they were able to make the Alcubierre jump back to Earth.

Sanctuary was a miniature planet where the crew would live on the inside. There was grass from Gertie, nourished by carefully calibrated grow lights, and they would tend their crops and maintain the ship like the home that it truly was. In case their attempt to secure the antimatter failed, its crew could survive in their close-cycle bubble for generations. Nothing like it had been constructed before. It was the perfect platform for a rebellion, but now Tannin wanted to leave it behind and unguarded. Thinking back on the conversation, he'd seemed more annoyed at the prospect of her revealing *Sanctuary's* existence to Carter than he was about a possible swarm attack from the Bwain, and that lack of concern concerned her. Not just a lack of concern, but he didn't even seem all that surprised.

A few dozen of her crew were adding the finishing touches to *Sanctuary's* exterior. They floated like shimmering ants across its surface, trailing streamers of plasma against the backdrop of its carbyne steel hull. They'd performed Herculean feats of engineering, and now their task was almost done.

"*Tranquility*," she said to the ship's computer. "General address."

She waited a moment for her cochlear implant to ping, indicating that the channel was open to everyone on board, then began her announcement.

"Attention all crew members. The *Fate's Winds* has made contact with a Bwain swarm, and they believe they're headed through The Gate toward Gertie. Captain Carter has kindly offered us amnesty to join them in coordinating a defense, and I have decided to accept. Please return to your duty stations and prepare to put us on battle footing. As for *Sanctuary*...," she said, pausing for a moment as she watched the nebula's light glimmering against its hull. It was truly beautiful, and the only life her wasted self would ever be capable of creating. "As for *Sanctuary*, secure it for our departure. We leave in two hours."

In the end it was all a question of trust, and the pirate in her trusted no one.

Chapter Ten

Personal Logbook: Captain Atlas Carter
Entry 20 – En route to Gertie

It's coming, Aida. We tracked a life pod just as we were about to test the security array. There was a young girl on board. We don't know who she is, but at least we know where she came from, and apparently she brought a whole world of trouble with her. Thing is, when I look at her I can't help but to think about all the orphans that poured into Belize when they were fleeing the *Narcos*.

I didn't protect either them or you when I had the chance, and I'll go to my grave hating myself for that. Even though I'll never be able to cleanse myself of the stench of those sins, it's almost like I have a chance to do it all over again. My crew...the girl...all the people on Gertie and Judgment...all their lives are in my hands now, and I will protect them, or give my life trying.

The man who fights without fear is strongest indeed. I'm afraid now. I wonder if I'll ever be able to forgive myself if I live? I wonder if history, or the ghosts of my past will forgive me if I die. Do I even deserve anyone's forgiveness after what I've done...what I allowed to happen? I guess it doesn't really matter. Forgiveness or not, my job now is to protect these people...whatever the cost.

* * *

The Fate's Winds
En route to Gertie

Aric studied the fusion reactor's readings for the fifth time that night. The *Fate's Winds* was at full power, and all systems were reading normal, but the sleep-defying nervousness he'd been feeling demanded an outlet.

The quantum vacuum's particle flows were within optimal levels, and the atmosphere interchange showed normal pressure and composition. He stopped at the small core of antimatter held suspended inside its carbyne Faraday cage by the most powerful magnetic field humanity had ever designed. His naked eye could make out nothing, not even a glow, but the capacity readout showed a green, fifty percent charge. Enough fuel to take them home to Earth in case they needed to run.

The sound of boot falls rang on the deck behind him. He turned to find Captain Carter ducking through the hatch. Quickly he snapped to attention, and Carter nodded in reply.

"At ease Mr. Keith. Having a late night are we?" the captain observed.

"Yes sir, I suppose you could say that. I just wanted to make sure that everything's ready," Aric replied. Carter glanced at the holodisplays, and tapped a knuckle against one of the glowing dials.

"And are you?" he asked.

"Am I what?" Aric asked stupidly.

"Are you ready?"

"Oh! Yes, I believe we are. All the readings are within optimal levels. The antimatter's steady, and there appear to be no major maintenance concerns at the moment. I *was* able to recondition the missile bay door motor, and..."

"No, Lieutenant," the captain said, interrupting him before he could continue. "I'm asking...are *you* ready?"

Aric swallowed, letting his eyes drift pass the glowing readouts. He'd become pretty used to getting the silent treatment from most of the crew since his disastrous attempt at command, so it took him a moment to put his thoughts together.

"Permission to speak freely?" he asked.

"Of course."

"I thought you were gonna leave me to die down there on Judgment," Aric said, his voice betraying the anxiety he felt over the thought, even now so far after the fact.

"Because that's what you did to Lieutenant Xiao?" Carter asked.

"Yes sir," he said. He could navigate engineering with his eyes closed, and he knew every nook and cranny of the engine room, but with the crew of the ship, and most especially her new captain, he still felt lost. "I wish I could take it all back. I let the anger I was feeling toward him affect my judgment. I don't think he'll accept my apology, but I have apologized to him, and I meant every word of it. There's nothing I wouldn't do for this crew, even if they do all hate me."

"Being in command gives you more opportunities than usual to make mistakes. No one knows what it's like until they're actually in that position, and yet they always seem so quick to judge. What they seem to forget is that even though we're in command, we're still just human beings, with the same flaws and failures as everyone else. The thing is, a captain needs to learn to hide those things away from his crew. They need to be able to look up to you, and to place you on some sort of a damn pedestal that no one has any business being on, because that's what creates discipline and loyalty. Your strength and your discipline makes them stronger. You see what I'm saying?" Carter asked. Aric's eyes fell to the floor for a moment as he considered the captain's words.

"Yeah, I do. I just wish someone would have taken me aside and explained all that to me *before* I took command."

"It's not really something you can learn at the academy. You just need to learn it like you do with most things in life. You learn it by making mistakes," Carter said.

"Did you make those kinds of mistakes after you became an officer?" Aric asked.

"We all make mistakes Mr. Keith. It's the ones that cost people their lives that are the hardest to live with," he said solemnly. Aric nodded at him sympathetically. He didn't know what had happened in his captain's past, but he'd been entirely correct when he said they were all flawed as human beings. In that moment, he could feel the burden of past regrets that the captain was carrying on his shoulders, and admired him for how well he kept those regrets hidden away from those under his command.

"Sir…"

"Yes?"

"Thanks," Aric said. Carter gave him a tight-lipped smile, and then turned to head back to the upper level.

"We don't always get a second chance in life, Mr. Keith, so you'd better make the most of it."

* * *

With little to do while they were in transit, Danny found himself spending long stretches of time at the girl's bedside in the med bay. Pandith had been hopeful that she'd recover quickly after her outburst, but two days had passed with no appreciable change in her condition.

She looked Japanese, he decided after a while. He tried to find some resemblance between her and his sister, but this girl's face was narrower, and her cheeks were lower. Regardless of the lack of similarity in their physical appearance, in his heart the pair couldn't be more similar. It made the burden he felt over his decision seem to grow heavier with each passing second.

"I think it's sweet how you watch her," Julie said from beside him. Her health had been improving rapidly thanks to Pandith's care. The orange tint of malnutrition had faded from her skin, and her cheeks finally had a little color to them.

"Thanks," Danny replied absently.

"If you ever want to talk about it…," she offered. Danny glanced at her, shaking his head. "You know, I told the captain about your transmissions. I'm sorry Danny. I really am. I just wasn't myself."

"I know. It doesn't matter," he said. Julie was taken aback by his apparent lack of anger over her betrayal. "You should probably get to your station. I'm not really good company these days."

"You know, you could be if you wanted to," Julie said as she left the med bay. "All you have to do is open yourself up a little."

The rescued girl shuddered, and her blanket slipped from her chest. Yawning, he rose to tuck the coverlet back over her shoulders. She looked so peaceful as he swept a lock of hair behind her ear, that he found himself smiling for the first time in as far back as he could remember.

"You can wake up now," he whispered. "You're safe here."

The girl's fingers fluttered under the blanket, and Danny's eyes widened.

She'd had spasms before, so maybe it didn't mean all that much. Then again, up until now she hadn't responded to anyone's voice.

"Are you all right?" Danny asked as he leaned in closer. "Can you hear me?"

The girl swallowed, and her eyes cracked open. They were bloodshot, and gummy with sleep, but there was life in them. She sucked in a deep breath, and squirmed as though she were trying to stretch.

"Pandith!" he cried. "Pandith, get in here! Hurry up!"

The girl focused her eyes on him for a moment, and then her face suddenly contorted into a look of terror that he'd never seen the likes of before. She screamed in Japanese as she thrashed against her blankets, and it took him a few moments to process and understand what she was saying.

"Slaves in knots!" the girl wailed over and over. "SLAVES IN KNOTS!"

She continued to scream and struggle against his efforts to restrain her until Pandith finally came running into the med bay, grabbed an injector from the counter, and then quickly pressed it against the side of her neck. There was a slight hiss as the injector shot the sedative into her, and a few seconds later she fell quiet once again as Danny laid her back down gently.

"Danny, what the hell happened? What was she screaming about?" Pandith asked. Danny glanced up at him for a moment, but then his eyes fell back to the girl once again.

"You'd better get the captain down here," was his only reply.

*　*　*

"She's sleeping normally now," Pandith said to the captain. Danny was still sitting at her side, holding her hand as he stared down at her with a level of concern that Pandith had never seen him show toward anyone before.

"When will she wake up?" Carter asked.

"With luck, she'll wake in a few hours."

"What do you think she meant by *slaves in knots*, Mr. Xiao?" Carter asked.

"I have no idea. Could it have something to do with the Bwain?"

"Who's to say?" Pandith answered. "We know so little about 'em, and every encounter we've had with them so far hasn't ended well for our side. How do you communicate with a species that only uses telepathy to communicate, and barely has even the anatomical capacity for speech?"

"If she remembers, and we can get her back to a coherent state of consciousness, then I guess she'll tell us what it meant. If not, then it still doesn't change anything about our situation. We'll..."

"Captain," Julie's voice suddenly interrupted. "I've got the administrator on the line. And, um...sir..."

"Yes, what is it?"

"Sir, I think you should take it in private. He's not very happy," she said anxiously.

"Acknowledged," Carter said as he glanced down at the girl once more. "You don't know it yet kid, but you're probably luckier than any of us right now. At least if you're asleep, you won't have to face what's coming. Anyway, take good care of her. I have to go listen to our bad tempered administrator bitch about whatever bug he's got up his ass this time."

"Sir?" Pandith said with a grin and he and Danny both looked at him with a mixture of amusement and shock.

"Let me tell you guys somethin'...off the record. The one thing you'll learn about the chain of command over the years is that the ones who bitch endlessly and expect the most from the people under them are the ones who spend most of their time sitting comfortably behind a desk, while everyone else is out fighting the battle. Now I'm not talkin' about the generals. I'm talkin' about all the politicians and bureaucrats. Nothing but a bunch of armchair soldiers who've never done a damn thing other than kissing enough ass to get into their lofty positions. You know, it's a crime that people like him have authority over us. Unfortunately, that's how our system works, so we're stuck with it...and with him. Anyway, take good care of her," he said as he turned and headed out of the med bay.

"We will Captain, don't you worry," Pandith called after him.

"Seems our captain doesn't have much use for civilian authority," Danny said with a grin.

"You can say that again," Pandith said as he grabbed a scanner from the counter, tapped a few of the controls, and then held it out over the girl's chest.

*　*　*

The Tranquility
En route to Gertie

"Our estimated time of arrival is four days, ma'am," her nav officer advised.

"Understood," Mephista answered in a dry voice.

She floated on the bridge with the rest of the third watch, technically off duty but unable to sleep. Her presence made this particular shift nervous, since they rarely saw her, but she felt more alive on deck with the crew than she did when she was alone with all of her pain and anticipation.

One of the mates floated a water bulb in her direction, which she accepted with a smile.

"Comms, prepare a recording for when we exit the nebula," she instructed after draining the plastic container.

"Recording now," the communications officer called back to her.

"Captain Carter, thank you for your kind invitation. This is Mephista, the captain of the *Tranquility*. I am hereby formally offering you the services of both my crew and myself for the duration of the conflict with the Bwain. I hope that we can let bygones be bygones, at least for a few days. If you'd be open to it, I'd very much like to meet you in person."

The comms officer, a young woman, turned to Mephista in surprise.

"That will be all. Please transmit the message, and let me know if we receive a response," Mephista said.

"Yes, ma'am," the comms officer said obediently as she tapped the controls in front of her to open a channel.

There was little else for Mephista to do with the ship under way. Her officers would conduct weapons drills, double and triple check that every hatch was battened and every missile armed. She took some consolation in the fact that she'd trained her crew well, but she still did not want to return to her empty cabin. It reminded her too much of the *Shift*. Mephista's thoughts drifted momentarily back to those days, and a resentment swelled in her that she knew she'd never be rid of.

In that first engagement back on April 12, 2125, the Bwain shot to wound, not to kill. They were like curious animals toying with a strange prey, but cruel all the same. The Battle of Judgment was named for its location near that planet in the Sword Belt. It was the sole reason that Mephista was still here.

"Captain, should I begin evasive maneuvers?" the *Shift*'s helmsman had asked when the first of the alien ships had appeared. She'd said nothing in response.

"Should we deploy chaff?" her weapons officer had asked. Again, she didn't respond. She followed her orders to the letter, and when the Bwain lasers began to peel open her bridge like an orange and melt her crew in front of her eyes, she felt an anger burn inside of her that was hotter than any sun.

"All hands, all hands," she called into her suit helmet as she fell back through the bridge's hatch. "The bridge has been compromised. Reserve bridge crew to secondary stations. Helm, begin evasive maneuvers, and get us back to the *Tranquility*'s fleet. Weapons..."

A massive, clanging impact shook the *Shift*, throwing her to the deck.

"Captain, they're gonna board us!" a woman's voice shrieked through her implant before the signal went all garbled.

The hatch at the far end of the corridor spun open. At battle stations it should have been sealed, but the crewman approaching her would no longer respond to orders. The left side of his face had been torn open, revealing his bloody teeth, and a madness that she'd never seen before shone in his eyes. He wailed in the corridor, wracked in unimaginable pain, but he continued to stumble forward with a plasma pistol in one fist, as if some other force was controlling him.

"Medical to corridor five," Mephista called. "What happened to you?" she asked as the man neared.

Behind him, a square of hull heated from dull orange to bright white, and then vaporized. The crewman gripped a railing, terror breaking through his madness. Two small, inhuman shapes in bulky suits clanged into the gangway. She saw scaled grins behind the Bwain's faceplates, and then she watched in horror as they scuttled along the deck. One of them reached a clawed hand toward Mephista, and the wounded crewman's arm rose.

That's when she realized the rumors she'd heard about the Bwain's telepathy were true. It seemed however that the creatures had an, as of yet, imperfect control of their abilities. Rather than lifting his pistol, the crewman raised the arm that was anchoring him to the railing. The second he let go, he was immediately sucked into space.

Unarmed, Mephista turned her EVO suit's inducers to maximum, and drove herself at the Bwain. They struggled as she knocked them off their feet, and squirmed around desperately, trying to get out from under her. The thrusters on her suit were still activated however, so they were both pinned down beneath her.

Somehow, the *Shift* was still miraculously under thrust. She could see the

Tranquility's battle group surrounded by the Bwain swarm through the gaping wound in the hull. The screams of her crew filled her ears as the sensation of a hot knife slid into her own mind, but she focused only on the skeletal bird faces that were mere inches away from her own. She could tell they were screaming, and she relished every last bit of the frustration and hate she felt from them.

She grabbed a hold of their suits, and then quickly reversed thrust so that she flew back up to her feet. With every bit of strength that she had, she smashed the creatures against the bulkhead, stunning both of them.

"Report," she called as she staggered backward.

"Have to hurt now," a slurred voice called back. "Have to die."

"Weapons, are we battle capable?" she asked, but the only response she received was the static and screams that filled her helmet.

The hatch in front of her opened once more. Two more crewmen in EVO suits staggered through, their metal fists matted with white bits of skull and hair. A steam of blood from one radiated toward the void outside the hull.

The Bwain pair struggled up beside the remaining members of Mephista's screaming crew. To them, humans were like puppets, to be used and manipulated.

Mephista blinked, trying to clear her head as her vision flickered. Pain filled her mind, and she quickly staggered back away from the hideous shapes before her. Her ship was finished...her crew dead. She reached the opening in the hull, but she hesitated. She was the captain. She couldn't abandon her ship.

"Please," she'd begged. "We mean you no harm."

"Harm," gurgled one of the lumbering, mind-controlled humans as he raised a fusion pistol.

Mephista hurled herself through the hole in the *Shift*'s hull, jetting toward the *Tranquility*, but the fusion pistol tore at her back, and the vacuum's chill filled her suit.

She floated powerless through the coal-black of space, her eyes fixed on the *Tranquility*'s airlock, while all around her human ships fell to the Bwain. She could have warned them. She could have fought, and as the oxygen fled her lungs and her suit's HUD faded, her only thoughts were of revenge.

*   *   *

Mephista shook her head slightly to jar her thoughts back to the present, and then she turned to speak to her executive officer.

"Mr. Higgs, I think I will turn in after all," she said. The third watch was the smallest, and the quiet onboard the ship was finally proving soporific.

"Roger, Captain. Have a good...," he started to say, but he was interrupted by the sudden squeal of the proximity alarm. The crew rocked against their tethers as the ship automatically adjusted its course to avoid a collision.

"Is it the *Sanctuary*?" Mephista demanded as she returned to her station.

"No ma'am," her nav officer responded. "It looks like..."

"What? What is it? Speak up!" she said impatiently.

"Honestly, I don't know what it looks like," he said, the uncertainty evident in his voice.

On the holoscreen, a flickering piece of what appeared to be a polished comet glimmered just in front of her bow.

"Scanning it now," the weapons officer called out. A few moments later he gave his report. "It's not made of carbyne steel, and its dimensions don't match anything we have in the database."

"Where the hell did it come from?" she demanded.

"I don't know why we didn't pick it up. It's like it just came out of nowhere," the nav officer said.

"No response to communications, ma'am. I'm detecting no electromagnetic signals coming from the object," her comms officer reported.

"Then it's a Bwain ship. Weapons, target and fire!" Mephista shouted urgently as she stared at the image on the screen.

The *Tranquility*'s magna-cannons thumped, but the strange craft flickered and disappeared just before the projectile's impact.

"We missed, and we've lost target lock," the weapons officer said.

"Find me that ship!" Mephista shouted. "Find out what it's doing. We have to..."

"Captain!" her nav officer called.

On the holoview, a massive ship flickered into view less than a single AU away. The bolted-on additions that studded its ancient hull were the tell-tale signs of Bwain construction, but underneath the modifications, she could see familiar lines. The vessel that faced her had once been a human ship.

"Oh my god," Mephista said, drawing a sharp breath as the strange ship's cannon thundered against the *Tranquility*'s hull. She knew then that their painstaking care and preparations had all been for nothing. "How could we have been so blind? Evasive maneuvers! Do it now!"

*   *   *

The Fate's Winds
In orbit around Gertie

"Explain to me how I'm to view your retreat and abandonment of the array as anything other than insubordination, Captain?" Tannin growled through the holoscreen.

"Administrator, in a situation where you're outnumbered, one withdraws to cover. In empty space, against a numerically superior enemy, there's nowhere to hide. In orbit, at least we have the ability to move to cover."

"While luring them directly toward our population center! Why didn't you run into the nebula?"

"We would have lost contact with you, sir," Carter replied evenly. "Your safety, and the safety of those down on the planet is my only priority."

The administrator's eyes narrowed. He seemed more worn than when Carter had last seen him. His hair hung in greased tangles, and a strange yellow color stained his beard.

"Your service record calls that into serious doubt, Captain."

"Sir, circumstances dictated that we postpone the array's trial."

"I AM THE ONE WHO DICTATES THE CIRCUMSTANCES, CAPTAIN!" Tannin thundered. "And right now it seems that your circumstances have changed. Effective immediately, I am relieving you of command. I would like to speak with Lieutenant Xiao, right now...if you please."

Carter sat stiffly in front of the monitor, his mind calculating. So *this* had been the administrator's plan all along. Maybe Aric had been right to leave Danny behind. Carter had gambled that his crew would be able to move on from their own struggles, and he didn't believe he'd lost that bet yet.

"Lieutenant Xiao, to the captain's quarters," Carter called.

"Roger," Danny's energetic voice spoke into his earpiece.

Carter studied the administrator's face on his holoscreen while he waited, trying to understand the motivations of the man who seemed to be dead set on becoming his adversary.

"You once said that there was a reason that we'd all been assigned to this system. May I ask what your reason is?" Carter asked. A sneer clawed Tannin's face.

"Don't think for a moment that I'm anything like you," he snarled. "You're nothing but a mass murderer. If your family hadn't died in Belize, Sol would have just hanged you and been done with it."

The stateroom's entry tone sounded. Carter rose on legs that were shaking with anger. He took a moment to steady himself before he opened the door to let in his supply officer. "The administrator would like to speak with you, Lieutenant."

"Mr. Xiao, effective immediately I am relieving Mr. Carter of his duties and appointing you as the captain of the *Fate's Winds*. Mr. Keith was ineffective in his tour as acting captain, but I'm sure you'll do a fine job. Your orders are to return to the array and ensure it is operational. Do I make myself clear?"

Danny looked up at Carter, a sick look paining his face.

"You'll do what's right. I have faith in you," Carter said.

"Tannin, what's happening? What's going on here?" Danny asked.

"Circumstances have dictated a change in command," Tannin said. "The crew will follow your orders now, won't they?"

"I don't know. I need a second to think," Danny responded.

"You what?" Tannin growled. "THE LAST THING YOU NEED TO DO

RIGHT NOW IS THINK!" he roared. "I expect you to..."

The transmission froze as Julie's voice overrode their implants.

"Captain to the bridge. All hands to battle stations. We're under attack!"

Carter tapped off the holoscreen.

"Captain, I...I don't...I mean, he can't be serious," he said with nervous anxiety.

"Later," Carter interrupted, as he dashed from the cabin with the younger man on his heels. "Right now, we've got bigger problems to deal with."

* * *

The bridge's holoscreen showed the pirate frigate they'd engaged ten days earlier. It was damaged in a dozen places, trailed atmosphere and gasses from what looked like three hull breaches, and its thrusters seemed to be struggling to maintain a linear course. Strangest of all, it was towing a massive, artificial sphere behind it that looked completely undamaged. Carter had no idea what he was up against.

"Ready to baste that turkey!" Ensign Purcell yelled. "Charge is at a hundred percent, and the bays are all hot!"

"Full offensive and defensive navigation solutions ready," Danielle called.

Carter zoomed his holoscreen, rotating the image to try and understand what he was seeing.

"Ms. Hoff, do a deep scan. I want to know if there are any other ships heading in this direction that are within one day's approach. Someone else attacked that pirate ship, and they might be headed this way."

"Transmission coming in Captain. It's a recorded message," Julie informed him.

"Put it on the speakers Ms. Ford," he ordered. She tapped the controls a few times, and suddenly Mephista's voice filled the bridge.

"Captain Carter, thank you for your kind invitation. This is Mephista, the captain of the *Tranquility*..."

"It's on repeat," Julie said. "I haven't been able to raise anyone."

"There may not be anyone alive over there," Carter said as he clicked a comms button. "Science Officer Granger to the bridge. We need to find out what the hell..."

"Captain!" Lieutenant Hoff shouted. "Coordinates 375, dot 108, dot 12. There's a ship coming this way that's less than two AUs away!"

Carter's holoview zoomed outward and above the *Fate's Winds* to show the signature that Danielle had found. The image of an ancient freighter barreling toward the *Tranquility* enlarged on his holoscreen.

"Get us to geostationary," Carter said. "Ms. Ford, contact the new ship."

"Channel open, sir."

"Attention incoming vessel. This is Captain Car...," he started to say, but a sudden scream tore through his ears in response that sounded like the pained cry of some sort of a raptor. It was certainly like nothing he'd ever heard come from a human throat.

"Captain, it's horrible!" Julie shouted with a pained look.

"Cut it off!" Carter yelled.

"Looks like the pirates did some damage, but it's still operational, Bryon reported.

Carter closed his eyes, breathed in through his nose and out through his mouth. There was time – not much, but a little – and he used it to examine his position. They were a tiny ship up against one, possibly two, much larger adversaries. He had no idea if he'd be fighting humans, the Bwain, or something else entirely, and yet the crew stood ready to jump in and fight.

"Mr. Granger, I need you to tell me what the pirate vessel is towing. Ms. Hoff, prepare evasive maneuver packages for projectiles and magna-cannons. Mr. Purcell, the second ship is our hostile. Target it, but don't fire until I give the order. Ms. Ford, try to raise someone on the *Tranquility*. Tell them we are not a threat but, we can't defend them. Are we clear?"

"Yes sir!" the bridge crew all called out in unison.

* * *

"It looks like a Frankenship," Bryon observed.

At first glance, the mining freighter did not appear to carry any weapons at all. As Carter zoomed in on it however, he saw what looked like a number of hastily retrofitted cannons, missile pods, and low-powered lasers stuck to its rusted hull.

"Ms. Hoff, has it adjusted course?" Carter asked.

"Yes sir, but it appears to be maneuvering erratically. The transponder has been disabled, but the tonnage and profile show that this is the *Ichikari*. I have no idea who's operating it."

"I do," a voice said behind them.

Carter turned to find Pandith standing there behind the survivor from the life pod.

"Mr. Pandith?" Carter said, his face registering slight bit of surprise as he glanced down at the girl, who Pandith had pushed there in a wheelchair.

"Sir, I think you should hear her out," Pandith said.

"There's something in their minds," the girl said. "It's controlling them. Driving them all insane. They aren't the same people anymore."

"What do you mean?" Carter asked.

"The Bwain are in their heads. They're controlling the crew," she said. Tears formed in her eyes, and her voice trembled. Pandith reached down and gave her a reassuring squeeze on the shoulder, and after a few deep breaths, she continued. "So many of them dead. It was horrible."

"Sir, they're targeting us!" Bryon called. "Magna-cannons and missiles."

"Don't let them get close!" the girl cried.

"Deploy countermeasures," Carter ordered. "Mr. Purcell, fire with everything you have. Ms. Hoff, execute your first evasive solution. Mr. Pandith, secure yourself, and your patient. This might not be pleasant."

G-forces pressed them all down toward the deck as the *Fate's Winds* rose vertically to avoid the angry red streaks of a dozen missiles that flew toward them on the holoscreens.

"Firing all weapons!" Bryon called.

The brilliant blue lance of the *Fate's Winds* laser stabbed into the mining ship, cleaving off a glowing section of its rear hull.

"That was their auxiliary generator and thrusters," Bryon said.

"Excellent work. Target missiles for the mid hull in two-degree clusters, and fire the lasers at will."

"She's massive sir, but that makes just makes her easier to hit," Bryon said with a grin as he executed his firing orders.

"We've cleared their missiles," Danielle reported.

"Well done. Continue evasive maneuvers on my mark," Carter ordered.

"Laser at fifty percent!" Bryon called, "Now sixty percent!"

"Ms. Ford, any word from the *Tranquility*?"

"No sir."

"They're entering Gertie's orbit," Danielle called. "It looks like they're gonna try to hide on the far side of the planet."

"Laser fire and projectiles inbound," Bryon warned.

On the holoscreen, the *Fate's Winds'* chaff lit with reflected laser fire, scattering the mining vessel's crude attack.

"No impact," Bryon called. "They can't touch us!"

That was Carter's niggling fear. *A ship this massive should have every advantage in the world against a corvette. What are the Bwain trying to do?*

"Evasive solution, Ms. Hoff," Carter ordered.

The bridge crew leaned hard left as Danielle threw the ship onto a new course.

"Firing!" Purcell called.

His second shot carved a massive gash in the center of the *Ichikari*'s bow.

"Anyone they had on the bridge is sucking vacuum right now," Bryon observed.

Carter studied his holoscreens. Something about the battle didn't feel right. Why give such a large ship such pathetic offensive capabilities? Unless...

"Captain!" Lieutenant Hoff screamed.

Unless it was a decoy.

"Brace for impact!" Carter shouted as three blurred streaks flickered in front of his ship.

* * *

The bridge shook and darkened. Carter felt the deck groan underneath his feet, and a depressurization warning blinked amber on his holoscreen.

"Mr. Keith, damage report! Mr. Purcell, near-field cannons! Sweep the area in front of us!"

When there was no acknowledgement of his command, Carter turned to see the ensign lying on the floor, a pool of blood spreading from his head. Carter leaped from his chair to take the weapons station. The laser was inoperable, but the magna-cannons still worked. He swept them out in front of the *Fate's Winds*, while Ensign Hoff desperately steered the ship away from whatever had struck them.

"Those things are coming around again!" Danielle shouted.

Carter still had no idea what the *Fate's Winds* was up against. On the screen beside him, the last of Bryon's missiles struck the *Ichikari*, erupting in an incredible explosion. The ensign must have struck the ship's reactor, and Carter glimpsed the ship listing off course. He twisted his cannons to starboard, slicing through the emptiness until the black of space itself crumpled and turned into a small, teardrop-shaped vessel that was shattered by his projectiles.

"Continue evasive maneuvers. We need to...," Carter bellowed, but he was interrupted as the *Fate's Winds* suddenly lurched, tossing the bridge crew into the air.

"We're losing gravity!" Aric said over the radio.

Carter tried his cannons again, but they were useless. He'd lost fire control completely.

"The weapons are offline," he said. "Ms. Hoff, get us to the far side of the planet! Now!"

"Thrusters are nonresponsive, Captain," she called. "I've only got attitude jets, or the Alcubierre!"

"Mr. Keith," Carter called. "Mr. Keith, respond!"

The engine room had gone silent. This was it, then. Carter could run to Earth, or he could fight. The green jewel of Gertie hung in view on the holoscreens, clear and peaceful below the shimmer of the strange vessels that were closing for another run.

"It's been a privilege to serve with all of you," Carter said. "Ms. Hoff, we're going to try and ram the vessels at these coordinates."

"Captain, they've disappeared again. I don't see anything," she said.

Suddenly, four brilliant streaks overloaded his holoscreens. When the computer filter brought them back up, Carter saw the wreckage of the other two mysterious vessels blossoming in the glow of superheated metal and atmosphere.

"What happened?" Carter demanded. "Where did that come from?"

"Captain Carter," the bridge speakers sounded. "This is Captain Mephista. You put up an excellent fight. It is our honor to come to your aid."

Part Three:
The Bwainsong

Chapter Eleven

The Fate's Winds

"Medical emergency in engineering, Captain," Granger's voice crackled through Carter's earpiece.

"Acknowledged. I'm on my way," Carter replied. Part of being a successful commander was understanding that even the most difficult battles were won by putting out the inevitable fires as they occurred, and in just the right order. "Pandith, I'll meet you down there."

"I'm already on my way," Pandith replied.

Now in his EVO suit, the captain made slow progress down the starboard side of the horseshoe. He kicked through mangled piping and cable, ducked under a collapsed ceiling, and climbed through a heat-warped section of decking. He finally emerged at a gaping gash in the hull where the mysterious Bwain ships' weaponry had torn through the *Fate's Winds'* defenses.

"Lieutenant Xiao, mark this location for exterior repair," Carter instructed.

"Yes sir," Danny replied over the radio. "I've got eyes on it right now."

Carter peered out through the gaping wound in hull, and saw Danny drifting past in an exterior survey of the ship. The edges of the carbyne steel panels glowed yellow with the nanobots' efforts to stitch the damage together, but most of the breaches were too broad for the tiny robots to repair in time. The crew would need to exact some of the major repairs on their own.

"Better make your way back toward engineering after you get done surveying the damage. We might need your help there as well," Carter added.

"Copy that. Sir, it looks like they were targeting the missile bays. They knocked out every weapon on this side of the ship. Our laser accelerator is gonna need to be replaced."

The captain triggered his inducers and floated over the missing area of the deck, eventually coming to a stop in front of an airlock hatch had sealed itself automatically. The electronics that should cycle open the hatch were malfunctioning, so he was forced to open the latches manually.

The hatch burst out at him as the air from the next section escaped through it. The force of it sent him flying back into a misshapen mound of carbyne that had been melted like butter in the attack, and then cooled into an unrecognizable form by the cold vacuum of space.

"Well that was a rookie mistake, ya damn moron," he grumbled to himself as he initiated his thrusters and righted himself once again.

Gathering himself, he climbed into the double hatch, moved until the depressurized side was behind him, and then he spun the interior hatch open.

"Thank God you're finally here," Granger said as Carter made his way into engineering. "I don't think Aric's gonna last much longer."

Aric was pressed against the hull a few feet off the ground. His face had gone gray, but his eyes were open and staring at the two EVO suited men that were facing him.

"It looks like shrapnel pierced the hull. His body stopped the depressurization but...yeah," Granger said sullenly.

"Captain...it hurts. It huts really bad," the engineer managed to say. His voice was weak, and he had a pained look on his face.

"Mr. Xiao, I need an emergency patch on the exterior of my location immediately! Mr. Pandith, please hurry. Time is of the essence."

Aric lifted a weak hand, beckoning the captain over to him. Carter stepped closer, taking the engineer's hand in his suit glove. The atmospheric pressure inside the engineering bay had turned Aric's body into a living cork, and Carter could see the tautness around the engineer's stomach as the interior air tried to force its way through the suffering engineer's torso.

"You were right," Aric said through clenched teeth.

"Try not to talk Mr. Keith. Danny's gonna get that hole patched up, and then we'll get you to the med bay," Carter said as he squeezed Aric's hand reassuringly.

"I just wanna say...that I'm proud to have served with you. With all of you," Aric gasped, and then his head drooped down lifelessly.

The port airlock unsealed, and Pandith rushed inside with his medical kit. In his haste to deal with the crew's many wounds, the engineer hadn't even bothered to put on a pressure suit.

"I'm at the damage site Captain," Danny called over the radio. "I see the rupture. Looks like we've got some kind of a fluid leak happening here."

"Understood Lieutenant. Please work quickly," Carter replied.

"Fusing the patch now."

"Oh my god," Pandith gasped as he dropped his emergency bag. "He's probably got severe organ damage. Our bodies have internal pressure too, and that pressure would have ruptured the skin and vented the fluids of his body out into space. That's what Danny's seeing out there."

"Yes, I'm aware of that. Is there any way at all that you can save him?" Carter asked.

"Halfway there," Danny said. "I just need a bit longer."

"I honestly don't know," Pandith said. Whatever I can even try to do for him, it's gonna have to be now.

"Almost there," Danny said, grunting with the effort of his work. "Ok, it's sealed Captain. You guys need anything else in there?"

Aric's limp body sagged into Pandith's and Carter's arms as the external vacuum released its hold on his body. A pink knot of flesh and muscle protruded from his back, and blood frozen into dark crystals crumbled from his flight suit.

"Hurry now," Carter urged as he handed Aric's legs to Granger. The two unsuited men would be able to move him more quickly to the medical bay. He opened the airlock for them, and they rushed through the hatch as quickly as they possibly could, leaving Carter all alone in engineering.

"Did you need anything else captain?" Danny asked again.

"That'll be all Mr. Xiao. You can return to your other repairs now. Thank you for attending to that so quickly. You may or may not have just saved a life."

"Captain?" Danny asked.

"Just attend to your repairs Mr. Xiao, and hope for the best."

"Wait, that's engineering. Is Aric ok?"

"It's not looking good," Carter replied sullenly. "Please, just attend to your repairs. Pandith and Granger are doing everything they can for him."

"Yes sir," Danny said hesitantly, and then the radio went silent again.

Studying the readings on the holodisplays, he found that the reactor was operating at full power, but some sort of a resonance issue had thrown the quantum vacuum out of alignment. The antimatter charge still glowed at fifty percent, which was enough for them to run home with their tail between their legs if need be, but it was a decision he really wasn't looking forward to having to make. It didn't sit right with him to just turn tail and run like that, but there was a distinct possibility that they'd be left with no other choice.

Sighing, Carter closed his eyes and rested his visor against the bulkhead. They'd been damn lucky that the Bwain hadn't destroyed them utterly, and he was smart enough to know they wouldn't be able to count on luck to save them again.

"Ms. Ford, please inform Captain Mephista that I'm going to take her up on her invitation."

*　*　*

Four of Granger's Majorana probes whizzed past Carter's faceplate as he exited the airlock in his EVO suit and began to float toward the *Tranquility*. The fist-sized satellites turned right with a brief pulse of their inducers, heading toward the roiling wound of the Orion Nebula. Carter had to hope that Granger would have a second breakthrough and figure out a way to track whatever the new Bwain ships were that had attacked them. He couldn't fight what he couldn't see, and the *Fate's Winds* would never survive another round with the Bwain unless they could even the battle, which was why it was now critically urgent that he meet this Captain Mephista face to face. She could have destroyed him at Judgment, but she didn't. Her message had seemed almost eager. He couldn't let himself trust her until he understood what she wanted, but something in her manner hinted that she was more than a simple pirate; and if that turned out to be the case, then his plan might just work.

As he used the suit's thrusters to guide him toward the *Tranquility*'s airlock, what he'd suspected during the battle became all too clear. Though the *Tranquility*'s SSC registration number had been painted over, the ship's name still blazed from its bow in tall, white, ten-meter high letters, as per SSC-regulations. Captain Mephista piloted a military vessel. The ship would have been big enough to hold a crew of two-hundred, and he wondered how many were left alive.

Drawing closer, he peered through the ragged gaps in the frigate's hull. There was a galley with its lockers burst open and emptied by the depressurization, rows of missiles protruding like teeth from a rent seam, the slow hiss of atmosphere from a lower deck. Dozens of her crew were at work repairing hull damage, and great stretches of the ship glowed with nanobots as they sealed the smaller wounds.

A short time later he entered the ship's airlock, and then reached behind him to seal the exterior hatch.

"This is Carter. I'm in airlock four. Exterior door secured."

A cloud enveloped his ankles, building into a hiss that he could hear outside his suit as the atmosphere refilled the chamber. The inner door unsealed, and he found himself facing a petite woman floating before him.

Her hair rose from her head in brown streamers, and the left side of her face was traced with several scars that spoke volumes about the battles she'd been through. In contrast, the right side of her face reminded him of those pictures of children with large, pleading blue eyes, that the SSC used in all its propaganda. This side of her face matched the voice he remembered so well from their first conversation; the other matched the ruin surrounding her.

Instead of an EVO suit or other exterior protection of any kind, she wore a fusion pistol on each of her hips, while her legs curled beneath her. The woman was paralyzed, and yet when she smiled he saw life buried behind the pain in her eyes, a sense of humor at his reaction to her appearance.

"Welcome Captain," she said. "Captain Mephista, at your service."

* * *

"We could offer you a gravity magnetron. My ship has a spare," Carter stated as he took the seat indicated.

"That won't be necessary," Mephista's engineer said.

Carter looked up at the *Tranquility*'s floating engineering officer in surprise.

"Our zero-G is intentional," Mephista said as she tapped the useless flesh of one of her thighs. "Obviously I wouldn't have much luck moving around the ship if we had artificial gravity turned on."

"I understand. My sympathies," Carter said. Her eyes flashed for a moment, but her humored calm quickly returned.

"I believe that we've come to the end of the rather meager list of spare parts and resources we can exchange," she said.

"There's just not enough, ma'am," her engineer interjected. "We need a dry dock. Maybe in the Antilles system, or −"

"Mr. Hart, we both know that the *Fate's Winds* is the only vessel with antimatter fuel for an Alcubierre jump. I suggest you limit your options to this system."

"Well then ma'am, with all due respect, there are none."

"What about your cargo?" Carter asked.

"That my dear Captain is off limits," she said.

"Then I'll head back to my ship," Carter said flatly.

"Leaving so soon?"

"I came here to discuss a plan to fight the Bwain. If you'd like to do the same, then we should speak in private. Or maybe you're just more comfortable using us as bait for their stealth ships?"

The insulted pirate officers glared at him. They were clearly loyal to their captain, but too well disciplined to act without her approval. Nothing about this pirate was what he expected, and he found himself intrigued when a small smile crept onto her face.

"Do you know more than you're letting on, or would you just like to get me alone for a few minutes?" Mephista asked, tilting her head slightly.

"I'd like to talk to you about exactly who you are, about why you didn't blow me out of the sky over Judgment, and about who's been letting you conduct your raids all over this system. After that, maybe we can come to an agreement," Carter said firmly, and then he stood there for a moment staring at her expectantly as she looked him over and considered her options.

"Fair enough," she said finally as she swung herself toward the room's exit and then pushed herself toward the passageway. She stopped herself using one of the handrails, and then glanced back at Carter with a strangely alluring smile. "Are you coming?"

*   *   *

"You act quickly, and without hesitation," Mephista said as she floated into to her stateroom. "You've obviously seen your share of combat."

Her quarters held little more than a bunk, a toilet station, and a holoterminal. The lone picture on the wall was of Mephista as a much younger woman, standing in front of her family as she wore the graduation blues of the academy. Her smile was bright, and her clear, blue eyes were accented by the color of her robes.

"I've seen much worse than combat," Carter answered.

Mephista drifted to her cabin's far wall, then faced him. "Then we may have more in common than you think," she said. "Tell me what you know."

"I know that Tannin was paying my crew member to sabotage the security array and submit false requisitions for material that it looks like went into building your…uhhh…cargo. I know that the administrator has been starving the people on Judgment intentionally, and that you've been helping him. I know…"

"Now wait a minute. I've never helped him to take innocent lives!" Mephista retorted, fixing him with a steady gaze.

"No? What about the *Mercy* then? Did it just blow itself up?" Carter asked. At this, Mephista spun away angrily to face the tiny port in her room, and stared at Gertie's verdant surface for a time before she spoke again.

"It was Belize City that got you sent out here, wasn't it?" she finally asked. It was almost more of a statement than a question in need of a response.

He studied her pale reflection in the black glass. He could see the sadness in her eyes. There was no malice in her question, so he chose to answer her truthfully.

 "Yes, it was. That, and what the *Narcos* did there because of me."

"And how much did those Narcos offer you to look the other way?"

"I don't have to answer that."

"Then neither do I," she said firmly as she turned back around to look at him once more.

Anger flared in him. For a moment, he remembered fighting the SSC brig guards when they'd caught him trying to hang himself, breaking one man's ribs for his right to die and be with his wife. It took him a moment to suppress those memories, and to once again regain control of his emotions before he answered. When he finally spoke he was calmer but he couldn't keep the hoarse tension from his throat.

"They offered me my family's life...but they lied. They slaughtered everyone because I let them do it. It's not a mistake I intend to repeat."

"So when you came here, were you looking for a fight?" she asked.

"I was *sent* here because it was the closest thing Sol could do to court-martialing an officer who was innocent in the eyes of the law. Seems to me that might be something you little bit about. What are *you* doing out here Captain, and just what exactly is that thing you're towing behind your ship?"

"You're right...at least in a way I suppose. I *was* innocent, but I wasn't sent out here like you were. And yeah, we've made our share of raids," she said through a small smile. "That is what pirates do after all, isn't it?"

"But you're not pirates, are you?" Carter asked. "This is an SSC ship. Your crew are all SSC officers, and you fired on your own," he added.

"I did not fire on my own!"

"I've reviewed every report from this system," Carter said. "In two years of raiding, your crew has never taken a life. Then one day, right out of the blue, you suddenly decide to blow the *Mercy* right out of the sky. It seems a bit odd to me that you'd destroy them, and yet you spared us in our encounter over Judgment."

"Captain, you're too smart to let yourself jump to conclusions," she said.

"Jump to conclusions? Well, let me tell you what I think happened, and then you can tell me how far I've jumped. I think Captain Green saw your secret cargo, and I think you destroyed the *Mercy* because of it. Now you've brought it here and I've seen it as well, so I want to know your side of the story before this goes any further. What is that thing for exactly?"

When Mephista finally turned around to face him, a look of sadness had crept back into her eyes.

"We're all the same out here, Carter. Stranded, without any way to get home. Administrator Tannin more so than anyone else. He used to be a Senator. Did you know that? He never told me what he did to get himself sent here, but he wants revenge against Sol more than anyone I've ever met. Not only that, he wants to get back home."

Carter considered Tannin's role and decided that he still didn't understand the corrupt bureaucrat. What could one man possibly hope to achieve, out in this forgotten realm?

"So, I suppose if we're gonna be working together, then you deserve an explanation, Captain...so here it is. The *Sanctuary* is a fully self-contained home," Mephista explained. "All it needs is antimatter to fuel the Alcubierre engine, and it'll take us anywhere we want to go in this galaxy. I intend to be aboard when she leaves this wasteland, and then I fully intend to hunt down the men who sent my crew and I to our deaths."

She floated there before him. Her eyes were wide, and her head was held high. He recognized the same damaged courage he saw in his own reflection...the same anger and hurt. There burned in her a need for answers that could only be found back on Earth. He suspected that deep down in her heart, she was still a Sol Space Command officer, just like him.

"All I ask from you is honesty, and I thank you for being honest with me," Carter stated with sincerity.

"My pleasure, but somehow I have the distinct feeling that you're gonna ask me for a bit more, aren't you?" Mephista asked knowingly. In spite of himself, Carter smiled.

"You're quite perceptive my dear Captain. Now, are you ready to hear my plan to keep us alive long enough to have a sit-down with Tannin?"

"I'm all ears," she said with a smile playing at the corner of her mouth as she floated back over to hover in front of him.

*   *   *

Mephista squirmed her way into one of the EVO suits in the airlock's ready room.

"Do you honestly think it all will work?" she asked. There was a twinkle in her eye, and he was struck by the fact that even in the face of lopsided odds, she still somehow managed to maintain a sense of hope.

He was beginning to understand why her crew was so devoted. Even he was starting to feel a sense of optimism in her presence.

"If we can get what we need, then yes. If not, then I guess we won't be around long enough to worry about our failure. Either that, or…"

"Or…you'll run?" She said as she floated to the porthole and stared out toward The Gate.

"I ran once before…a long time ago," he said as he turned and stomped toward the airlock's outer door and reached for the hatch. "People died because of it, but I'm the one who has to live with what I've done."

"Regrets are burdensome, aren't they?" she observed as she followed him into the airlock.

"Yes, they are. They more certainly are," he said with a heavy sigh.

Chapter Twelve

The Fate's Winds
In orbit above Gertie

Danny Xiao lay in his bunk, exhausted from the seventeen hours he'd spent patching the hull. He had raw skin where his EVO suit had chafed, and his hips and shoulders throbbed against the mattress. Given what he was about to do however, the pain felt appropriate.

He tapped the small holoscreen above his pillow, and slowly entered his personal code. Falconi had never asked him why he'd never received a single reply to all the recorded messages that he'd asked him to deliver to Ursa Major. He wouldn't have answered anyway. It was already too hard to face the fact that the one person he wanted to talk to more than anything in the world, would never again be able to respond.

The most recent image he had of Nuo had been taken two years ago. His sister's body had kept growing toward adulthood even as her mind had atrophied. Her jaw hung limply open, a string of saliva stretching between her lips and the feeding tube. She lay in her hospital gown, pale skinned and amorphous. She was like a creature that was alive, and yet had no life at all. The photographer had turned his sister's head away from the camera in an effort to hide the massive gash that had collapsed the right side of her skull during the Bwain attack on their colony ship.

He'd always wondered how the alien swarm had chosen his family's stateroom. What had made their laser cross billions of miles of emptiness to strike his sister as she played checkers next to him? One minute, he'd been laughing as he hopped his king over her pieces. The next he'd looked up, and half of his sister's head had disappeared.

"Danny, help me," she'd uttered as her body toppled over. They were the last words she spoke to him.

He'd screamed in the cabin's thinning atmosphere, pulling his sister with him into the corridor where he found his parents cleaved in two. He'd have died as well if it hadn't been for an SSC medic carrying life bags with emergency breathing masks.

His parent's money had put Nuo into a hospital where they said they could regrow her brain, but Tannin's money had kept her there. Nuo had said other things, her good eye struggling to focus as her lips formed words that had no grammatical connection; but she was still alive, and still responding to the treatments.

"Hey sis. I don't know when I'll be able to write again, so I wanted to send you at least one more message before things go all to hell. Unfortunately, the Bwain are on their way here to attack us. We don't know how much of a chance we'll have against 'em, but I'll tell ya this right now. If we go down, we're not goin' down without takin' some of 'em with us. Oh, and on top of that, that administrator that I kept calling your uncle is...well, we don't need to talk about him right now. I guess you'd be more interested in what's been goin' on with your brother," he said, pausing for a moment to force back a sob before he was able to continue. "We got attacked by a couple of Bwain ships already. We had some help and somehow managed to stop 'em, but then I had to help fix the ship. We all did. I dunno, I guess I don't really have a lot to say right now. Whatever happens, I just want you to know how sorry I am...for a lot of things. Mostly I'm sorry that we'll never get to finish that game of checkers we were playing. I was kickin' your ass and you know it. Anyway, I love ya sis. If you don't hear from me again, I just want you to know how much I love you."

As those final words left his mouth, he reached up and tapped the display to stop the recording, and then he buried his face in his pillow and cried himself to sleep.

The emotional and physical exhaustion he was feeling sent him into a deep, and much needed sleep. A sleep that was later interrupted by a chiming sound, announcing that someone was wanting to enter his cabin. He slipped out of his bunk and opened the door to find Captain Carter waiting there for him.

"Are you ready?" the captain asked.

Danny reached back and tapped the send control on his holoscreen that would upload the recording to a queuing system that would hold it until Falconi next entered the system, at which time it would upload the message to his ship's messaging system for delivery. The way things were looking however, it was questionable whether or not Falconi would ever be able to return.

"I'm ready for duty, Captain," he said.

"Come on, we've got work to do," Carter said as he led him off down the corridor.

*　*　*

Gertie
Landfall

At least twenty militiamen ringed the administrator's residence in the heart of Landfall, glaring at Hal from behind their plasma rifles. He'd spent two days traveling to every farm outside of the town, and though he felt justified in what he was doing. He was absolutely terrified, and it didn't help that he'd been having lots of bad dreams and headaches thanks to the havoc his newfound sobriety was wreaking on his body.

"Mr. Yellowknife, are you expected?" the militia's captain asked.

"*Expected?* You know I'm on the Council. What is this?" Hal called out to Vartan.

"I'm afraid things are different now."

"What the hell do you mean by that?" Hal demanded, his fear giving way to a sudden flash of annoyance.

"Last night we had some people in town that got into it. I don't know if it was nightcrawler or somethin' else, but there was one hell of a fight, and two men were beaten to death. The administrator's gonna make sure this place doesn't fall apart," Vartan explained. Hall studied the militiamen for a moment, noting the mistrust he could see in their eyes.

"Are you sure that's what he's doin'?" Hal asked as he pushed past him and forced his way into the cold halls of Tannin's home.

"Now wait a minute Hal! Hey, you can't go in there!" Vartan said as he turned and chased after him.

Hal burst into the reception hall just in time to see Tannin's assistant, Phuri, slam a door closed in panic. Hal caught a brief glimpse of a younger SSC naval officer he didn't recognize in the office as well.

"I'm sorry," Vartan called from the doorway. "He just barged in and…"

"What the hell is all this?" Hal demanded as he pushed open the door that Phuri had closed in an apparent attempt to hide something. "Murders? Your house under armed guard? Just what the hell's goin' on here Tannin?"

Sweat shone on Tannin's face, and his eyes seemed to wander around aimlessly, not really focusing on anything in particular. His mouth moved, but no words passed his yellow-stained beard.

"The administrator…he's not himself," Phuri stammered.

"And who are you exactly?" Hal demanded of the third person in the room.

"Acting Captain Danny Xiao," the other man said. "The administrator has relieved Captain Carter of his command of the *Fate's Winds*."

"Tannin, would you explain yourself?" Hal asked.

Phuri looked over at Tannin, unsure of what to do. The administrator shook his head, and his focused appeared to return for just a moment. He seemed to recognize Hal for the first time since he'd come in, and took two steps forward in greeting. He stopped short however, and fell still once more.

"He may see," Tannin said, though the words coming from his mouth seemed to come from a distant voice.

"See what? I...," Hal started to say, but just then the side door opened, and a creature that Hal had only ever seen before in a holoimage came shuffling out.

If it resembled anything, Hal found, the Bwain looked like a vaguely humanoid, feathered dinosaur. The creature's lizard arms ended in oversized clawed hands, and the feathers that ruffled its torso and limbs varied their colors between the gray-brown tile and the light purple of the sky outside, almost as if it were some sort of a chameleon. Its clawed feet scraped across the floor as it walked toward Hal, its gait alternating between a series of stiff jerks and fluid bobs, while its reptilian head swung back and forth to taste the air. A membrane blinked open and closed across its eyes in rapid succession, while its throat churned and its beak clacked as if it were hungry.

"Tannin, what the hell is this?" Hal whispered.

Beside him, Vartan half-raised his pistol.

"No, it's all right," Phuri insisted, holding up his hands in a placating gesture.

The Bwain faced them, turning its head to one side as parrot-like caw issued from its beak. "I not hurt you. I help."

"One of the beauties of this planet is the abundance of mushrooms that Victor's xenobiologists found during their initial flora survey," Tannin said in the same distant voice. "We know so little about the Bwain, except that they are a truly ancient race that has spanned the galaxy for more millennia than humanity has been in existence. Yet here, on this backwater planet, we found the gateway to our greatest rivals' thought-language."

Phuri handed Tannin another one of the small yellow mushrooms. The Administrator swallowed without chewing.

"What does it mean when it says it'll help?" Danny asked.

"Gentlemen, we are on the edge of human space," Tannin reminded them. Suddenly, he seemed to be a bit more alert, and less dreamlike and vague. "My job is to preserve this colony from any and all threats while it develops. Before we came here, we knew the Bwain might be close. You have no idea how close they've been."

"Are you saying they've been here, on this planet?" Hal asked, his eyes wide with surprise. "They've been here all this time?"

"No," Phuri replied. "This one just recently arrived."

"Oh my god, was that what we saw in the sky last night?" Hal asked.

"It might have been," Captain Xiao said.

"The Bwain have other technology, but very little remains. Their ships are incredibly ancient. They don't have the gifts of manufacturing and agriculture that we have, Hal. They're low on food. They've come in peace, so they can learn and build with us."

"Peace," the creature squawked. The feathers at its throat flashed the same yellow color as Tannin's mushrooms.

"These things have attacked humans literally *everywhere* they've appeared," Hal pointed out. He continued to stare at the Bwain before them, as though he still could not believe what he was seeing.

"Misunderstandings," Tannin said vaguely. "You'll note as well that we have slaughtered their swarms each time we've encountered them. The Bwain have a history that's entirely different from ours. They do not share our same collective cultural understanding, and without any way of communicating with each other, there was no path toward peace. That is, until now. The mushrooms allow them to communicate through me, which means that I can be the one to broker a peace between our two respective peoples."

"So what you're saying is, I was making parts for *them*?" Hal asked, angered by the deception. He turned to Danny. "Is that what your orders were for?"

"It's our peace offering," Tannin replied. "I'm sorry for lying, but you'd have refused if I'd have told you the truth."

Hal stared at Danny, trying to read the boy's reaction. The officer seemed stiff, and unusually in control of his emotions for a man so young.

"My people were promised quite a few things by invaders once," Hal said. "They ended up being massacred, or force-marched to useless scrubland in Oklahoma. How do we know we can trust 'em?"

The Bwain lifted its arm to its chest, taped the scaled feathers there, then tapped its head. "Trust," it said.

Hal felt something shift behind his eyes, the glimmer of a headache, as if he'd had too much nightcrawler the day before, but he was seven days sober. This was something else.

"There are other intelligent races in this universe, but not all of them are friendly," Tannin said. "You may not believe it right now Hal, but the Bwain are our future."

* * *

Personal Logbook: Captain Atlas Carter
Entry 26 – In orbit above Gertie

I don't know if I can trust her Aida, but I need Mephista's help. You always had the right sense about who to trust. I was too open...too naive. I think Danny will do what he knows is right, and I think the crew can rally through this whole thing in spite of their fear, but this Mephista...the way she looks at me...

What would you think if I took up with her, eh? Would you say my crippled inside and her crippled outside were a good match? I think you probably would, though I feel like I know you less and less now for some reason. I've been trying to catch what little sleep I can during the repairs, and when I do, you no longer come to me. There's just nothing there, and then I wake up covered with sweat, and with my heart pounding in my chest. Is it a good thing that you're not in my dreams anymore? Is it progress, or are the Bwain digging into my mind like Kaylee warned us about?

When I told Mephista about what the Bwain can do, she said she knew first hand, and then she said that what the creatures discovered in *her* mind would be enough to send them back to whatever Sol-blasted rock they evolved from.

Maybe it would, and maybe I can learn to trust her. You know, I think you'd have liked her. She's got the same kind of a fire in her that I used to see in you. I guess that's a part of what makes me want to trust her. I just hope for all of our sakes that the trust I'm placing in her isn't misplaced.

* * *

The Fate's Winds

"Do you think Aric will make it?" Danny asked from down on Gertie. Julie was routing his signal to Granger's implant as the science officer floated slowly away from the *Fate's Winds* at slower than walking speed, careful not to get too deep into the battle's debris field. With all the sharp, jagged edges out there, he was scrupulously careful to avoid tearing his suit.

"Pandith says his odds are less than thirty percent," Granger answered. His HUD filled with red and yellow cautions as the computer led him through the wreckage of the Bwain ships. He'd spent fifteen hours in his suit making exterior repairs to the *Fate's Winds'* hull, and his skin was crawling with the desire to get back into the ship's open air environment. However, he had one last task to complete before heading back to the airlock. It was an experiment that might just tell him more about the Bwain, and how they'd seemingly just appeared out of nowhere.

"You know, Aric's a pretty tough guy," Granger added. "He's a good engineer too. I think he'll recover."

"I hope so," Danny said sullenly. "Julie, are you still on here? I need to talk to the captain next."

"I thought *you* were the captain now?" she asked quizzically.

"I am, as far as they know down here on Gertie, but this is serious Jules," Danny said.

"Ok, I'm putting you through now."

"You take care of yourself down there, Danny. Don't you sit there worryin' about us," Granger said as he scanned the debris field.

Finding what he was looking for, his inducers lit up and pushed him toward what looked like a chunk of gray glass. It floated among shards of the *Fate's Winds* hull that still glowed with the nanobots that were trying to repair the damage. The science officer slowly worked his way closer to it, pushing smaller fragments away with his gloves until he was finally able to reach the meter-wide shard of debris.

"It's not me I'm worried about," Danny replied from the surface.

"Oh, I think we might be okay," Granger said as he tethered the chunk of metal to his belt and turned back toward the ship. "We may just have a trick or two up our sleeves."

* * *

There were clicks and a brief hiss of static as the call patched through. Bryon and Carter could hear Danny's tinny voice through the bridge speakers, and they could barely believe what he was telling them.

"A Bwain?" Carter repeated. "On *Gertie*?"

"That's right, sir," Danny confirmed. "I stood in the same room with the thing. It's telling Tannin it wants peace."

"How the hell did it get past us?" Bryon asked. He wore a tight bandage over his forehead and was still slurring his words a bit from his concussion during the battle.

"It can camouflage itself," Danny said. "Sort of like a chameleon."

"That may be Danny, but up here, their Bwain-brothers weren't just using biology." Granger said as he stomped onto the bridge. The tall man hadn't even bothered to change out of his EVO suit, and he was carrying a strange, shimmering piece of material that he tossed onto the deck in front of him.

"What's that?" Carter asked.

"Watch this," the science officer responded. He pulled a power coupling from the deck's relay line, touched the cable to the metal, and the material shimmered out of view before their eyes. When he lifted the coupling, it reappeared.

"It's some kind of cloaking device," Danielle said as she stared at it with wide eyes. "And it's just activated by a regular old electrical charge?"

"Yep," Granger said.

"But how the hell could the Bwain have developed cloaking technology?" Carter asked as he studied the strange material. "They don't have the manufacturing skills that we do. Not even humans have come close to this."

"I can't answer that, Captain, but I can show you where these things are." Granger said as he brought up a holoimage.

Carter watched as Granger's familiar multidimensional representation of the Majorana particles enlarged. The data was more refined by additional probes, and he quickly zoomed in on a series of jagged streaks that ran perpendicular to the main bulge of readings.

"Look at these four streaks, Captain," Granger pointed out. "They came in about a day ago, headed right for us. If I recall, there were three kills, but it looks like there was a fourth that headed right for Gertie."

"Cloaked, but no longer invisible," Carter muttered to himself. Then, he said, "My god Granger, you did it! Excellent work!"

"But the swarm is only a few days from the array," Danielle warned.

"Danny, are you gonna be able to get us what we need? We're short on time up here," Carter asked.

"I'll be moving Heaven and Earth, sir."

Carter studied a holoview of Gertie. The green planet glowed like an emerald against the blackness.

"Is that what you promised them, Tannin? A planet of their own while you slipped away and left the rest of the humans to die?" he huttered to himself quietly.

"You know Danny, when the administrator finds out what Mephista's about to do, he's gonna be furious. You be careful down there. We're all counting on you."

"Yes, sir...and thank you for trusting me," the lieutenant replied.

* * *

Gertie
Outside of Landfall

Hal sighed as he trudged up the path and found Victor sitting with his back against his crate.

"You're out of clean glasses," the engineer called.

"I'm not here to drink," Hal replied tersely.

Hal passed by him on his way in, but he didn't invite his friend inside. The wind moaned around them, and Victor's hair fluttered across his eyes.

"Awww, come on. Take a load off and ease your mind," Victor urged.

"I'm not really in the mood right now Vic."

"Come on Hal, what's eatin' you?" Victor asked. Hal scowled at his friend, if that's truly what he was, as though he were being deliberately obtuse.

"Ok, well…for one thing, that alien claims that it came here in peace. A representative of the *Bwain*, a species that massacres humans every damn chance they get, now claims that it wants peace with us. Are you really gonna sit there and tell me you actually believe that crap?

"I believe in the administrator," Victor said flatly. "Regardless of anything else, he's kept us all goin' out here."

"Damn it Vic, he *lied* to us!" Hal objected.

"So what's our alternative, Hal? We've got one little ship against a whole swarm of Bwain? Cooperation is our only hope of surviving this whole thing!"

"Cooperation, or *collaboration*? What are they getting in return for sparing our lives?" Hal asked.

Victor waved to the printing station control console, its lights flashing mutely.

"A few sheets of carbyne, some molecular lattices...who cares?"

"Did it ever occur to you that maybe the only reason they want our help is because we keep *winning*?" Hal asked. "We've struggled to keep them at bay, but what happens when they get their hands on our technology?"

"Hal, that's not gonna happen. We've been assured that it..."

"*Assured?*" Hal snorted. He gazed out at Factory 22. The printing station was producing, but he'd taken care to mark it offline with a malfunction. It paid to be cautious, given what he was planning.

"Hal..."

"You know, when I came out here I thought we'd really be building something. Something good. Something that would last. What have we got now, huh? A corrupt and useless administrator who's out for his own ends, and we're helpin' some murderous alien race to achieve whatever their sick objectives might be. It's all *lies*, Vic! It's nothing but a bunch of deceit and duplicity!" Hal said angrily. Victor stood, ready to put his friend straight.

"Look, I know this is a shock, but you have to..."

"Get the hell off my porch," Hal demanded. He waited for a moment to see what Victor would do, and then he reluctantly pointed his fusion pistol at his friend's face. Victor's hands rose in front of him defensively as he started to back away slowly.

"Where'd you get that pistol?" he asked.

"The same place the militia got 'em, I would imagine," Hal responded, a new determination reflected in his voice.

"This isn't over, Hal. You can't do things like this without consequences," he said as he continued to back away. He took about ten steps back, and then he turned and headed back toward town.

Hal watched him go, and a part of him regretted having to take such an action against someone who heretofore he'd considered about the best friend he had on this God forsaken world. Unfortunately, there was no undoing it now, and he wasn't sure he would, even if he could.

"Screw this, I need a nap," he grumbled to himself as he turned and headed back into his crate.

*　*　*

Hal woke to hammering on his trailer door and prepared himself to meet the militia. No doubt it would be Captain Xiao himself who'd take him to Judgment. He was somewhat reassured by the fact that he'd been able to talk to several of the farmers before he'd gone to bed, so they knew what to do, regardless of what happened to him.

"I'm unarmed," Hal called out to whoever was on the other side. "I'm coming out."

The banging continued, until the metal reverberations set his teeth on edge.

On second thought, Hal lifted his pistol from his end table. What was the point of starving to death when he could go out with a bang? He threw back the door and aimed his weapon's glowing muzzle at the face of Captain Xiao. The young SSC officer threw up his hands in surprise.

"Hey! Whoa there Hal! I'm alone. I'm not armed, and I'm not here to hurt you," he assured him. Hal stared at him for a moment, absolutely dumbfounded.

"What the hell are you doing, son?" Hal asked as he glanced around to make sure that Danny really was alone.

"Listen...I think we need to talk," Danny replied somberly.

Chapter Thirteen

Gertie
Aboard the Fate's Winds

Captain Carter woke up screaming. He'd been dreaming of Belize City again. The first flashes of gunfire sparkling below him, the rockets and tanks demolishing whole blocks...it was utter chaos. He'd been floating in the air just above the city as the concussions battered his face, and the shrapnel sliced through him. Wounded and dying, he tried to fly faster toward Aida, and his house on *Calle Boxer,* but the flames and smoke caught him. They pulled him down and choked him in a blackness so thick he could not even call her name.

He raised the lights in his cabin and looked around wildly for a moment, trying to shake himself of the horrific images that had plagued his sleep. He'd fallen asleep in his flight suit, and his knuckles were raw from punching the deck above his bunk.

He laid there for a while, letting the adrenaline rush recede a bit before he finally got up and washed his face. He stared at himself in the mirror for a moment. He looked terrible, and the lack of sleep wasn't helping matters.

He wet his fingers and then rubbed his eyes, trying to regain a little of the focus that had eluded him since he'd woken up.

"You used to be a handsome devil. What the hell happened to you?" he asked with a wry grin as he tapped a button that caused his sink to retract back into the wall. Just as he was about to change out of his flight suit, his stateroom chime rang.

When he opened the door, he found Kaylee standing there in the hallway, looking incredibly worried. The girl had wrapped a blanket over her ill-fitting flight suit, and offered him a reflexive bow that he politely returned. Finally recovered from her ordeal, she looked much healthier than the shivering victim that he'd rescued from a life pod, not so long ago.

"I was awake, and I heard you yelling," she stated without preamble.

"I was having a nightmare," he said. "I'm sorry if it frightened you."

"They taught us to comfort the men on the *Ichikari*," the girl said. She stepped toward him, offering an awkward embrace. "Would you like me to..."

"No...," Carter said as he took her hands and gently lowered them back to her sides. "You don't need to do those things anymore. Things are different here."

"I'm sorry. I shouldn't have asked," Kaylee said, lowering her eyes with a look of shame on her face.

"How are you feeling?" Carter asked, not only to push past the awkwardness of the moment, but because he was genuinely interested in how she was doing.

"I'm feeling much better now, thanks. I haven't been able to sleep though. Mr. Pandith gave me some sedatives, but I don't want to take them. Not yet anyway," she said. Just then, a thought ran through Carter's head.

"Wait – were you in the med bay just now?"

"Yes," she answered.

"And you could hear me screaming from an entirely different deck?"

An anxious look pinched Kaylee's face. "I was awake. I heard you, so I came here to see if you were all right."

Carter squatted down to face the girl at eye level. Her brown eyes were watering, and she tried to turn back down the corridor away from him.

"It's all right, Kaylee, I'm not angry, but I'd like to ask you a few more questions. You might be able to help the crew. Could you do that for me?" he asked. The girl brushed away the tears from her cheek, then smoothed her face into a placid mask.

"I fought on the *Ichikari*," she said, feeling a small measure of pride at her own survival. "You and your people have been good to me, so I'll do whatever I can to help."

Carter invited her into his cabin, gave her a hot drink, and listened for nearly an hour as she navigated through the awful tale of the attack on the *Ichikari*. Even though it was still early, as soon as he'd heard her story, he knew he had to take her straight to Granger.

* * *

When Kaylee began repeating her story, Granger had been thumbing sleep from his eyes, but by the time she finished, she had his undivided attention.

"So?" Carter asked. "What do you make of this 'mind control' stuff?"

"It's certainly possible," Granger said, looking up at Carter. "If my theory is true, our consciousness is all somehow connected. That would include the Bwain."

"What do you think they want?" Carter asked.

"Well, they're an alien race. We have no context for understanding their desires, in the same way they don't understand ours. To them, we might not even be viewed as intelligent, and I –"

"Control – they want control," Kaylee stated flatly. "They know we are smarter. The others – they were smarter too, but the Bwain escaped. They were slaves before, but not now."

"What do you mean?" Carter asked her. "What others?"

"The Bwain aren't smart enough to build things. They need slaves to do it, just how the Bwain's masters did. They want to make us slaves, but humans don't want to be slaves, so they tried to take us over," she said as she looked up into Carter's eyes. "It all begins with bad dreams like yours."

"Captain, what does she mean?" Granger asked.

"It means that I need you to figure out a way to block these Majorana particles, Mr. Granger, and you'd better do it quickly. Otherwise, what happened to the *Ichikari* is gonna happen to us as well."

"How much time do I have?" Granger asked, turning his attention back toward Kaylee.

"I still can feel pieces of them," she replied. "I think they've already started."

* * *

Gertie
Landfall

"What do you want to show me?" Tannin asked the creature he'd come to think of as The Voice.

The Bwain kneaded its clawed hands against his shoulder. He'd found the creature oddly animal-like in its grooming, as if evolution had brought its race into space, but had nevertheless left its social habits unchanged. No matter, the glimpses he'd seen of the Bwainsong had shown him wonders far more incredible than the creature's simple manners.

"Need know why," it said. "Need know what come."

The creature's head snapped from side to side, then tilted at the mushrooms Phuri brought. Tannin sat down in an overstuffed chair he used for the purpose, lifted two of the mushrooms from the box, and swallowed them whole. The mushrooms were quite bitter, so he tried to avoid chewing them if at all possible.

"Yes, soon," the creature said in a far-away voice. "Yes, now."

The last image Tannin saw before falling into the dream was the Bwain hovering over him, its feathers glimmering like a kaleidoscope. Then he closed his eyes and allowed himself to enter into The Voice's vision.

A part of him still felt as though it were sitting there in the physical world, but that feeling became secondary to what he was experiencing in his mind. He was sharing in the thoughts of millions of Bwain, all woven into an intricate fabric that spanned the universe.

The Bwain had spread across vast distances, but in relative terms, they were not overly numerous. They lived in swarms, clustered around the very old, very large ships they called Bwainhomes. The race had no planets of their own, and had long ago forgotten where they'd even come from. After over a millennia spent in nomadic isolation, they hungered after what Tannin could give them. They wanted a habitable planet with earth and sky, ore and metal, machines and people to make new things, and to teach them how to fix the things that they'd forgotten how to fix. The Bwain desired nothing more than a permanent home, with the whole of their hearts.

If Tannin was the one to establish a profitable peace with the Bwain, how could Sol deny him a return to Earth? They'd willingly offer him the full wealth and glory he deserved. Of that, he had no doubt.

A subtle urging from The Voice focused Tannin's attention inside another Bwain's senses. The vision was disorienting at first, but the mushroom's chemicals allowed him to let his consciousness blend in with the creature's own. It was currently standing in a large room, along with a group of other aliens. The Bwain were swaying, making some kind of rhythmic chirping sound as they knelt in front of the impossible vision that was floating in the center of the room.

This, Tannin realized, was what the Bwain would bring to Gertie. It was what had sustained them. It had given them life, and even consciousness, just as it had done with so many other species. It was a source of the most *immense* power, but there was something else. There was a concept in his host's mind that he couldn't quite understand.

Tannin sputtered awake in his chair, fighting the mushroom's hold on his mind.

"What is that?" he spat through his yellowed lips. The Bwain bobbed backward, cocking its head. "You never told me what you were!"

"Showed," the Bwain said. It bobbed its head, clattering against the tile.

"This power. Where did it come from?" he asked.

Phuri handed the administrator a glass of water. Tannin sipped, trying to wash the bitter taste of the mushroom from the back of his throat. His mind's eye still fired with the last of the chemicals, and a part of him could see the threads that connected The Voice to the others of its kind, the golden knot that bound them all.

"What was it, sir?" Phuri asked cautiously.

"It's power, Phuri. Raw, unadulterated power. It's the way they communicate with each other, but there's something more to it. I don't quite understand…"

"I show. You understand," the Bwain said as it reached its claws toward him once more.

* * *

Danny shaded his eyes, watching the *Fate's Winds'* orbiter soar high into

Gertie's rose-colored sky until only its contrail remained. Then he hefted the ancient rifle Hal had handed to him and turned toward the distant fields.

"You want to be up there with them, don't you?" Hal asked.

"Yeah, I do," the young officer said.

"So will I if Tannin finds out what we're doin'. That bastard's as cold and as cruel as the day is long."

Danny studied Gertie's low hills, the grass bending in the wind. It could have been a vision of heaven as seen through his sister's eyes. That thought caused a hollow feeling in his stomach that he had no time for at the moment.

"Do you think this will work?" he asked.

"Your science officer sure seemed to think so," Hal said. "I mean, there's not a lot of room for error, and it's not something that would come with the manual for your ship, but with the components we just sent up there, at least there's a chance."

"I meant this," Danny said as he gestured to his rifle. It was an antiquated powder-and-cartridge design. Unfortunately, it was the best Hal could print without access to radioactive materials.

"Oh, you mean our little adventure?" Hal asked. He was pushing two hovercarts along in front of them, their loads of weaponry covered in tarpaulin. If anyone saw them, or the militia questioned them, it would be impossible to hide their guilt, but the Bwain's arrival had forced his hand. "How the hell would I know what's gonna happen? I'm just an engineer with a taste for the old firewater. Lucky for you, I've been workin' really hard to kick the addiction lately, otherwise I'd be more or less worthless in this whole thing."

"That's good. I'm glad you are," Danny said. Hal nodded, but didn't respond.

"Have you seen combat, son? I mean, aside from your run in with the pirates, and then that nastiness with the Bwain?" Hal asked after they'd walked in silence for a while.

"Yeah, I have."

"I thought you might have," Hal said. "On Earth, we've got recordings of the tribal elders from the twentieth century talking about fighting the white man. Not many took the time to watch 'em, but I did. They had the same look that you do sometimes. Eyes that have seen too much."

Danny nodded, looking back at the thin ribbon of exhaust from the orbiter that was fading into the sky.

"Tannin will see the contrail," he noted.

"Yeah, I'm sure he will, but he'll also assume that you're on it, going to get him his antimatter. That's the nice part about being a double agent."

The supply officer lent a guiding hand as the whirring hovercarts drifted over the grass. He seemed to be wrestling with something in his head.

"Do you want to talk about what's really on your mind?" Hal asked. For a time, he heard only the grass whispering, but then Danny suddenly spoke with a rush of emotion.

"Tannin found out that my sister was nearly killed in a Bwain attack on our colony. I bankrupted myself to keep her on life support. I joined the Academy because of her. I traded everything I could on the black market so I could make enough credits to keep her alive...and then he approached me with more money than I'd ever made, just to help him falsify some records. Of course I said yes. I mean, who wouldn't say yes when the life of someone they love is on the line? I thought...well, I don't know what I thought, but the more I helped him, the more he had me under his thumb."

"Why'd you decide to stop helping him?" Hal asked, curious about what could cause such a dangerous and sudden shift in loyalty.

Danny jogged up a rise, scanning the path ahead with his binoculars to make sure it was clear.

"I decided to stop helping him, because she's never gonna wake up. She'll never even know me...," he said, trailing off as the emotions welled up inside him. It took him a few moments before he was able to continue. "He thought I'd stay loyal, and that I could be bought off like some crooked politician. That's what I hated the most about the whole situation. He didn't treat me like a human being. I was just a tool to be used for a specific purpose, and then disposed of when I wasn't useful anymore. That bastard was gonna leave me on Judgment for Christ's sake! If it wasn't for Captain Carter, I'd either be dead right now, or I'd still be stuck on that God forsaken planet."

Hal clamped a comforting hand on Danny's shoulder, and smiled at him sadly.

"Don't feel too awful bad, son. He was using all of us," Hal said as he clamped a comforting hand on Danny's shoulder, and smiled at him sadly.

"I can't live in the past anymore," Danny said as he attempted to shake off all the guilt he'd been feeling, and the memories that had been haunting him every day since the attack that took his family from him.

"It's not a good place to be, that's for sure," Hal agreed.

"That ship up there...that's my family now, and I'm damn sure gonna do whatever I can to make sure they don't end up like my real family did," he said firmly. "We may all end up dead when all this is done and over with, but it sure as hell won't be because we didn't try to fight."

"Well kid, I guess if there's a bright spot in any of this, at least you're not alone in this fight," Hal said reassuringly.

"I know. I just hope it's enough," Danny said as they continued on to their destination.

*　*　*

The Fate's Winds
Medical Bay

After the absolute cold and vacuum of space nearly took his life, ironically, it was cold water on the back of his neck that finally returned Aric to consciousness. He felt the chill curl around his throat and dribble down over his shoulders. Weakly, he brought a hand up and tried to wipe it away.

"Mr. Pandith, come quick! He's awake!" a girl's voice called.

Aric opened his eyes and found himself lying face down, staring at the gleaming deck of the med bay.

"Aric, can you hear me?" Pandith asked. Aric tried to lift his head, but the strain on his back was too much.

"I'm here," he mumbled into the table.

"Oh my God, I can't believe you're awake," Pandith said as he squatted down next to him. Aric could just make out the Malaysian's smiling face through squinted eyes. "Captain to the med bay, stat! Our patient is awake!"

"Jeez, I feel like I've been run through a meat grinder. What happened to me?" Aric groaned.

"Your back still isn't fully healed, so you need to be careful. Kaylee, help me if you could with the bandages please."

"Ok," she said as she moved closer to the table.

"So basically what happened is that there was a rupture in hull at the engineering bay, and the depressurization tried to push you through the hull breach," Pandith explained. "You lost a lot of blood, and even parts of some of your organs to the vacuum. I was able to treat you with accelerated stem cells to repair the damage, but it was an extreme trauma to your body. If I'm being honest, I wasn't all that sure you'd be able to recover."

"We survived?" Aric asked in surprise.

"Yes, we did, Mr. Keith," Captain Carter said as he entered the med bay. "You made an excellent cork in a rather nasty hull breach."

"Funny," Aric groaned. "Least I was good for somethin' I suppose."

Carter's scarred flight boots came into Aric's view just as the captain squatted down to face him.

"The real trick now is gonna be *staying* alive. How are you feeling?"

"I've been better, sir."

"It'll be weeks before he can move, sir," Pandith added. "I'm honestly surprised he's even awake this soon."

"Well, I'm glad about it," the captain said. "I've got an engineering problem, Mr. Keith, and we've got a whole lot more of those Bwain ships headed right for us."

"How many is 'a lot'?" Aric groaned.

"As near as Granger can tell, all of 'em," he said. Aric gulped weakly as he tried to process what the captain had just said.

"Now, here's what I need from you Mr. Keith, and believe me, I wouldn't be asking if it weren't absolutely necessary."

"I'll do what I can Captain. Just don't expect me to jump through any hoops anytime soon," Aric said with a weak laugh that was quickly followed by a pained grunt.

"I wouldn't think of it Mr. Keith," Carter said, smiling to himself in spite of the seriousness of the situation they were in.

* * *

"They've never shown command of materials like this before," Granger was saying as the other crew members entered the bridge. "I mean, multidimensional stealth technology? It's absolutely unheard of. We've never had any reports that would indicate that they've reached this level of technology."

"A few attacks at the edge of human-occupied space don't really tell us everything there is to know about another life form," Julie noted.

"True," Granger conceded. He shook a piece of glassy, gray metal in the air. "Think about it. Every other encounter we've had with them has shown us that we're at least two centuries more advanced than they are when it comes to manufacturing capability, and yet now all of a sudden they show up here with something that's way beyond anything that humans have ever produced. Tell me, how does that happen?"

 "So what are you saying?" Bryon asked. A lengthy scar arced above his right eyebrow, and he winced as he sat on an overturned crate. "That they've got allies out there somewhere that are feeding 'em tech?"

"I don't know," Granger said. "Pandith and I need more time to…"

"You may not have it, Mr. Granger," Carter said as he joined them on the bridge.

"Attention on deck!" the science officer bellowed.

"At ease," Carter said as he took his seat and pulled up the holoscreen. It showed a very pale and wan looking Aric waving to the bridge crew from down in the med bay. "Our first order of business is to welcome back Mr. Keith."

A smile crept over Aric's face as the crew clapped and cheered. Kaylee stood beside him, bowing and clapping.

Suddenly Aric's expression changed. "Where's Danny?" the engineer asked.

"Mr. Xiao stayed behind on Gertie to help the local population," Carter informed him. "Fortunately, he was able to help us out with our supply situation, and we're on our way to The Gate as we speak."

"Captain," Aric whispered. "I..."

Carter merely held up a hand. He knew Aric wouldn't divulge his suspicions about Danny in front of the crew unless he felt the situation was desperate, and this certainly qualified. He looked meaningfully at Aric through the screen as he interrupted what the engineer was about to say.

"Mr. Xiao is committed to communicating our needs to Administrator Tannin." Carter added.

Aric nodded, satisfied with the answer. He hoped that Danielle hadn't noticed this little exchange. She would be all over him with questions as soon as he was out of bed. The thought of it actually made him smile. Anyone talking to him about anything would be more than welcome after his exile in the med bay.

"Now, I've called you all here because we've got to make a decision, and after what we've all been through, it's only right that we do it together."

"What is it?" Danielle asked.

"You've all been working night and day on this ship to get it repaired, and you've all done one hell of a good job. Mr. Purcell has informed me that our offensive capacity is being steadily being restored but unfortunately it's still diminished."

"They hit our starboard side pretty good," Bryon said. "I've only got the port missile bays right now and the laser's at less than fifty percent."

"What about the *Tranquility*?" Julie asked.

"Captain Mephista and I have made an arrangement. We're going to be fighting together, but if our goal is to save lives we need to keep the *Tranquility* in orbit around Gertie. If the Bwain get past us, she'll be the only thing standing between them and every colonist in the system."

"If?" Bryon repeated. "Beg pardon, Captain, but what chance do we have?"
"We think we may have a solution to that problem," Granger said.

"That's right – but, again, in order to do it, we need to make a decision." Carter paused to study their faces.

"What is it, Captain?" Danielle asked. Carter met their eyes, one by one before he answered.

"What we have to decide is...whether or not we ever want to go back home."

*　*　*

Danielle, Julie, and Bryon sat together in the galley discussing the question that the captain had put to them. Their conversation was frequently interrupted by long bouts of silence as each reflected on how they felt about the situation.

"I mean, I think it sounds all right, at least compared to some of the alternatives," Bryon reasoned. "Besides, there's something vaguely romantic about going down with the ship."

"Romantic?" Julie scoffed. "Hmm, let's think about that for a minute, shall we? We've got hordes of angry, mind-controlling aliens coming at us as though their lives depend on it. Then when they get here, we get to watch our ship get sliced apart by lasers, and ripped to shreds by magna-cannons. Then, if we're *really* lucky, we'll die by getting sucked out into space rather than by tearing each other apart on the ship in a mind-controlled frenzy. Yeah, that all sounds wonderfully romantic," she said, rolling her eyes a bit. "Don't you have a family or anything Bryon? Aren't there people waiting for you back home?"

"Yeah, I do actually. As a matter of fact, I got a really big family with lots of cousins that are scattered all over the galaxy at this point. The Purcells are adventurers."

"Yeah well, the Fords aren't," Julie said with a hint of sadness in her voice. "We're...I mean...I don't even know what we are, but I do know that this isn't what I signed up for. I don't think I can do it."

Danielle was toying with an orange that she'd found on the grass in the day room while she'd been sweeping the ship to clean up damage after the attack. To her, it was more than just an orange. It was a little piece of home.

"How much time would they have?" Danielle asked.

"Who?" Bryon asked in return.

"If we run...how much longer will it take the Bwain to find Earth? They don't have Alcubierre drives, but what if they learn to build 'em? The colony's computers could tell 'em how, and there'll be people down there that they'll capture and use to help 'em with the manufacturing. I mean, it's only a matter of time before they can make their way to Earth, and then what?" she asked. They all contemplated that dreadful prospect in silence for a moment.

"I honestly have no idea," Bryon said finally.

"You know, a few days ago I would have said we don't owe anyone anything, but think about all the good we've done since the captain arrived. We were nothing before, and now I feel like we have actually have a chance to do something great. I don't know about you guys, but I'm in. I'm not gonna let him down after all he's done for us," Danielle said firmly. Bryon nodded in agreement, and then they both turned their attention to Julie, who was shaking her head slowly. Suddenly she stopped though, as a thoughtful look took over her features.

"You know, he could have court-martialed me over the whole diet pill thing, but he didn't. He helped me when I passed out in his cabin, and then let me return to duty without ever saying another word about it. I just don't know though. I mean, what if we all die? Then what? What would we have really accomplished?"

"A lot more than we'll have accomplished if we just turn tail and run," Bryon said. "If I'm gonna die out here, then I wanna go down fighting."

"Me too," Danielle said. Julie let out a heavy sigh as she looked back and forth between them.

"If we all get killed, I'm never speaking to either of you again."

"Fair enough," Bryon said as he and Danielle both smiled at her.

* * *

The Tranquility
In orbit over Gertie

"How'd they take it?" Mephista asked.

"Some better than others," Carter replied through her holoscreen.

"I think there's probably a lot of us that head out into space because we don't ever wanna go back, don't you think?" she asked.

Half-smiling, Carter looked down at his hands for a moment, and then back up at her.

"And what would you do?" he asked.

"I think I've already answered that."

"Ok, let me ask a different question. What would you do if your injury hadn't happened?"

It was her turn to fall silent. In truth, it was a question she'd long ago pushed behind the realities and decisions of life as a renegade captain. She knew her crew felt the tug of home more strongly than she did, so it was far easier for her to deal with being so far away than it was for them.

"You know, I think I'd retire to a planet with lots of coastline. Get myself a nice, big boat, and sail a different way," she said. Carter nodded, his suspicions about her confirmed.

"My science officer has a pretty good read on the Bwain swarm's course and speed from the data he's gathered with his probes," Carter said. "They'll be through The Gate in roughly about fifty hours or so."

"How many ships?" she asked.

"The last probe we sent has cameras and instruments to help figure that out, but the Bwain have been catching some of the satellites. The best I can tell you right now is that there will be quite a few."

"Then I guess it's time."

"I know what this means to you," he said. Her eyes watered, and she dabbed at them for a moment before she could continue. "Tannin never wanted to leave, did he?"

"I think he did, but I don't think he meant for anyone else to come with him," Carter said. He could tell how used she felt in the whole situation, but it was an avenue of conversation that he chose not to pursue. Tannin had used a lot of people, but that time was coming to an end.

"I wonder what the Bwain will think about their new home?" she asked.

"Hopefully they won't have much time to think at all," he said. She tried to smile, but her trembling lips wouldn't cooperate. "You listen to me Carter. You be careful out there. I don't want anything to happen to you," she said in a soft, sincere voice.

"You do the same Elise," he said. She cut the transmission and closed her eyes, taking a deep breath in an attempt to control the emotions that were boiling up inside of her.

"Your orders, Captain?" a voice asked gently through her implant.

"Begin the acceleration," she said. "Three orbits should do it, and then we'll have to see if Carter's still alive."

Chapter Fourteen

Gertie
The planet's surface

"They're coming," Danny hissed as he pulled Hal to the ground.

Five colonial militia pounded through the late afternoon sun toward Dax and Lisa's farmhouse. The low building sat on a few hectares of farmland that had been planted with soybeans, corn and wheat. Danny peered through the grass, and watched as Dax ran inside and slammed the door. The militia's distant shouting floated over the hill.

"How good of a shot are you?" Hal asked.

Danny slipped the rifle from his shoulder and sighted in on the loose ring of militia surrounding the house. "I've never fired one of these before," he admitted.

"Neither have I," Hal said as he belly-crawled to the crest of the hill. "But then again, I've never led a coup against a colonial administrator either."

The engineer dropped his head, closed an eye, picked out his target, and then squeezed the trigger. The rifle punched backward into his shoulder, nearly jumping out of his hand. Hal's eyes widened for a moment.

"Be careful kid, you need to hold on tight to that thing!" he reminded him, though it was hardly necessary to mention it.

Danny didn't say anything in response. He just stared down the sights and picked out another target. The men had heard the shot, but they didn't know where it came from, or what it was for that matter. They were so used to using plasma weapons that hearing a shot from a normal rifle was totally foreign to them.

This time, Danny's target was a man with a bandanna tied around his forehead. Slowly he squeezed the trigger, and the rifle roared once again. When the smoke cleared, he saw the man clutching his stomach as he fell to the ground, howling in pain.

Wild plasma bolts shot overhead. Hal took a death grip on his rifle and began squeezing the trigger in rapid succession. Two more militia fell, and Danny saw the house's door crack open.

"Hold your fire!" he cried to Hal as Dax flew out behind the last two soldiers with a spade in his hand. The farmer swung at the backs of their heads, and before they even had a chance to react, both men fell to the ground in crumpled heaps.

Danny scanned the area once again, trying to see if there were any more members of the militia on the way, but Hal was already charging down the hill.

"We did it Dax!" Hal whooped. "We did it!"

"Hell yeah we did!" Dax cheered as he waved the spade high over his head.

*   *   *

Hal's elation had faded by the time they'd finished burying the bodies. Covered in sweat, he leaned heavily on Dax's spade and stared at the farmer.

"I honestly didn't know what they were gonna do," he said. It was the closest he could come to an apology.

"You might have just saved our lives, Hal," Lisa said as she swiped at a loose tendril of hair, and then tucked it deftly behind her ear. "It's just that..."

"We knew these men," Dax finished for her. "We knew all of 'em."

"I did too," Hal admitted as Dax brushed dirt from his hands, picked up the fusion pistols the militia had dropped.

"Maybe we could have talked to them," Lisa suggested. "Maybe Tannin would see reason."

"I'm afraid that ship has sailed," Hal said. "Listen, things are so much worse than we originally thought. The lieutenant here is from the *Fate's Winds*, and he's going to tell you guys some stuff that you both need to hear."

* * *

Danny set aside the sweetened tea that Lisa had brewed for them. The delicate clink of brittle porcelain was the only sound in the silent farmhouse. Night filled the windows, and the moths crawled all over each other on the solar lights that were mounted to the ceiling.

"So, Tannin is actually bringing the Bwain here," Dax finally muttered in disbelief.

"It's real now," Lisa said. "It's really happening."

"But what do you think going after Tannin's gonna do, Hal?" Dax asked. "It's not like he's flying any of those Bwain ships himself."

"No, he's not, but this is *his* plan. He's been lying to us for years. He's been arresting innocent people like you and sending 'em to die on Judgment just because they found out things he didn't want 'em to know."

"And the two of you helped him," Dax said. "Why should we trust you?"

"Well...," Hal said, but then he paused for a moment, not really sure how to answer the question. "Well, I guess you don't have to. I mean..."

"You don't need to trust us," Danny said, quickly interrupting him. "You just need to make a decision about what side you're on."

"What would you know about any of this, boy?" Dax asked acidly.

"Dax!" Lisa objected.

"It's all right," Danny said. "I'd ask the same thing. I guess I'm the only one who's ever been paroled from Judgment. When I was, it was much more than just getting my life back. Captain Carter showed me what it meant to live for the right reasons. I believe in him. Even if he doesn't come back from The Gate, and even if the Bwain tear through the *Tranquility* and surround this planet, I'm still gonna fight Tannin. For myself, for all of you, and also because my captain is up there fighting for what's right, and he needs our help."

Dax and Lisa reached for each other's hands. Long shadows crept down their faces, and it took a moment before Danny realized they were nodding.

"All right, Hal," Lisa said. "We'll help you. What do you need us to do?"

*   *   *

The Fate's Winds

"It's insanity, that's what it is," Bryon said incredulously. Danny's laser accelerator had arrived from Gertie, and Bryon was welding a section of it against the repaired hull plating, squinting against the bright white of his plasma torch.

The ship was headed toward The Gate at maximum thrust. They were trying to beat the Bwain to the nebula's exit, and Bryon had volunteered to be hard tethered to the hull while performing Aric's repairs. One wrong move, such as an accidental loosening of the spider-steel linkage that was anchoring him to the hull railings, and he'd be ripped from the hull and left tumbling far behind the ship in an instant. He knew that Carter would circle around to retrieve him if that happened, but still...he didn't want to embarrass himself in front of the ladies.

"The concept has been demonstrated in numerous lab studies," Granger said through Bryon's implant.

Bryon rested his glove on the accelerator coil. The laser system was basically a giant electromagnet that used mirrors and magnetic fields to condense photons into a super-dense, super-high-velocity plasma, and his repairs needed to be flawless. The positioning matched the schematics on his HUD, and when he tried to push and pull the assembly it wouldn't budge.

"Does this look like a lab to you, Granger?" Bryon retorted as he pulled the last piece of accelerator toward him and positioned it to link with the thick tubes of the laser's firing nozzle. The *Fate's Winds* was still in a pretty sorry state, but at least she'd be able to fight. In any case, for what the captain had planned, it just might be enough.

"Space is the greatest of laboratories, Bryon," Granger said. "It's the source of life itself, and everything in the physical universe."

Bryon didn't respond. He was too busy concentrating on his plasma welds as the nanos surged against the barrier he'd erected. He finished a few moments later, and then extended his tethers a few feet from the hull to study his work. Everything looked ok, so he took a second to stare off into the onrushing nebula, and the mysterious, invisible aliens that lay beyond.

"Hey Granger...are you afraid of what's coming?" he asked.

"Emotionally I am, but intellectually I'd have to say that I'm extremely curious to see what happens."

"Yeah, that's cool...I guess," Bryon said as he released the nanos and began packing his equipment. "I'd just rather have more than one ace up our sleeve, and it'd be helpful if that one ace that we did have wasn't an experimental one."

"Oh, so you and Danielle still aren't speaking then?" Granger asked.

"Yeah, we are. I thought we were anyway. Why?"

"Because apparently you haven't heard the good news. We've got *two* aces up our sleeve now."

"Oh? Do tell," Bryon said as he made his way back into the ship.

* * *

"The laser repairs worked, Aric. Your instructions were perfect!" Pandith said excitedly.

"I kind of assumed so, since I didn't hear any explosions," the engineer half-joked. He'd grown extremely weary with his uncomfortable position in the med bay, and the fact that he couldn't help the rest of the crew to prepare for what was coming was affecting his temper. "I'm still worried though."

"About what, Mr. Keith?" Kaylee asked.

The girl bobbed underneath him, holding up a water bulb for him to sip on. He smiled at her kindness, and she flashed her pearly white teeth in return. It was widely known that Kaylee had developed a crush on her patient, and the crew rarely let him forget it. Kaylee seemed to be a natural nurse, and he wasn't planning to let her down until *after* he was released.

"I should be at my station," Aric grumbled. "What the hell good am I to anyone if I'm stuck in here?"

"There's nothing we can do about that," Pandith said. "It'll be weeks before you're fit for duty again, even with the cellular therapy.

"It is all right, Mr. Keith," Kaylee assured him. "You won't be stuck in here forever."

Aric smiled at her appreciatively. Reaching out an arm, he ignored the pain that rippled down his back and ruffled the girl's jet-black hair.

"That's true, isn't it?" he agreed. "I guess I shouldn't worry so much. We actually turned out to be a pretty damn good crew after all. It just took a good leader to show us what we were capable of."

"You can say that again," Pandith agreed as he grabbed a medical scanner from the counter and hovered it over Aric's back to check on his progress.

* * *

"That's it, Captain. We're in position now," Danielle informed him.

The bridge lights were dimmed. It was the third watch, and Carter had volunteered to relieve the rest of the crew so they could get some rest. Danielle had stayed at her station, because she wanted to personally monitor the final details of their positioning. The Gate yawned before them in the holoscreens, like a wedge of blackness in a furious sea of multi-spectral colors. Out of that emptiness would soon come a fury more lethal than anything that any of them had ever faced before.

"What's the array's status?" Carter asked.

Opening a new holoscreen, the lieutenant showed him every mirror in the cluster. Six of the mirrors were still in transit, with countdowns above them that showed when they'd reach their new positions.

"Six hours away from full deployment, Captain."

"Good work Ms. Hoff. You can stand down now and get some rest. You've certainly earned it."

"Sir, would you mind if I stayed?" she asked.

"Of course not," he said, smiling at her warmly. They're not wrong when they talk about the loneliness of command you know. Truth be told, I'd get pretty bored if I had to sit here all by myself."

She smiled her thanks at him, but then her expression suddenly turned serious.

"Have you...uhhh..."

"Have I what?" he asked.

"Have you had the dreams?" she asked.

"Yeah, I have. I think we all have," Carter said. Danielle just nodded, and then turned her attention back to the readings on her holoscreen.

"Does it scare you?" she asked, without looking back around at him.

"A little I suppose, but there's nothing wrong with fear Ms. Hoff, as long as we don't let that fear control us, it can actually make us sharper, and more effective. Just to put your mind at ease though, Granger began working on a solution to that whole situation as soon as he finished with the antimatter."

"Well I hope it works, because I don't know how much more of this I can take," Danielle responded.

"I hope so too, believe me. Now, why don't we see what's out there?" he suggested as he pulled up Granger and Pandith's experiment. The main holoscreen was suddenly filled with the now familiar yellow blotch that represented the Bwain swarm. Carter rotated the angle several different times, trying to spot anything he might have missed. If there was one thing he'd learned from the *Narcos*, it was that there were almost always weaknesses that could be exploited, if one could only find them.

"We've had some data loss, Captain," Danielle said.

"What do you mean?"

"We used to have readings from forty probes, but now there's only thirty-six reporting back. Crap, another one just went dark," she said anxiously.

Carter double-checked her readings, and found that the holes in the data were widening.

"The Bwain have discovered more of the probes," he noted. "Ms. Hoff, make sure we're recording. We need to get as good of a read as we can on the Bwain's course before we lose the ability to track them all together."

"Acknowledged. All data streams are being recorded."

"Good, let's see what the last one has picked up so far." Carter said as he tapped a button on his holodisplay and switched the view on the main screen to the visible light cameras that Granger had placed on the most recent satellite.

"Oh my god!" Danielle exclaimed.

For a moment, Carter couldn't understand what the probe was showing them. A giant section of the nebula seemed to writhe and twist, but when he zoomed in to get a closer look, he realized the truth. A massive swarm of hundreds of Bwain ships swirled through The Gate toward the probe. None were alike, and they ranged in size from that of the *Tranquility*, all the way down to a fighter-sized craft. Weapons jutted awkwardly out of every ship like antennae on a bug's head.

The ships seemed to be jockeying for position, flying as if they were each unaware of the trajectory of all the others. It was more ships than he'd ever seen in one sector all at the same time, and quite possibly more ships than humanity had ever assembled.

Dani did her best to hide her fear. This was a moment to be professional. She needed to be strong for her crewmates, and for her captain.

"They're just twenty-four hours away now, Captain," she informed him. "Captain, what do we do?"

"We hope for a miracle, Ms. Hoff. Or, on second thought...we might just have to make our own."

* * *

The Tranquility
In orbit around Gertie

The bridge was a place of quiet concentration, as each crewmember struggled with the enormity of the threat that they would soon face. Mephista spoke with Carter on a secured channel after she'd retreated to her stateroom to receive the call. If there was to be yet more bad news, she'd prefer that her crew hear it from her directly.

"This will probably be the last time we can speak," Carter's holoimage said.

"I appreciate the update," Mephista said solemnly.

"Have you received any word from the planet?" he asked, the image crackling slightly.

"No, but we're monitoring. Tannin hasn't returned my calls," she said. Carter frowned slightly as he considered that for a moment.

"What do you think he's doing?" he asked.

"If your lieutenant is doing the job you sent him there to do, then the crooked old bastard is probably fighting for his life right about now," she said, earning her another one of Carter's half-smiles.

"Are you enjoying this, Captain?" she asked.

"In a strange way," he conceded. "I suppose that part of me feels like I should just have just joined my wife and given it all up months ago," he said. Mephista recognized the pain, and knew it all too well.

"But now?"

"Now I'm in deep space, with a dedicated crew of remarkable misfits, getting ready to defend all of humanity from impending doom. To be honest, it feels as though this is a battle I was meant to fight. It's the reason I'm still alive, even when I wanted to give everything up not all that long ago."

Mephista studied the controls in front of her and swallowed hard. It was eerie just how similar Carter's thoughts were to her own.

"I'm glad I let you live, Captain. Don't make me regret that decision by screwing this whole thing up."

"Never," he said, smiling at her once again.

"The pain won't ever get any easier to deal with, but eventually it just starts feeling like it gets farther and farther away. Just don't let it become the dominant force in your life. I wouldn't want to see a man like you lose yourself in it, if you know what I mean," she said. Carter nodded, a look of determination hardening his face.

"You take care of yourself. Watch over that planet, and your crew."

"You too," she said. A second later, the screen went dark, and she was left alone in her stateroom.

*   *   *

Gertie
On the outskirts of Landfall

In the dead of night, keeping low and silent, just as real soldiers would do, sixty some odd farmers crept up the hill overlooking Landfall's western outskirts. Danny knew how easy it would be for disaster to strike. They'd only have one shot at this, and if Hal's intelligence was to be believed, they were already outnumbered by at least three to one.

"That's his house?" Danny asked.

Hal squinted at the double crate at the end of the straggling dirt road. Pressing night vision binoculars to his eyes, he zoomed in on the two militiamen who guarded the entrance.

"Yeah, that's it. Looks like those are the only guards."

Lisa nodded beside him, and then she looked back around at all the nervous faces behind her.

"Is everyone ready?" she asked. Only a handful nodded. The others all stared off into the distance, or mumbled prayers to whatever deity they happened to worship. Danny slithered back down the hill, and then jogged back over to them.

"Remember, these are real guards, with real weapons. Once we begin, there's no turning back," he reminded them. "Oh, and don't forget what I told you about Judgment. When the time comes to take him down, don't hesitate. You just think of what he's done to your friends and family, and then you pull that trigger."

"The lieutenant's right," Hal agreed. "If we want this to be *our* colony, then this is what we have to do."

The farmers' faces hardened, and they pressed their rifles into their shoulders. This time, even more heads nodded in agreement.

"All right, then," Hal said, readying his weapon as the others did the same. "Let's go make us some trouble."

* * *

The first guard yawned, rubbed his eyes for a moment, and then shifted back and forth in an effort to try to clear the fatigue from his body. It was a pleasant night, and as he stared up at the sky, he studied the nebula, and glanced around from one horizon to the other, trying to spot some shooting stars, or anything else that might of interest.

"Did you hear something?" the other man asked.

"I wasn't listening," the first said through a sudden yawn. "What did you...hey!"

He tried to turn at the sharp jab in his back, but hands seized him and turned to flatten him against the house wall. A gag slipped into his mouth, pressing against his tongue.

"You'll want to be quiet," a man growled threateningly into his ear. "This will all be over soon."

The raiders wore the earth-stained overalls that were typical amongst the farming class, and many had rubbed black dirt on their faces. They were carrying some kind of antiquated weapons that the guard recognized from period movies, and the whole scene was so surreal he almost thought he'd fallen into the strange dreams that had recently plagued his nights.

"What do you want?" the militiaman's partner asked before the men muffled him.

"We want you to let us in," one of the farmers said.

In the glow of the few plasma pistols the raiders carried, the militiaman found himself pressed toward the crate's door while they pushed his hand up to the code panel. Reluctantly, he entered the access code, and the door slid open, allowing a small pool of light to spill out. Vartan had been having trouble sleeping lately as well, so he was still awake at his holoterminal when they entered.

"Don't you even knock anymore?" he grumbled. His weary face filled with surprise however as the farmers entered. He tried to draw his pistol, but it was too late. Hal and Danny's raiders had already rushed inside, and they quickly pinned the militia's captain in place with their rifle barrels.

"Don't move, Vartan!" someone growled.

"Hal? Hal, is that you?" the militia captain spluttered. "What the hell do you think you're doin'?"

"I'm saving this colony," Hal announced. "Now on your feet. You're coming with me."

Chapter Fifteen

The Fate's Winds
Outside The Gate

Carter slipped Granger's delicate copper mesh over his head. Instantly, the fogginess and irritability of his exhaustion faded, only to be replaced with a greater sense of clarity than he'd felt in days.

"Wow, this thing actually works!" he said with a look of happy surprise.

"The headgear creates an electromagnetic field that negates Majorana particles," Pandith said. "It's crude, but we believe it will block the Bwain's ability to affect our minds."

"You have enough of these for the whole crew?"

"Yes, sir," an exhausted Granger acknowledged.

"Outfit them immediately," Carter ordered, "And then I want you to get a message to the *Tranquility* about these. I want everyone wearing these, and their combat EVO suits at all times."

"Yes sir. I'll get right on it," the science officer acknowledged.

"Ms. Hoff, how are we doing with the array?"

"The last mirror's coming into place now, Captain."

"Excellent," Carter said, smiling to himself. It was all coming together, just as he'd hoped. Pulling it off would be a different matter entirely, but at least their preparations were nearly complete.

While he waited, Carter studied the data from the few probes that the Bwain had missed. The yellow blob had resolved into what looked like a series of pulses, and that worried him. He was about to enter the unknown, and the fact that he was losing his ability to see where the Bwain were and what they were up to worried him quite a bit. His advantage in the boxing ring had always been intelligence, but you couldn't outsmart or outmaneuver what you couldn't see. A blind fighter was useless.

"Mr. Purcell, I'd like to prepare another practice run. On my mark..."

Bryon was punching buttons to bring up the simulation when Dani yelled out from her console.

"Captain, look!" she called out urgently. On the holoscreen, a jagged streak of yellow arced out toward one of the mirrors closest to The Gate. "One of the Bwain's stealth ships is inbound toward the array."

"Awww crap. Do the Bwain see the mirrors?" Carter asked.

"I have a missile solution," Bryon called.

"Fire at will, Mr. Purcell. Ms. Hoff, get that mirror out of harm's way.

"Yes sir," they both called out in unison.

On the holoscreen, three missiles arced toward the shimmering emptiness of one of the Bwain's stealth ships. The mirror fired its inducers as Danielle tried to push it out of the Bwain ship's course, but the satellite had never been intended for maneuverability, and as such it was too slow in lumbering itself out of the way. Carter watched the mirror clip the scout ship, and then float off out of position, tumbling in a random fashion as it went.

"Captain, I've lost control of the mirror's induction thrusters," Danielle called.

"Five seconds to target," Bryon announced a second later.

The missiles erupted against what a moment before had appeared to be empty space. Sections of suddenly visible hull scattered in the explosion.

"Kill confirmed, Captain," Bryon reported.

The entire bridge stared at the listing mirror on the holoscreen, watching all their plans collapse right in front of them.

"Sir, if we don't get that mirror back into position, the array won't fire properly," Granger said.

"Mr. Pandith, come with me to airlock one," the captain ordered as he jumped out of his chair and headed toward the door. Everyone else, you know the plan, and you know what you need to do. I just want you all to know that I believe in both you, and your ability to carry out this mission to a successful conclusion. Stay strong, believe in yourselves, and maybe we'll still have a shot at surviving this whole thing."

"Captain," Julie called after him, "What are you gonna do?"

"I'm gonna fix that mirror, or die trying," he replied with absolute determination.

* * *

The nebula in front of Carter swelled like an angry muscle shot through with dark veins and white tendon. He pushed his suit's two inducers to their maximum and pulled up the damaged mirror in his HUD. Granger's best estimate for the Bwain's arrival at The Gate was displayed at the top of his face shield. They only had about twenty minutes left before the aliens would reach their trap. He just hoped it was long enough for them to do what they needed to do to fix the mirror and get it back into position.

"*Fate's Winds*, are you reading me?" he said.

"Roger, Captain," Julie called back to him over the radio.

"Focus your telescope's, coordinates on 495 by 733 by 10."

"Understood. What are we looking for, sir?"

"Mr. Granger," the captain said, "I think the Bwain are early."

His suit's exterior optics had a limited telescopic range, but he patched into the *Fate's Winds'* data stream and brought up the telescope's feed in his HUD.

Ship after ship emerged from the darkness of The Gate, following a twisting course that made it look as though they were rotating around the eye of a storm. The ungainly vessels were blunt amalgamations of technology that no human would ever have designed, patched and pieced together from what looked like dozens of sources, but they could fly, and there were hundreds of them.

"Oh my god, it looks like a meat grinder," Bryon said over the comm.

Carter focused on the mirror in front of him. In spite of the kilometers dwindling on his HUD, the satellite didn't seem to be coming any closer.

"How long to do I have, Ms. Hoff?" Carter asked.

"Maybe ten minutes, Captain. It's not gonna be enough time."

"Well, then we'll just have to do our best," the captain's steady voice responded. "Oh, and Mr. Purcell..."

"Yes Captain?" Bryon said.

"When the time comes, regardless of whether I'm in the way or not, you are to fire your weapons without hesitation. Do I make myself clear?" the captain said firmly.

"Yes sir," Bryon answered. "If I could just make one request though Captain. Please hurry the hell up."

In spite of himself, Carter smiled, as he felt another piece of Aida fade away. The pain was still there, but as Mephista had said, it was farther away now, more gentle. It had been replaced by the love, loyalty, and admiration of his crew. They were his reason for living now, and he found that even though the desire to join his wife someday in the hereafter was still with him, he wasn't in any hurry to rush it. She'd be waiting for him...whenever he happened to get there.

"Acknowledged Ensign," Carter called back to him. "Believe it or not, I'd actually like to survive this whole thing."

* * *

Gertie
Landfall

The administrator's eyes blurred open. He tried to call for Phuri, but his tongue stuck in his throat. He knew he was lying down, but he didn't know where. There was no sensation of time or self for a moment, only a strange roar in his ears that he could not place. It was often this way when he swam back toward consciousness from a period within the Bwainsong.

"Sir," Phuri said from somewhere above him. A straw passed his lips, and Tannin drank the cool water that it offered. "Sir, you need to come quickly."

Tannin was annoyed. These returns to his physical self were all too jarring. He longed to stay in the incredible expanse of the Bwainsong rather than the pathetic nothingness of his normal life. The Bwain had spoken throughout the galaxy before life on Earth had even begun to rise from its primordial ooze. They were an ancient and marvelous species, but his own species continued to call him back to the pale shades of their own reality.

Hands helped him to sit up, and he found he could finally focus his eyes. He was in his chamber, facing the worried lines on Phuri's forehead.

"What is it?" he demanded.

"Sir, there's a revolt in progress," Phuri informed him.

"A what?" Tannin shouted as he threw off his aide's hands and kicked out from under the sheets. He forced himself upright on unsteady legs, staggered to his chamber doors, and then quickly threw them open.

His mind was unprepared for such noise and violence, and he winced at the roar that pummeled his ears. The Bwain's footsteps were clicking back and forth in front of the windows, and Tannin joined his ally to assess the situation.

It was morning, and in the growing light he saw his militia battling in the streets against a mob of colonists that appeared to be armed with a mixture of fusion and antique weapons.

"Hal...," Tannin muttered.

"What this?" the Bwain asked.

"A mistake that will cost a lot of humans their lives. Phuri, get me Vartan! Now!" he demanded.

"I've tried sir, but he hasn't answered," Phuri responded nervously.

"And what about the rest of the militia?"

"They're fully engaged, sir. All of our reinforcements have already been sent."

"No...this can't be," Tannin said, his voice trailing off in disbelief.

There were dozens of shooters on the streets from both sides, but as Tannin watched in absolute horror, more and more of the colonists joined the rebellion. They were unarmed but furiously swarming his soldiers and dragging them to the ground. They beat at the militia with cooking

Pans, shovels, and whatever other weapons they could find. As his men were pushed back toward his residence, Tannin pounded his fist on the wall.

"No! I will not let this happen! Phuri, we're going down there right now."

"But...but sir," his assistant sputtered with a terrified look in his eyes. "What can we do?"

Even in his anger, Tannin recognized his aide's point. His gaze settled on the Bwain as the creature's head snapped toward him.

"*You*," Tannin said as he pointed at his ally. "What can *you* do?"

"We will help," the creature squawked as it bobbed from side to side, flicking its eyelids.

*   *   *

Danny ducked behind a cluster of barrels as two plasma bolts whirled overhead, stripping the roof off a house that was behind him. A militia patrol had seen the farmers moving into town, so what had started out as a small raid had quickly turned into a full-blown battle. Everywhere he looked, he found nothing but chaos.

Hal crashed into the barrels next to him, sweating and gasping for breath. "What I wouldn't give for a drink right now," the nanoengineer gasped.

In spite of himself, Danny had to smile. He rose to one knee and quickly fired at the two militiamen who were guarding the front entrance of Tannin's home. Unfortunately, the smoke that billowed up out of the ancient weapon obscured his vision, so he had no idea if he hit them or not. The compound was only sixty feet away, and what little remained of Vartan's militia had been pushed back to nearly indefensible positions in the building's plaza.

"The drinks will be on me when this is all over," Danny said through ragged breaths. "Only if we win though. If we lose, then you're buyin'."

He sprinted past Hal toward a doorway where two other farmers had taken cover. Suddenly, a sharp pain stabbed into Danny's skull and sent him skidding into the building's wall. At first, he thought he'd been shot, but when he felt his forehead, there was no wound. He tried to stand and reach the doorway, but his vision blurred, and he could only manage to crawl toward where the farmers were writhing on the ground.

"What's happening?" Hal called from behind him. Danny turned, fighting the stabbing sensation in his mind. He tried to see the engineer...to call out a warning, but he had somehow lost his voice. As a strange darkness fell, he couldn't muster up enough strength to tell Hal to run.

He knew what would come next. It was the same thing that Kaylee had experienced on the *Ichikari*. Only this time, there were no life pods.

* * *

The Fate's Winds

"He's not going to make it," Danielle said in a worried tone.

"Now come on Dani, just stay calm. The captain knows what he's doin'," Bryon said from behind her.

"But there's no time, and there's way too many of them," she pointed out. "What are we gonna do?"

The Bwain ships filled the holoscreens with a swarm of churning metal. An inset video feed showed them the captain's tiny suit in the foreground of the Bwain's grinding fleet, and she silently urged him to move faster. She'd laid in every possible course and evasive maneuver she could think of, so there was really nothing left for her to do now but to wait as patiently as she could, without losing her mind.

"Captain, they're gonna be within range in five minutes," Bryon said.

"I understand, Ensign," the captain called from his suit. "Use your best judgment, and that goes for all of you. You know what to do. We can stop them, so don't spend time questioning yourselves. Just remember the plan, and execute it, just like we talked about."

Danielle knew they still had the option to withdraw to Gertie. If they left now, they'd stay out of range of the Bwain's weapons. They'd stand a better chance fighting alongside the *Tranquility*, using the planet for cover.

"Captain," she asked. "If you can't get the mirror repaired in time, do we withdraw?"

There was only the whine of static over the comms. The nebula's interference had affected the captain's transmission, so Julie had to make a few quick adjustments to clean up the signal.

"You can always run, Ms. Hoff," Carter told her. "There are times however when you won't be able to run far enough away from the consequences you leave behind.

"Danielle," Granger's voice spoke in her earpiece. "Just so you know, we don't have the ability to make a jump."

Danielle didn't answer. She simply watched the captain hurl himself too late toward the tumbling mirror as the first sparkles of the Bwain's weapons flashed.

"Incoming," Bryon said. "Deploying countermeasures."

Danielle's hand hovered over her nav controls. How long would they survive if they ran? Who else would pay the price? She thought for a moment about what the captain would do, and then she reached out a hand and started tapping her controls.

* * *

"Evasive maneuvers," Carter heard Danielle say through his earpiece. The Bwain fleet was close enough now for him to see their missiles whizz by, and the magna-cannons hurl their deadly payloads. In a few minutes, their fleet would pass maybe a half of a kilometer above him. If he zoomed in his HUD, he could even see inside some of their ports, but none of the creatures were looking back. Apparently, they still hadn't noticed the mirrors.

"It looks like standard projectile weaponry," he reported.

"Captain, how long do you have?" Bryon asked urgently.

Checking the tumbling mirror, which seemed to grow to the size of a house as he approached, Carter's stomach dropped. "Ten minutes. I'm already at max thrust."

"But not close enough," Bryon stated.

"Roger that," Danielle said. "We're wait one…"

It took everything Carter had not to throw off his trajectory by spinning in his suit and looking back at his ship. He'd lose precious seconds as his thrusters readjusted, but the curiosity he felt was tearing at him.

"Sir," Danielle called. "I've got a large signature coming from what looks like Gertie. It's moving very rapidly."

"Thank God," Carter said, smiling to himself. "Mr. Granger, how does its trajectory look?"

"The acceleration and kinetic energy may be enough, sir. I don't have an exact target point yet, but Captain Mephista's crew did an admirable job."

"There's a lot to like about how that pirate runs her ship," Carter said.

"It's gonna get pretty hairy for you right about when you get to the mirror," Bryon's voice broke in.

Carter focused on the satellite rising in front of him, and forced his eyes to stay straight ahead. No matter what came next, he still had a job to do.

"I knew the risks when I put on the suit Mr. Purcell. Besides, it's gonna be one hell of a view."

* * *

Carter's stomach lurched as his inducers decelerated and brought him into a spin to match that of the mirror. There was little time to waste.

"The mirror looks intact," he said, swallowing to clear his throat. "The only damage is to the starboard thruster array.

His magnets engaged automatically, drawing him toward the spinning assembly of carbyne steel and electroglass. Once his attitude matched, he focused on the satellite to calm his stomach, while ignoring the massive battle that was about to begin above him.

"Captain, it's coming," Danielle warned.

As quickly as he could, Carter detached the inducers from his suit, worked his plasma torch free, and clambered hand over hand toward the damaged section of the mirror. He cut away a twisted piece of the structure to create a smooth surface, and then began positioning the thruster according to the instructions on his HUD.

"I'm attaching the thruster now," he reported.

"Captain! Watch ou...," Danielle started to say, but then the transmission got cut off.

Without thinking, Carter looked up just in time to see a massive white flash engulf the entirety of the space above him.

Chapter Sixteen

The Orion Nebula
Outside The Gate

The *Sanctuary* was traveling at nearly a quarter of the speed of light, accelerated by Captain Mephista's use of Gertie's gravity, as well as its own plasma thrusters. It struck the center of the Bwain fleet in an impact so enormous, that it registered on the *Fate's Winds'* systems as a small supernova.

Bryon watched the explosion ripple through the cloud of ships, consuming all but a handful of the densely packed vessels.

"A direct hit," he said, watching it all play out in complete and utter awe.

"Julie, inform the *Tranquility*," Granger said from beside him.

"Targeting the remaining ships," Bryon said. His fingers moved as if they were beyond his conscious thought. "Missiles away."

He couldn't believe it had worked. An entire ship, used as an interstellar battering ram. It was unheard of...audacious, and even a little crazy, but the plan had worked. Now their enemies were off balance and scattered by the enormity of the explosion. Bryon could barely breathe as he watched his missiles destroy their respective targets.

"I think we did it, Captain!" he shouted excitedly into the radio.

Danielle clamped her arm against his shoulder to get his attention. He looked at her, and the words she spoke dragged him kicking and screaming back to reality.

"The captain. He's still out there," she said solemnly.

* * *

Carter floated beside the mirror, helpless. The explosion's shockwave had forced his suit to shut down, and in his haste to get the job done, he hadn't taken the time to tether himself to the satellite. A handhold gleamed mere inches from his glove, but in the vacuum of space, the chasm was insurmountable.

"Damn it," he grumbled into the echo of his helmet. Suddenly his visor flickered, and air whirred against his throat as his HUD flashed back to life. As soon as the comm system was reactivated, the very first things he heard were the excited shouts of his crew.

"Direct hit!" someone squealed. "We did it!"

Carter relaxed, realizing for the first time the amount of tension he'd been carrying. As soon as his inducers flashed green, he pushed forward to the mirror and tethered himself to its square hull.

"The captain! What about the captain?" a voice sounded in his ear.

"I'm still here," Carter said as he surveyed the impact's aftermath. "Dunno how, but I'm all right. My suit shut down on me after the blast, but it fully operational now."

Above him, the nebula had gained a new shower of dissociated gases and dust. Chunks of flickering metal and electronics swirled out from The Gate, but the impact had nearly obliterated the entire mass of ships. If he ever saw Administrator Tannin again, he'd have to thank the man for commissioning them such a wonderful weapon to use against his allies.

"Sir, I think you can come on back now," Bryon called. "It looks like we were all worried about nothing. Oh, wait a minute..."

Carter zoomed his HUD toward The Gate once more. It was flashing red and green, picking out strands of energy and rapid changes in the radar feed.

"Do you see that?" he asked.

"Oh my god, there's another wave!" Granger said nervously. "Captain, it looks like that was only the first of 'em. You gotta get that mirror back up and running, before it's too late!"

"I'm doing everything I can," Carter said as his gloves flew against the mirror's hull. He welded the new inducers into place, and then brought them online. Moments later the thrusters had synched up with the satellite's nav computer. He made final weld, and then pushed away from the mirror to gain a safe distance before he tapped into his HUD to monitor the satellite's status.

"Ms. Hoff," he called. "Repairs are complete, at least as best as I can tell. Give it a try."

"Acknowledged," she replied. A few moments later, blue-white streaks of plasma poured from the newly repaired attitude control system. The mirror's spin slowly corrected until it finally drifted into the ideal position and attitude.

"It worked Captain!" she cried. "It worked!"

"Copy that. Now I'm gonna repair the mirror itself." Glancing at the Bwain ships above him, it looked to his naked eye like this wave was coming even more quickly, and that the ships were much larger than the previous ones. "Granger, any idea how many waves there'll be?" he asked.

"No sir. I wish I could tell you more, but they've gotten most of our probes. Hopefully, if the antimatter weapon enhancement works, we should have enough power to hold them off. We're in the right position."

"Wish me luck then," Carter said as he magnetized himself to the satellite's dish. The electroglass was so highly polished he could see his perfect reflection seventy times in its facets. The surface looked like a giant steel drum, and without his HUD he never would have noticed the small pings that Danny had made in the damaged panel.

"Hurry Captain. You've got less than five minutes," Danielle said.

"Copy. I'm working as fast as I can," he said as he passed a command through his suit to the satellite's main control systems. The magnet behind the mirror suddenly released, allowing the electroglass block to float free. He tethered it to his waist, and then brought out the replacement. Once he'd slid it into the mount, he triggered the magnetic locking system once more to secure it into place. A few moments later his HUD flashed a full green for the satellite's status.

"Captain," Danielle said excitedly. "I'm showing mirror 17 as fully operational."

A cheer cut across the channel as Carter's inducers lifted him from the line of fire.

"I'm clear," Carter said. "Fire when ready."

"With pleasure, sir," Bryon acknowledged. "Oh, and be sure to lower your visor. It's gonna get awfully bright out there."

"Acknowledged," Carter said as the visor on his helmet quickly slid down into position.

*   *   *

The holoscreens showed the Bwain ships screaming toward them like the crooked roots of some mammoth tree. There seemed to be some kind of pattern to their movements, but for the life of her, Danielle couldn't figure it out. She assigned a subroutine to record and analyze their flight paths for any future value the data might provide.

"How many ships can they have?" she asked.

"There's no way to know," Granger said. "There are no records of any Bwain sightings of this size in the SSC's database."

"They'll be in range in thirty seconds," Bryon said. "Laser at one-hundred percent, and holding."

"Copy," the captain said from his distant location as he continued backing away from the mirror. "Good luck...to all of us."

A heavy silence fell over the bridge. Danielle realized that she was holding her breath as she stared at the holoscreens, hoping desperately that their insane plan, and retrofit they'd done would work.

"Firing now," Bryon said.

Brilliant plasma streaked from the *Fate's Winds* laser port, reaching out toward the first mirror in the array. The laser's hue was tinged by Aric and Granger's reconfigured antimatter, surging across the blackness of space in a malevolent yellow. Even with the holoscreens automatically dimming its brightness, the beam was painful to watch.

"One-third of the mirrors are active," Bryon called.

The laser was pinging back and forth between the circle of mirrors that Danielle had spent hours adjusting with Granger's help, so that it formed a massive lattice of fire across the mouth of The Gate.

"Two-thirds now."

"They're less than twenty kilometers from the array," Danielle called. "We've only got about ten seconds."

"Almost there...," Bryon said.

The last mirror was the one the captain had repaired, the one that had never worked for them from day one thanks to Danny's tampering. When the laser struck the satellite, it ricocheted back to the first laser at a perfect angle to form an impenetrable barrier of plasma.

"Full deployment!" Bryon called. "Antimatter is holding steady!"

The first of the Bwain ships struck the barrier, and Danielle recoiled in horror at what she was watching. Traveling too fast to adjust their trajectories, the massive ships wilted like paper in a fire when they sailed through the array. After passing through the searing plasma they emerged little more than sagging, molten blurs, stripped of all recognizable shape

"My god," she gasped.

"Captain," Bryon called. "I don't know if you can hear this but it's working. It's working!"

Something came back over the captain's channel, but there was too much interference from the plasma, and Danielle couldn't make it out.

Checking her data streams, Danielle saw that another problem was developing. She couldn't see beyond the laser's wall, and without the probe data she had no idea if the Bwain were still coming or not. Twisted hulks were still passing through the defenses, but her readouts showed that their numbers were gradually becoming fewer and fewer.

"How can I tell when it's over?" she asked.

"Without the probes, I don't think we can," Granger replied.

"We're just gonna keep fryin' those bastards as long as they keep on comin'," Bryon said eagerly. "I could do this all damn day!"

"Purcell, remember that this is a brand new array, and it's just been repaired," Carter screamed into the static in his helmet. "Make sure you watch your power distribution!"

If Aric had been at his station, he might have been able to stop the firing in time. If Captain Carter had been on the bridge, or if his transmission could penetrate the electromagnetic field created by the blast of supercharged plasma that had decimated the Bwain fleet, his orders might have changed things.

The laser accelerators were never meant to handle such a powerful energy source, so as the firing continued, the heat built up inside the conduits until a weak weld finally gave. The nanos fought to keep the repairs stable at the microscopic level for as long as they could, but even they were no match for the super-laser. As a result, the suddenly unfocused plasma beam erupted through the *Fate's Winds'* hull and out into the cold dark of space.

* * *

Alarms flashed everywhere on the bridge. The ship lurched hard to port, threatening to throw the bridge crew to the deck.

"I've lost the laser," Bryon screamed as he held onto his station's tether.

"Shut it down!" Danielle shouted to him. "We've got a hull rupture on the starboard side."

Bryon banged the controls, and the antimatter-fueled beam died at once.

"We're losing atmosphere in the starboard horseshoe, and the day room as well," Pandith said over the radio. All crew members, get your helmets on."

Danielle slammed her EVO helmet over her flight suit and twisted the seal.

"I'm bringing us back to position," Danielle said as she furiously worked her controls.

"Are there any more of 'em?" Bryon asked.

Granger flipped through his readings, cycling the holodisplays as quickly as he could through every detection frequency.

"God damn it! Can you hear me?" the captain's urgent voice rang in their helmets. "There's something else coming through!"

* * *

The crude oval above Captain Carter was massive, easily the size of a moon. Tapered at its front, it resembled an ancient jet engine as it passed through the dormant mirrors without a scratch.

"Launching every missile we've got left," Bryon said. As Carter watched, the projectiles streaked through space and struck the object with less impact than a mosquito that had just flown into an elephant.

"You need to run," Carter called urgently. "Get back to Gertie and do what you can."

"But, sir, we can't leave you out here," Danielle protested.

"That's an order, Ms. Hoff," Carter barked as he triggered his inducers. He rose up and away from the mirror that had done so much good, its cooling electroglass quickly dwindling behind him.

"What are you gonna do Captain?" Aric asked with a weak voice.

"I'm gonna try to buy you guys some time," was his only reply before he went silent.

* * *

"I've never seen a ship that big before," Danielle said as she turned the *Fate's Winds* and plotted a course for Gertie.

"It's moving fast," Bryon said.

"Come on now, we all need to focus. We don't know what that ship can do and we need to be on our...," Granger said, but he was interrupted when a streaming lance of light bathed the bridge in a blinding spray. Danielle felt the deck fall away from her, saw sparks and explosions rip from the overhead. For a moment, she felt pity for the screaming, wounded soul that she could hear somewhere nearby, but then a horrific realization hit her. The cries she heard were her own, as they echoed on the inside of her helmet.

Chapter Seventeen

Gertie
Landfall

Danny woke with the taste of vomit in his mouth. He lay sprawled on his side in the dirt, and he realized someone was screaming at all of them. He blinked for a moment and tried to sit up, but hands held him down.

"It's better if you don't," Hal said.

Orange sky wheeled overhead. They were on the street in front of the administrator's compound. Scarred and bloody militia patrolled in front of them, but they seemed more worried about the Bwain that slunk beside them than about any of the farmers. The citizens were clearly terrified, but if what Kaylee had said was true, they should have all turned violent. He should still be in crippling pain, unless the Bwain were learning how to control human minds, and the *Ichikari* had just been an experiment.

"Now, many of you are clearly ignorant of history," the administrator bellowed. "Colonial uprisings always fail. They've failed for the past seventy-five years, just as badly as you've failed today."

"Hal," Danny whispered. "Hal, we need to..."

"Keep him quiet!" one of the militia hissed.

Hal nodded, patting Danny on the chest. The engineer was missing a finger, and a plasma wound had scorched a chunk from his shoulder.

"I kept this rat's nest operating," Tannin said furiously. "I established order. When a threat to this colony came, when people like the SSC and our buddy Hal over here would have squandered our lives by trying to fight a superior power, I negotiated with them to bring you peace. And this is how you repay me?"

Tannin looked unhinged. A sickly yellow drool dribbled from his mouth, and his hair stood in greased spikes.

"Hal, we need to kill that Bwain," Danny whispered.

"With what?" Hal whispered back.

"I told you to stay quiet!" the militiaman shouted again as he stomped toward Danny, seized his collar, and hauled him over to drop him in a heap at Tannin's feet.

"Well, if it isn't Mr. Xiao. I'm afraid it looks like our little arrangement won't be so profitable after all," he sneered as he turned to the militiaman. "Give me your sidearm."

"Peace!" the Bwain squawked, alarmed at his actions. "You said *peace*! I said *peace*!"

Tannin aimed the plasma pistol at Danny's forehead. "Say hello to your sister for me," the administrator said, but just as he was about to pull the trigger, the Bwain suddenly screamed like a rooster that was being slaughtered.

When Danny opened his eyes, he saw Tannin moving over toward the alien creature. It had bent backward onto the ground like a collapsed ostrich, and its head snaked in the dirt.

 "What's going on?" Tannin demanded.

"The swarm!" the creature croaked. "The swarm dies!"

"Oh my god, Carter actually pulled it off!" Danny exclaimed. Tannin stomped back toward him, fury tearing at his face.

"What did you say?"

"He had a plan to deal with your friends Tannin. He knew what you were up to. Your friends are done for."

Tannin's face fluttered with a strange mix of fear and rage. Then he lifted the pistol and pointed it at Danny's head once more.

"That may be kid, but you won't live to see how it turns out."

"Sir!" Vartan suddenly shouted. He sounded absolutely terrified.

"God damn it! What now?" Tannin snarled.

The militia leader pointed skyward, toward the rolling streams of drop ships churning the sky.

"I don't understand," Tannin muttered. "Where the hell did they come from?"

Danny didn't wait to find out. He kicked at Tannin's legs, lunging to catch the man's pistol when the administrator fell. The second Tannin hit the ground, the rest of the farmers rose up as one to rejoin the fight.

*   *   *

The Gate

The massive Bwain ship blotted out the stars, but as Carter hurtled himself through the swarm's debris, the features of its hull came more into focus. Once it had been a series of triangular cylinders, constructed in alien proportions that swelled and shrank at a dozen points along the hull. Whatever the ship's original lines and intentions were however, the entire vessel looked as if it had been built and rebuilt numerous times over the past several eons. The giant plasma cannon that had struck the *Fate's Winds* was one of thousands of appendages that extended from various alien ships that had all been blended into the hull of the main ship through a series of patchwork repairs. Bubbles and tears throughout the ship's hull made it seem incredibly ancient. Unfortunately, when he used his HUD to search for airlocks he found no functioning entryways.

Carter had no idea what he'd do when he arrived at the ship, but if the Bwain had destroyed the *Fate's Winds*, then all he needed was revenge. Nothing else mattered at this point.

"I'm one-hundred meters from the ship," Carter called just in case his crew were still alive and listening. "Seventy-five now. Just in case anyone can hear this, I just want to say that..."

Before he could finish his transmission, a chunk of debris struck his face shield, shattering the electroglass and throwing him off course. Cold sucked against his cheek as his oxygen rushed past his face and out into space through cracks that glowed red with damage. He clamped a glove to his visor, trying to stop the loss of atmospheric pressure. What remained of his HUD flickered with warnings, but even without the computer he knew the damage was far too severe for the nanos to repair in time to keep him alive. The only option left if he wanted to stay alive was to get aboard the Bwain ship.

Reorienting his inducers, Carter pushed for the ship. His right eye began hurting as the vitreous fluid rushed to the front, and suddenly he lost half his vision. The vacuum sucked at his breath and whistled against his ears.

The Bwain ship was fifteen meters from him, then ten. He aimed for a jagged tear in the hull, and triggered his magnets as soon as he landed on the Bwain ship's surface. His plasma torch spiked on, and he hacked at the hull in front of him to widen the entrance. His lungs felt squeezed and his breathing was labored at best. His grunts of effort grew more and more distant as the metal glowed first red, and then white beneath his torch. He left the tool to float back at his side and punched at the panel until it snapped loose. Then, with the desperate feeling of asphyxiation tightening around his throat, he slid into the ship.

* * *

The Fate's Winds

Aric sparked an emergency lantern from the med bay's survival kit, fighting the pain in his abdomen and back.

"The life pods!" Kaylee was yelling from Pandith's arms. "We have to get to the life pods!"

"This ship doesn't have any, Kaylee," he said. "It's too small."

"Then what can we do?" she cried.

"This is Aric to anyone on the bridge. Do you copy?" he asked. There was no response.

"Aric, I'm not getting anything from the environmental controls," Pandith advised. "Whatever hit us, it killed the ship."

"All right," Aric said, wincing at the excruciating pain in his back. "Helmets on."

Pandith slapped his helmet down, then knelt to help Kaylee. Aric could barely stand, and when Pandith finished with Kaylee he helped Aric get into an EVO suit, which was no easy task in his condition.

"Take her down to the orbiter," Aric said. "I'm going to the bridge to see what happened."

"Aric, you don't have the strength for that," Pandith said.

"I'll manage," he grunted as he headed out of the med bay. Each step brought a new wave of pain, but he had no other choice. As far as he knew, he and Pandith were the only members of the crew who were still alive, and Pandith had to take care of the girl, so that just left him to see what he could do with the ship.

Using his suit's inducers instead of his muscles, Aric found he could glide through the airlocks with minimal effort, and it was certainly a lot less painful than walking. The most direct route from the med bay was straight through the day room, but the room's airlock opened onto absolute devastation. Most of the garden's plants and topsoil had been sucked into space, and the remainder had crystallized into a hideous stream of freeze-dried life.

He pushed ahead as quickly as he could, trying to ignore the nightmarish shadows that his inducers cast against the flickering walls.

"The orbiter's still intact," Pandith called to him over the radio.

"Copy that. I'm just making my way to the bridge now. The day room is a total loss. Not much left of it," he replied as he approached the hatch that led to the bridge and saw that the control panel was blinking red.

"I'm surprised there's anything left of the ship after that hit we took," Pandith said."

"Yeah well, the bridge is depressurized," Aric said. "I'm gonna try to get in there to see what happened," Aric said as he tapped the door controls. The door motors groaned and shuddered, but the door didn't open.

Gripping the latches with his hands, his body roared with pain as he forced them open manually. The corridor depressurized as the door opened, and nudged him on through to what used to be the bridge, but was now nothing more than the open darkness of space. The bow of the ship had been torn off entirely. The bridge ended raggedly, just a few feet in front of the weapons station. It was lit by showers of sparks and flickering holoscreens that sent a hollow feeling flooding through him.

"Aric?" a weak voice called. Aric brightened his suit light and pointed it higher.

"Oh, my god! I can't believe it!" Aric practically shouted.

Following protocol, the bridge crew had tethered themselves to their stations. It might have been enough to save them, but he couldn't tell how many of them still lived. Only Danielle was conscious, waving weakly at him as he coasted toward her.

"What happened?" Aric said.

"I don't know. Whatever hit us fried our suits. All I have is line of sight broadcast left. My boots are fused."

"Bryon, Julie?" he called. "Granger?" But the three others slumped at the end of their tethers.

"I don't know," Danielle said. "I heard Julie earlier but, I don't know if she's still alive. I don't know if any of 'em are."

He shone his lamp on her and recoiled in horror.

Danielle's foot had been sheared off by debris. The suit had done the best it could to tighten around her and form a tourniquet, but he could see gray bone sticking out the bottom of her leg. He tried to lift her from under her arms, roaring in pain as his inducer pushed against his body, but her remaining boot's magnet had locked her onto the deck.

"All right, I'm gonna get you outta here," he said, forcing himself to remain calm.

"No Aric, you have to leave," she said weakly.

"That's not gonna happen," Aric said firmly. "Be right back."

He floated to Bryon, inspecting the weapons ensign's suit for signs of damage. Bryon's suit had a few small punctures that the nanos seemed to be repairing. His eyes were open, but he seemed concussed, and his boots were locked down as well. Next was Julie. She had a large gash across her stomach, and Aric could see gray flesh underneath. He had little time left to save them, so he needed to find a way to release their boots before it was too late.

 The emergency kit was mounted to the far bulkhead, so he used his inducers to help him reach it. Inside he found a roll of suit mesh, and a plasma torch. Then he turned back to Julie and wrapped the mesh around her torso, praying that her nanos were still intact enough to repair her suit. As soon as he'd finished wrapping her up, he knelt down and began to cut the decking from the bottom of her boots.

Bending at his waist brought instantaneous pain. Aric's HUD flashed bio-warnings, but he gritted his teeth and traced the plasma flame around her boots just as quickly as he could.

"Pandith, listen to me," he gasped.

"Yeah Aric, whatcha go up there?" Pandith replied quickly.

"I've got two, or possibly even four survivors. Gonna be coming your way as soon as I can get 'em free."

"Copy," Pandith answered. "You need me to come up there and help?"

"No, just get the med bay prepped. We've got some bad injuries to deal with. We need to at least get 'em stabilized before we can move 'em off the ship."

"All right, I'll get everything ready. I just hope we have enough time."

"Me too," he said as he released the second of Julie's feet from the deck, and then grunted with pain once again as he floated back over toward Danielle.

"Thanks Aric, but just go ahead and leave me now. I can't feel either of my legs," Danielle's weak voice whispered.

"Not a chance," he said firmly as he knelt down once again and set about the task of cutting her remaining foot free. "I mean, if I leave now, then you and Bryon are gonna miss out on the chance to have a whole brood of beautiful little obnoxious babies together someday. I can't have that on my conscience now, can I?"

"Yeah, right," she said, wincing in pain as she laughed weakly.

"Don't worry. If there's a way to get us all outta here alive, then that's what we're gonna do, no matter what it takes. You just rest now and let me work," he said.

* * *

The Bwainhome

Carter had cut into a darkened corridor. The strange deck in front of him had been twisted long ago as the result of some sort of an impact. He could barely see, and barely breathe as he flung himself toward a series of concentric triangles that were flickering around what could have been a hatch. The door was twice his height, as if it had been built for a much larger species. Carter beat at the triangular handles in front of him, twisting and turning the strange alien shapes. A sucking need for oxygen paralyzed his lungs. His vision flickered, and he felt his muscles weaken. For a moment, he thought he saw Aida's bright shape above him, and all he wanted to do was to go to her, but that was not to be. Suddenly, and much to his surprise, the hatch opened up in front of him.

Gasping, he tumbled inside the Bwainhome, and then pulled the hatch closed behind him with the last bit of strength he had left before he collapsed down upon the deck. Mist drifted over him, and there was a sound like a whisper that swelled into a hissing. He choked, wheezing in one breath and then another as the airlock pressurized, and the ship's atmosphere fell over him like a blanket.

He pulled off his helmet and filled his lungs over and over again with his newfound ability to breath. It took some time before the choking pressure in his chest finally began to recede. The air in the ship smelled vaguely of methane but it was otherwise breathable.

Whatever else happened now, he was committed to his current course of action. The *Fate's Winds* was gone, and he had no way to leave the Bwain ship. He'd come to the Sword Belt alone, and that's how it would end. "It won't be much longer now," Carter muttered, and images of his beloved wife flashed through his mind. "I promise I'm coming to you Aida. I just have one last thing I have to take care of first."

He suddenly remembered Granger's mesh, and realized that it had remained on his head when he pulled his helmet off. He let out a sigh of relief as he reached up and touched it, pressing it against his temple, just to reassure himself that it was still there. Then he realized that if it had come off with the helmet, he'd have probably been incapacitated by the thoughts of countless thousands of Bwain, penetrating his mind like needles would pierce one's flesh.

Once he'd gotten to his feet, he moved to the opposite door and lifted the triangular controls in the same way that had opened the first hatch. This one responded immediately, and allowed him passage into the outer corridors of the Bwain ship. He had one mission, and that was to stop the ship from reaching Gertie. Now he just had to figure out how to make that happen.

* * *

The passageway before him was at least twice his height and decorated with strange, hand-carved runes that were burned into a purple, faintly glowing metal. The corridor inexplicably stretched and shrank at different points, as if the ship's builders were under the influence of a powerful hallucinogenic or something while they were designing it. The effect was dizzyingly foreign and difficult to fathom.

Carter took a moment to take stock of his current situation. His suit was largely intact, and though he still carried his tools, the best he could do for a weapon was his plasma torch. Holding the cutter in front of him, he made his way up the gangway, fully expecting multitudes of aliens to come sprinting at him through the dim light of the passageways...but that didn't happen. In fact, there was little of anything. No other hatches, no variation, just the impression of an artery that was running slightly upwards along the ship, pulsing in a way that he couldn't quite understand.

He had no destination, and no sense of where he was on the ship. All he knew was that he'd keep going until he found one of the Bwain, and then he'd use his plasma torch to make it tell him where the ship's bridge was. This was the *Narco* way, and he was about to deliver a double helping of it to the Bwain...if he could only find them.

After traveling for what felt like at least a kilometer, he finally reached another triangular hatch, and popped open the entrance by lifting its center lever.

The door opened to reveal shimmering purple and black feathers flapping in front of him. For just a split second Carter froze at the sight of the Bwain that was only about a meter away from him, but then his reflexes took over. He struck the creature in its abdomen, knocking it hard to the deck. The creature squawked and beat at him as he fell with it, but he was bigger than any Bwain, even without his EVO suit, so it was an easy matter for him to pin it to the deck.

"You understand me, right?" he growled. The Bwain's membrane flicked over its eyes while its head wobbled back and forth on its long neck. Joints that seemed to be located in odd places heaved against his gloves, but his grip on the creature was firm.

"Where is your bridge?" he asked. "Where is your leader?"

The creature stilled, then seemed to focus on him and grew incredibly agitated. It struggled with all of its strength to free itself, but Carter shifted a knee to its neck, and the Bwain stilled.

"Where's your captain?" he demanded again.

The Bwain coughed, thrashing its head under him. Worried that he was choking it to death, Carter let up his knee.

"Go...up," the creature croaked.

Then it jabbed its long neck at him and seized Granger's cowl in its beak.

Before he could stop it, the alien tore the mesh, and the full, disorienting mass of the Bwainsong forced its way into his mind. Screaming, Carter triggered his plasma cutter and drove its blade into the alien's chest. The creature's dark feathers and deep red blood vaporized instantly, but Carter barely felt it shudder and die underneath him. He dropped the torch and rolled off the alien, grasping his head in both hands, trying to force out the pounding assault of the Bwainsong.

* * *

The Fate's Winds

Aric wrapped a line of spider steel around the four members of the bridge crew, cinched the cable to his waist, and then triggered his EVO suit's inducers. The suit had just enough thrust to push the bridge crew down the port side of the horseshoe, and he let out a sigh of relief when Pandith and Kaylee met him near the midpoint of the day room entrance. Kaylee was able to take Julie from him, while Pandith took Granger and Bryon from him.

"Danielle's in the worst shape," he said through panting breath as he gently pulled her around so that Pandith could have a look at her.

Pandith's helmet scanned the nav officer, and Aric could see the concern in his eyes.

"The cold will be better for her leg," Pandith said. "Get her to medical, and gather every first aid kit you can find. I'll meet you there," he called as he dropped down the ladder to the cargo bay. "They're all in bad shape. We need to attend to them as quickly as possible."

"Pandith, you need to take Danielle first," Aric said.

"It's all right. Don't worry about me," Danielle mumbled.

Aric wrapped an arm around her waist and jetted further down the horseshoe toward the med bay. He rested her just inside the cabin's hatch while he cracked open the supply cabinet, pulled three emergency medical kits from it, and then tethered them to his belt. When he tapped his inducers to head back over to her, the ship's lights suddenly blazed back on.

"What's that?" Pandith's garbled voice called.

"I don't know," Aric said. "I think maybe the computer restored emergency power somehow?"

Suddenly, Aric's HUD scrolled with thousands of lines of code. The *Fate's Winds* computer was trying to download something to his suit. Disoriented, he rammed into the bulkhead and a bolt of pain shot through his spine. If his inducers hadn't been working, he would have collapsed before reaching Danielle.

"Aric, are you seeing this?" Pandith asked.

"Yes," he groaned. "What is it?"

"There's something else out here with us. Something different than the Bwain ship. It has the same dimensional phase characteristics, but...wait a minute."

The deck shuddered as Aric finally reached Danielle. She was unconscious now, and inside her suit, her skin had turned gray. The lights blacked out once more, leaving him alone with the glow of his suit lights.

"We gotta get outta here Aric!" Pandith cried.

Aric wrapped Danielle in his arm and flew her off down the passageway. "We're coming!" he cried. "Wait for us! We'll be there soon!"

* * *

Even with the inducers, Aric was barely able to carry Danielle down the ladder to the cargo bay. The pain was tearing through him, and it took everything he had to hand Danielle's body over to Pandith.

"Let's get the hell outta here," he gasped as he reached the orbiter's hatch and handed the first aid kits over to Kaylee.

"Aric, the bay doors won't open," Pandith practically shouted. He squatted to lay Danielle down on the orbiter's deck as Kaylee tended to her. "There's no power. We need to do it manually, but we couldn't lose the atmosphere in here until you arrived."

Aric stared at the four prone shapes before him. Pandith and Kaylee were their only hope.

"They need you here," Aric called. "Close up the orbiter and I'll take care of the door."

In agony, Aric turned his suit to jet toward the manual crank at the bottom of the cargo bay that would open the bay doors. He slipped open the control's cover, wincing at the pain that was burning through his waist, and jerked on the crank. The gearing didn't budge. He put all of his strength against the handle and could feel his torso tearing. Then he remembered that he could use his inducers to help him.

He cranked up their thrust, and the lever started to move as the bay doors cracked open. He held on tight as the atmosphere swept around him, and then cranked up his inducers again to help him with the crank.

It was hard work, and Aric was sweating and coughing as it went. It took some time for him to realize that he was coughing blood onto his faceplate.

"We're almost clear," Pandith said.

"Roger," Aric gasped.

"Aric, are you okay?"

"I'm...," he tried to say wearily. "I'm..."

The *Fate's Winds'* lights blasted on again, but this time, a great groaning and shuddering wracked the ship. Aric felt the deck underneath him warp, as if something was trying to tear the ship apart. Once more, his HUD filled with unintelligible data streams, and a strange whine rang through his cochlear implant.

"What is that?" Pandith shouted.

"I don't...I don't know," Aric choked. The bay doors clanged and groaned, and he kept grinding the gears. "You need to get the hell outta here," he finally managed to say.

"But Aric...," Granger protested.

The crank slammed to a full stop, and the bay doors had opened to the vastness of space. Aric slid down against the box, feeling the warmth in his stomach begin to cool.

"You go ahead Pandith. Get the others outta here," he whispered. "I'm just gonna stay here for a while."

"Aric...no. Come on, you have to come with us," Pandith begged.

"I'm done. Tell Kaylee I'm sorry, and tell Danielle...," he whispered, but then he fell silent and still.

"God...Aric," Pandith said, hesitating for a moment before he gathered the others and got them into the orbiter. "Kaylee, you get them secured into their seats while I fire this thing up."

"All right," she said as she dutifully followed his orders.

A few moments later, as his eyes fell closed, his last sight that Aric saw was the orbiter breaking from its magnets as it launched, and then sailed away from the crippled ship.

* * *

The Bwainhome

The dead Bwain carried a strange weapon, a kind of double-bladed knife. Carter had no idea how it worked, but it had a trigger that just fit the pinky of his suit glove. He pressed the weapon to his skull. Without the cowl's protection from the Bwainsong, the visions were both appalling and unending, and he had to find some way to stop them.

Over and over again he saw his house in Belize City crumble into fiery rubble. He saw the plasma bolt strike the *Fate's Winds* and tear it to pieces. He saw Danny lying in a heap with a pistol against his head on Gertie. There were visions from what must have been other times, other places. One was of a massive creature, dozens of meters tall, striding across a field of broken eggshells with legs like muscled girders. Another had a dirty man in bear skins emerging from a cave and growling through rotten teeth, and yet another had a woman knitting fabric, forming the thread by hand and looping it into an endless knot.

Then there was an image of himself, with his wrists chafed by iron shackles, and what looked like a smoking flintlock pistol in his hand. He was staggering forward with greenish blood on his hands and torso. As he approached himself in the vision however, he realized the man he was seeing had different features, and wore the breechcloth of a slave from Earth in the 1800s.

The visions were too much for him. They were like a pressure that was building in his mind until it felt as though it would burst. He needed to end the pain.

"Aida, I'm coming!" he grunted as he squeezed his eyes shut, pressed the points of the Bwain's weapon against his temples, and then...a hissing sound came from the corridor. Looking up, he saw two more Bwain lurching toward him. They wore a kind of dull armor that protected their torsos and throats, and they approached at a halting lope. Their heads swiveled at him, and their claws ticked against the metal. Carter pointed the Bwain weapon and squeezed the trigger. Purple bolts lanced out at the creatures, spilling their blood against the deck.

Carter stared down at the weapon in his trembling hand, and began to question himself.

"Gertie needs you, and Mephista's still out there somewhere. What the hell are you doin' just giving up like this?" he said to himself.

Grinding his teeth, he bore down and then staggered upright. Pushing his anger hard enough, he found he could hear his own voice amidst the cacophony that was resonating in his head. Suddenly he could remember more than the pain, and his head began to clear.

The first Bwain he'd killed had said that the bridge was up above him somewhere. The alien passageway sloped upward, which was the direction he needed to go, so he followed it past the pair of gurgling Bwain that he'd just shot, not even pausing for the few seconds that it would have taken to end their suffering. There was much more revenge to be had before things were all said and done, and he was going to get every last bit of it that he possibly could. Enough to avenge his doomed crew, and the crew of the *Ichikari*. Enough to avenge Danny's family, and enough to avenge the countless other humans whose lives the Bwain had destroyed. This was his time now, and before he took his last breath, he was damn sure going to make sure they paid the price for what they had done.

* * *

The next hatch opened onto a broad hall lit by massive triangular fins. An open staircase along the far wall led up to another deck, and he could see a strange golden light pouring down from the landing.

The next section at the top of the stairs appeared to be some sort of a social area, with dozens of Bwain milling around in groups amongst what could have best been described as market stalls, offering everything from machine parts, to feed grains, to any number of other strange, alien items.

Wild shots cracked over his head as soon as he was spotted. At least a dozen Bwain who were dressed in a similar fashion to the two he'd just killed were stalking toward him, but many more in the chamber tried to hide. They either shimmered as they attempted to camouflage themselves, or spread their wings and flapped into the room's dark corners. Carter returned fire, slipping behind a pillar that climbed toward the ceiling at odd angles. Suddenly, the doors at the far end of the room sprung open, and a phalanx of Bwain charged in and started firing at him as well.

Even though he was struck by the horrible visions that seemed to drip from his mind's eye into his reality, Carter was better built for combat than the aliens were. Their jerky movements sent their shots too wide or too far at the last moment. They just couldn't seem to hold themselves still long enough to aim their weapons properly.

He also noticed something else as he ran between the room's pillars for cover. The aliens seemed to be terrified of him. Even those who were armed and were clearly either soldiers or security personnel, squawked and ran when he approached. It seemed so unlike the actions of all the others that he'd encountered, that he was reluctant to kill off the ones who were still shooting at him. Many threw down their weapons and attempted to cower in the corners, as if they were waiting for him to execute them. Something strange was going on here, and Carter wished the pain in his head would disappear, even just for a few seconds, so he could reason it all out.

When the fighting stopped, Carter winced as he worked a knuckle against his temple. Somehow, he knew his destination was up the next staircase. The Bwain had been half-heartedly protecting it, as though they were trying to prevent him from accessing whatever was up there, so there was obviously something up there they didn't want him to get to.

He left the cover of his pillars, watching the Bwain from the corners of his eyes. There were hundreds here in this chamber, and they settled into a strange bow as he passed, their feathers flashing white as he passed.

The staircase was heavily worn and claw-scratched, but he didn't encounter any more resistance on his way up. His visions grew much stronger as he climbed toward the light, replacing his vision of the ship for seconds at a time.

He saw the first Bwain ships sail up into the sky from a far-off world, looping in drunken arcs as they climbed. Then his visions changed. He saw their first visions of humans in their strange, sleek looking ships. "*Want*," he heard. "*Need*."

His visions changed again. This time, he saw a landscape of thatched huts, and oxen in the fields. It looked like ancient Europe. There was a group of farmers who were pale and dirty, gibbering in fear as they offered up wooden replicas of a knot design.

Carter reached the top landing with no memory of the two-story climb. He shook his head, trying to clear it, and then looked up to find a great door, at least fifteen meters high standing in front of him. Golden light leaked from the entryway's seams, and the two sides of the door cracked open as he neared.

For a moment, he couldn't tell if what he saw was a hallucination, or if the surreal had somehow come to life. He saw an endless form of golden light, coiled and writhing like a snake that was neither alive, nor dead. It was an endless knot of gold braid, hovering before a pedestal that was built from twisted shapes, much like those in Granger's multidimensional simulation. Without understanding how, Carter knew that this form had been created longer ago than any memory. It was the giver, taker, and recorder of life. It was eternal, as that was its destiny.

Dozens of Bwain surrounded the pedestal, their colors changing from black, to gold, to a smattering of other hues in rapid succession. Carter raised his pistol, and they all quickly cowered down, turning their backs to him. No purple fire reached for him.

He'd spared the Bwain who'd run from him, so he couldn't bring himself to kill these particular Bwain either.

"What is this place?" Carter called out to them. "Who are you?"

A hissing cough rose through them. He had trouble making out the word with the clamor in his head, but then it suddenly hit him. The word was *Bwainslayer*.

"What? I don't understand."

One of the creatures rose and shuffled toward him. He swung his weapon at the alien, and it turned its head away in fear, but kept inching toward him in an almost pathetic crawl. The individual was obviously afraid, but the group needed him to do its bidding. Slowly, Carter lowered the pistol. The Bwain's claw hand took his forearm and gently tugged him forward.

"*Save*," Carter heard, but the word hadn't come from the creature's mouth.

The spinning knot in front of him gave off a heat, and Carter felt himself sweating. The edges of the thing blurred, and wherever he tried to focus he found he couldn't quite make out any detail. Glancing upward, he saw that there was no ceiling in the room. There was only what appeared to be a massive star map.

"*Bwainhome*."

"That was your home?" Carter asked.

"*Find*."

"You're looking for your home? A planet where you can live?" he asked. The creature's head bobbed, but it still wouldn't look at him directly. They were only an arm's length from the knot, and Carter forced the creature to stop. "What are you trying to tell me?"

The creature's head bobbed. Around it, a dozen colors flashed from the other creatures.

"*Save,*" he heard.

Suddenly, a vision struck him with a force and power he could not resist. He was back in his helicopter, only this time he pushed the stick forward and roared toward Belize City. Dozens more filled the air around him, raining destruction down on the *Narcos*, and rescuing the citizens who had fled their homes.

Tears rushed down his face as he recognized *Calle Boxer*, but instead of Aida on his rooftop, he saw a single Bwain. A pathetic, bedraggled, and tired looking creature. A traveler of many miles, somehow a prisoner in a way that he did not comprehend. What was clear however, was that whether they be human or alien, they had all come to the Sword Belt to be freed.

He would get back to Earth, and find more than just answers to his own questions. He would find answers for them all.

"I understand now," Carter said, nodding slowly.

Then he took a deep breath, and thrust his hand into the endless knot.

* * *

Gertie
Landfall

The fight seemed even, at least at first. Two of the militia dove for Danny and knocked him away from Tannin, so that the administrator could escape up the stairs and into his compound. Hal snatched the fallen plasma pistol, and then rolled onto his stomach to find a target. Both conventional shots and plasma rang out. Farmers, colonists, and militia all screamed in pain, fear, and loss as they fell.

Danny was wrestling with one of Vartan's men when the orbiters thudded into the middle of Landfall. Their hatches cracked open, and heavily armed men in the uniforms of SSC marines sprinted into the fray.

Without any idea of who was who, the marines took down everyone they could with magnacuffs. Those who could still run, scattered in an attempt to avoid capture.

Kicking the militiaman to the ground, Danny let the man scuttle away, and then raised his bleeding hands in the air.

"I'm from the *Fate's Winds*," Danny called. "I'm with Captain Carter!" A pair of the marines jogged to him, keeping their rifles trained on him until Hal struggled to his feet behind him.

"Drop that pistol," one of the marines barked at Hal.

"Danny?" the engineer asked. "What's going on?"

"It's okay Hal, go ahead and drop your weapon," Danny said as he brushed himself off. "These men used to be pirates, but they're the good guys now."

*　*　*

Tannin screamed from his compound window where he'd barricaded himself. Danny ignored him as the newly arrived orbiter's hatch swirled open, and a woman came floating out on a hovercart. He stood and snapped to attention with the other marines, and when the woman reached him, she smiled.

"Lieutenant Xiao, I presume," she said.

"Captain Mephista."

The pirate captain was a petite woman tucked into the cart's lone seat so that she sat nearly chest-high to him. She studied the bodies in the streets, the scared look on many faces, and with the most interest, the Bwain, who was curled up on the ground, cowering in fear. When she spotted the pathetic creature, she pushed her hovercart toward where the alien sat dejectedly in the dirt, under the watchful eye of a dozen soldiers.

"You can take over minds, can't you?" she asked. The creature gave no sign that it had heard her question. Its chest heaved, and its features rippled to a sad brown.

"The Bwain can save this colony, Mephista!" Tannin howled from his window. "You have no idea what you've done!"

The pirate captain glanced up at the administrator for a moment, and then shook her head.

"Can you understand me?" she asked as she turned her attention back to the Bwain. The alien nodded without looking at her. "Good, then you can understand this. I'm going to execute you and your entire race for what you did to me and my crew back on the *Swift*."

She held out her hand, and one of her marines handed her his sidearm. The fusion coil glowed white hot as her finger charged the weapon.

"You've always been a traitor Mephista!" Tannin screeched. "You could have had everything you wanted, and now we're all stuck here! We're all gonna die here!"

The captain smirked, then shook her head. To Danny, she seemed almost sad as she looked at the Bwain once again.

"Ma'am?"

"Yes Mr. Xiao?" she asked, aiming her weapon.

"What do you want to do with Tannin?"

"One thing at a time," the captain said as she sighted on the Bwain's chest.

Suddenly, the Bwain flashed in a series of brilliant colors. Its neck jerked upright, and it met the startled pirate's gaze.

"Mephista, you're not gonna believe what happened, or where I am," it said in a raspy voice. She lowered the weapon, her eyes narrowing suspiciously.

"How do you know who I am?" she demanded.

"This is Carter. I'm with the Bwain on their ship. You wouldn't believe what I've got to tell you."

* * *

Mephista's hovercraft hummed quietly next to Danny as they watched together. The steps of Tannin's compound were scorched by laser fire, but at least the bodies were cleared away now. Some were being buried by solemn teams of colonists and ex-militia, dragooned into service by their new commanders. Others were being treated by corpsmen attached to the marine detachment from the *Tranquility*. As Mephista watched it all play out, she once again found herself pleased by the dedication and absolute professionalism of her able crew.

As the streets were gradually cleared of debris and abandoned weapons, one question still remained.

"Who's gonna preside over Tannin's trial?" Danny asked her. "I mean, we can't wait around on this. Someone has to pay, and it's gotta be him, right?"

"I'd suggest that Captain Carter preside over it, but he appears to be indisposed at present," she said as she reached up and tied her hair back in a neat ponytail.

"Guess that makes you the interim colony administrator then," Danny said.

She was already way ahead of him. The need for a swift trial, as well as the public dispensing of justice, was wholly inarguable. The colonists had been through so much, between all the lies, the betrayal, and the threat of mind control and annihilation. These were forced on them by their corrupt lunatic of an administrator.

"Yeah, I guess it does. Let's go see the prisoner and find out what he has to say."

* * *

Tannin was bound to a metal table by magnacuffs, in a small courtyard within his compound. Marines and armed colonists surrounded the area, keeping guard. The bedraggled, defeated old man was snarling at them savagely. That is, when he wasn't begging them for mercy.

A marine sergeant noticed Mephista's arrival, and crisply saluted.

"All secure, ma'am. Two casualties to report, both already prepping for evac back to the ship."

"All right, thank you," Mephista said as she returned his salute. It always felt odd to deliver this time-honored gesture from a seated position, but her useless legs gave her little choice in the matter.

"Who's this?" she asked of a prisoner who was sitting in the corner of the courtyard, opposite the spitting, seething Tannin.

"That's Vartan," the sergeant explained. "He was the captain of the militia under Administrator Tannin. He's been very forthcoming since his arrest."

"Has he?" Mephista asked, her scarred face curling into a smile.

"A summary of our findings," the sergeant said, offering Mephista a portable holoscreen tablet. "There's quite a firm case against Administrator Tannin."

"I think it would be more proper to just refer to him as plain old Tannin now, don't you Sergeant?"

"Yes ma'am," he responded. After he snapped her another quick salute, he headed off to get started on organizing the court proceedings.

Danny spread the word, and colonists began arriving from all over Landfall, taking seats in the compound while they spoke animatedly in anticipation of what was to come. Only hours before, they were rebels with targets on their backs. They were wanted men and women who were considered traitors to their local government, but they saw it differently. They had risked their lives for the promise of something better than Tannin's hapless, self-serving reign. Now they would watch as justice prevailed, and this whole, sad affair could finally come to an end.

"I see no need for undue formality," Mephista began, her voice amplified through speakers that were wirelessly linked to her implant. "We stand at the very edge of human-occupied space, and as such, we can dispense with the letter of the law, in favor of something more...appropriate."

The crowd loved this. Sections of seating in the compound, especially those where injured colonists and their families were seated, began braying for blood from the very outset. She waited for them to quiet down once again before she continued.

"Administrator Tannin stands accused of having abused his position, and there's not a man, woman, or child here today who doesn't have some kind of grievance against him."

More jeering and threats emanated from the crowd. Danny mumbled to the marine next to him.

"I guess this is what it sounds like just before a lynching," he said. He hoped Mephista would retain the air of decorum they'd agreed was essential to these proceedings. Otherwise, they might as well have just thrown Tannin to the crowd and let them deal with him.

"We will be brief, and we'll give the accused an opportunity to explain his actions under cross-examination," Mephista promised, silencing the crowd with a noticeable increase in the volume of her amplified voice.

The crowd booed as she turned to address the prisoner.

"Tannin, would you please explain to these people the reasons for your inviting the Bwain to come to Gertie?" she asked. He had never looked older, or more scared.

"I made a deal," he began in a shaky voice. A marine walked over to place a microphone on the table to which Tannin was shackled. As soon as it was set, he repeated his initial statement once again, and his words reverberated around the compound. "I made a deal with the Bwain. They needed a home, and I needed protection from the corrupt empire of Sol, so we agreed to help each other."

"And what role was the crew of the *Fate's Winds* to play in this?" Mephista asked. Danny stiffened in his seat.

"Don't you dare, you old bastard," he muttered under his breath.

"The ship was to be disabled, and its antimatter fuel transferred to the surface to provide energy for our colony as it expanded."

Mephista waited for him to continue as she hovered quietly in the center of the compound. "And?"

"And...a mole I planted on the *Fate's Winds* was assigned to destroy the security array, which would have prevented the Bwain from coming through The Gate," Tannin added, but Mephista wasn't about to let Tannin drag someone else into this mess to share the blame with him.

"It should please you all to know that this mole that Tannin speaks of renounced his allegiance to the administrator, and fought heroically against the Bwain with his crew. Not only that, but he fought at your side during the uprising."

This seemed to satisfy the crowd. Danny was relieved beyond words not to have been identified, although his remaining crewmates that were currently recuperating on the *Tranquility*, would know the full story soon enough.

"It may interest you to know Tannin that the array was made functional, and destroyed countless Bwain ships on their way through The Gate. Please, do continue with your story though. What did you do then?" she asked. Tannin was shaking like a child waiting in the wings at the school play.

"The Bwain thought that I'd betrayed them. That I intentionally acted to wipe 'em out, but that wasn't true. I just wanted to give 'em a chance for a secure future. Once the *Sanctuary* was destroyed by your act of utter madness...," he said, but he quickly found himself interrupted by a volley of abuse from the crowd.

"We sacrificed our route out of this system to stop the Bwain hordes from rampaging through human space," Mephista explained to the crowd. Tannin tried to stand, but the shackles jerked him back to his seat.

"You don't understand! The Bwain aren't the enemy!" he cried. A nearby marine approached and threatened to whack Tannin with the butt of his rifle. The crowd urged him to strike, but Mephista stayed his hand with a gesture.

"Yes, we know that now," Mephista explained. "We've seen evidence of a much greater threat. The captain of the *Fate's Winds* is, at this very moment, on the Bwain mothership. He has established a line of communication with them, and will return to us when he's able."

A round of applause broke out, and there were brief chants of "Carter! Carter!" from the more enthusiastic sections of the crowd. Again,

Mephista raised her hands to silence them before she turned her attention back to Tannin.

"These decisions were not yours to make. You were administrator of this colony, not the dictator of this planet's future," she said. The crowd noisily agreed. "You took it upon yourself to decide not only the fate of this planet, but the fates of both my crew, and the crew of the *Fate's Winds*. Not only that, but not once did you ever consult the long-suffering colonists about your plan to provide a home for the Bwain, who I need not remind you have a history of unspeakable violence against humans."

"It was all nothing but a chain of misunderstandings, caused by a lack of communication between our two species!" Tannin insisted.

"But you were able to enter their Bwainsong," Mephista pointed out. "You alone could see their true nature. What a pity then that you did not invite others to witness these spectacles."

"Lies!" someone in the crowd bellowed, and the rest of the crowd around him took the word up as a chant. A stern growl from a nearby marine quieted them down so that the trial could continue.

"The others weren't equipped to deal with it," Tannin explained desperately. "Their minds weren't ready for it."

"You lied to the Council!" Hal shouted as he stood defiantly in the midst of the seated crowd. "You could have told us what was going on, and allowed us to advise you, and arbitrate this whole thing, but you just *had* to take all the power for yourself!"

They chanted Hal's name now, until the marine swatted at a few members of the noisy crowd and the noise died down once more.

"Autocracy...dictatorship," Mephista said as if the words left a vile taste in her mouth. "These are not the traits of an administrator. They are the tools of a self-serving monster who would spend the lives of those he was entrusted to protect, all to further the prospects of an alien race that we barely understand. You have committed murder, and endangered the security of human-occupied space. We must now decide the punishment for these crimes."

The crowd was in absolutely no doubt as to what the punishment should be.

"Death!" was the unanimous call, along with various suggestions as to how the sentence might be carried out. Danny found himself impressed by the range of options put forward, but knew that Mephista would take the most direct action in order to bring it to a decisive conclusion.

"Tannin, you have failed and betrayed both this colony, and humanity itself. You will die for what you have done," she said as she drew her sidearm. "Do you have anything more you'd like to say?"

He either didn't, or just couldn't find the words. He gaped at her with widened eyes, as if he could not believe what was about to happen.

A single blast rang out, and Tannin was flung back with a large, burning hole in his chest. The compound erupted in cheers of relief, and a newfound sense of hope for the future. Danny knew as he watched the crowd hug and congratulate each other, that there was going to be one hell of a party to celebrate not only their victory, but the end of the corruption that had plagued them for as long as Tannin had ruled.

He saw Mephista promptly heading out of the compound, flanked by four marines, and he followed her out into the deserted town.

"Captain?" he called out from behind her.

Mephista wordlessly dismissed her guards and beckoned Danny to walk with her toward the little rise at the edge of town. The sun was beginning to set, and behind them, the noise of the raucous party told them there would be a long, and unforgettable night to come.

"Have you heard anything more from Captain Carter?" he asked

"No, not since his warning before the trial. He seemed certain that there's something a hell of a lot more dangerous out there beyond The Gate than the Bwain. Tannin knew it too, and I have no doubt that there'll come a time when we'll have to deal with it."

"Not today, though," Danny said.

"No, not today," Mephista agreed. "Your friends arrived safely aboard the *Tranquility*, and our med teams are looking after them. I'm sorry, but your friend Aric...he didn't make it. Apparently he was instrumental in saving the lives of the others though, so at least he died a hero. That's more than most men can claim."

Danny looked down, and let out a heavy sigh. "Thanks for telling me. He and I had our share of problems, but we'd pretty much worked it all out. It wasn't anything that was spoken. It was just sort of an understanding between two guys who both had regrets about how they'd acted. I think that if he'd have survived this whole thing, we might have even ended up being really good friends at some point. It's nice to hear that he was so brave at the end."

Moments later, they were joined by the shuffling, feathered form of the Bwain. Neither of them had noticed the creature at the trial, or the execution which was now so rowdily being celebrated throughout the little colony. It seemed to watch the sunset for a few seconds, and mirrored the dimming light with its chameleon-like abilities.

"Justice," it said after a long moment of silence.

"Damn straight," Danny muttered.

"Is that what you want?" Mephista asked.

"Want peace," it squawked. "Want friends."

They both looked at the strange alien and felt something close to pity.

Perhaps Tannin could have been at least partially right, and these strange, but seemingly intelligent creatures were simply misunderstood. After all, this was the first time in recorded human history that they had had even this much up-close contact with the Bwain, and there was still so much to be learned about them and their culture. Perhaps they deserved a chance to prove themselves after all. Carter's presence aboard the Bwainhome, and his recent discoveries about their past were certainly a starting point.

On the other hand, there had been a long history of death and destruction caused by the Bwain. It would take a lot of time. and a great deal more knowledge of these alien creatures for the humans to come to terms with their losses.

Maybe someday they would be able to forge some sort of an agreement to allow for a peaceful co-existence between the two species. In fact, the very survival of their respective species might just depend on it in the very near future. That is, if Carter was right about the greater threat that they could both potentially be facing.

Unfortunately, the emotional scars ran much deeper than physical ones. The healing would take time, and each individual would have to come to terms with the reality of the future before them.

"What else do you want?" Danny asked the creature.

The Bwain shuffled slightly, and its head lolled from side to side. The sun crept lower, and the sky became a glowing red-orange color. The alien seemed to sigh, and then uttered a single word in response.

"Home."

About the Author

J. Channing is an engineer and manager for a semiconductor company in Boise, Idaho by day and a dedicated entrepreneur and freelance writer by night. Born in Butte, Montana, he spent most of his childhood roaming around the northwest, living in eighteen different locations before getting through high school. When not at his day or night job, Channing is also actively involved in the community, with his church, and as a small business owner. He utilizes his business ties and proceeds to give back to the local community, having raised funds for Boise area charities.

J. Channing has been interested in military history, time travel, World War II, and weapons technology since he was a small child. The original story concept for *Forever* was outlined on one of his many solo bus rides from the Seattle area to Helena, Montana. It was adjusted and improved over decades and was finally, as a labor of love, completed. The book is a fulfillment of a story that has played out in his head hundreds of times; he hopes the world enjoys it as much as he always has.